D1648429

STONE HILL

Phantoms Reborn

DEAN RASMUSSEN

DARK VENTURE
PRESS

For more information about this book, click or visit:

www.deanrasmussen.com
dean@deanrasmussen.com

Stone Hill: Phantoms Reborn

Published by: Dark Venture Press, 15502 Stoneybrook West Parkway, Suite 104-452, Winter Garden, FL 34787

Cover Art: Mibl Art

Developmental Editor: C.B. Moore

Line Editor: C.B. Moore

Proofreader: Roth Notions

❀ Created with Vellum

This novel is for Mom and Dad.

The time had come.

Brother David was giddy. Elated. Even rapturous as he unlocked the back door and escorted Brother Andrew inside the kitchen.

"Are they gone?" Brother Andrew peered toward the front entrance.

"The house is empty," Brother David said. "You only have to do as we planned."

"The guards out front?"

"They won't hear a thing."

"Mrs. Crane?"

"Bertha is spending the evening at the hospital. She won't be home until tomorrow. I'll provide you with cover, so just stick with the plan and this will be over within moments."

"What if he wakes up?"

"He won't wake up. The medications have made him drowsy." Brother David guided Brother Andrew through the living room to the stairs leading up to Pastor John's bedroom. "He's an abomination now. Once you see him, you will understand."

"He is still my pastor."

"Not anymore." Brother David moved in closer to Brother Andrew and whispered only inches from his face. "Darkness is consuming him. That hideous growth has spread through his body. Your actions are merciful, so there is no need to be afraid. Stick to the plan."

Brother Andrew nodded and bowed his head as if he'd said something shameful.

"It is God's will that we destroy him," Brother David whispered as he crept up the stairs.

He leaned into each step slowly to keep the boards from squeaking. Brother Andrew stayed close behind him. Halfway up the stairs the handrail squeaked from the weight of Brother David's hand. He yanked it away and froze for a moment as his heart thumped hard against his chest. No need to panic. Even loud conversations might only cause Pastor John to rustle in his bed. Everything would proceed without a hitch. The plan was impeccable.

Brother David stopped at the top of the stairs and let Brother Andrew take the lead. The hallway light was off, but in the dim glow coming from Bertha's open door at the end of the hall, he caught sight of the knife in Brother Andrew's clenched fist. A large military knife to complete the task quickly. Brother Andrew's military experience would assure success. Excitement surged through Brother David. Finally, it would happen.

They opened the door to Pastor John's bedroom as if a sleeping bear were inside. He lay face up with the covers pulled up to his chest. His mouth hung open as if gasping for a breath. The patches of black skin were clear across his chin and neck. So unnatural and disgusting. The darkness would soon swallow up his face.

Brother Andrew recoiled with wide eyes. He turned back to Brother David. "Oh my God," he whispered. "Is that him?"

Brother David shook his head. "Our pastor no longer occupies that thing on the bed. This is an abomination."

"I never imagined..." Brother Andrew's whispers trailed off.

"You understand now."

Brother Andrew nodded.

That thing lying in the bed needed to be destroyed. It was God's will. Brother David was the rightful pastor of the temple, and only this horrid creature stood in the way of his leadership.

"Be strong," Brother David whispered, nudging Brother Andrew forward.

A rush of coolness filled the room as the air conditioner kicked in.

The floor squeaked as Brother Andrew stepped toward the bed, but the steady drone of the air conditioner drowned out the sound of his footsteps as he inched closer toward Pastor John.

Brother David took a deep breath and glanced out into the hallway. They would have plenty of time to finish the task, but there was always the chance that one of Pastor John's guards or associates might make an unannounced visit.

Brother David's heart beat faster as Brother Andrew stumbled and bumped against the edge of the bed. The sound of Pastor John's breath rose as he let out a moan and shifted slightly. Brother Andrew paused and looked back. Brother David gestured for him to keep going.

Moving up alongside the bed, Brother Andrew held out the knife over his Pastor John's chest.

Brother David clenched his fist and thrust down an imaginary knife as if he were committing the murder himself. *Plunge the blade through its heart.* He stepped closer to get a better view. He smirked and nodded. *Do it now!* He wanted to scream the words. *Push the blade down!* It would only take a moment.

He couldn't blink. The knife hovered above Pastor John's chest as Brother Andrew shifted forward and raised it in anticipation of the blow. Brother Andrew stopped.

Pastor John's eyes shot open, and he threw his hands over his face to shield it. A black swarming cloud erupted from the patches of darkness on his neck, chin, and pushed out from below his shirt.

The mist pooled in the air between them, then swirled up toward Brother Andrew, a million tiny particles of black light. It streamed like liquid, encircling Brother Andrew's arms and torso like an anaconda snake. He swung the knife through the black mass, but the blade passed through it without effect.

Brother Andrew let out a scream. It cut short a moment later. He shuddered as the churning mass poured into his open mouth. A gurgling erupted from his throat as the black cloud disappeared into his body. He tilted his head and wobbled as if on the verge of collapsing.

Brother David stumbled backwards, gripping the edge of the open door behind him to keep from falling. Every muscle tensed as his heartbeat raced. Something had gone wrong. He shivered as a surge of horror swept through his body. He couldn't look away. But Brother Andrew lifted the knife over Pastor John's chest once again. If he could only swing it down. *Push the blade into the abomination's chest!*

Brother Andrew convulsed. His clothes and skin were ripped apart, revealing a ghostly, churning black form that twisted and tore through his flesh. Blood sprayed across the bed and pooled on the floor. Brother Andrew's intestines and organs were squeezed out between his bones until his skeleton cracked and shattered. The mangled flesh and splintered bones snapped away piece by piece, slapping down against the bed sheet, until all that remained of Brother Andrew was an unrecognizable pile of mangled meat on the bed and floor.

The monstrous pulsing mass of darkness floated in the air above Pastor John, taking on Brother Andrew's shape and size as it shed the last remnants of flesh. But as Brother David backed away to the edge of the door, it morphed into a swirling cloud of particles, and another human form. Pastor John's.

The form floated silently above Brother Andrew's blood and flesh as it slurped down the side of the bed. It craned its head around as if seeing the room for the first time. A guttural groan strained from its throat.

Brother David moved back slowly. Pastor John's form turned its head to the side, peering at him from its peripheral vision.

His blood chilled. If he moved, the thing would see him. He held his breath and prepared to bolt down the stairs if the thing turned in his direction. As he slipped his foot back around the edge of the door, the creature morphed again into a flowing mass of black fragments. It swirled above Pastor John's body, then compressed and merged with the black patches of skin on Pastor John's neck and upper chest.

Pastor John's gaze remained fixed on the ceiling, still wide open.

Brother David stumbled back. His hand thumped against the wall. Certainly, that thing had heard him. No more time for stealth.

He raced to the staircase, his legs a weakened mess. His heart pounded as he bolted down the stairs, stomping onto every other step. That thing hadn't seen him, had it? He wasn't so sure. Its eyes, or whatever ghoulish thing it used for sight, had never locked onto him.

He absentmindedly headed for the front door. No, no, no. What was he thinking? He couldn't go out the front. The guards would see him. His mind whirled as he headed toward the back door. His only way out. He gasped for each breath.

"Who's there?" Pastor John's voice called from the top of the stairs. "I will find you."

"No," Brother David muttered as he hurried through the living room. "It's God's will. It's *my* temple."

Brother David slammed his shoulder into the wall next to the door as he fumbled with the door handle. He wobbled and glanced back before racing outside, catching sight of Pastor John's shadow far behind him, near the stairs.

Trembling as he rushed through the humid summer's evening air, Brother David darted through the back gate. His truck was parked a block away. Those other abominations, the phantoms roaming the streets and fields of Stone Hill at night, would be his only obstacle to freedom. His fear drained away as he ran.

He would destroy the abomination to save the temple. "I will make this right."

Still humming with dark energy, Pastor John alerted the guards about the traitor who had made an escape out the back door, then returned to his room and observed the sprawling mass of flesh and bones spattered across his bed and the floor. His own clothes were soaked. It would take the housekeeper a long time to clean it all up, but she would keep quiet about the matter. She was reliable and responsible. Loyal as all his followers should be.

His insides still burned with rage as he went into the bathroom and cleaned himself up. One of the traitors had gotten away. The assassination attempt had startled him, but a coup was to be expected. Every leader who rose to a greatness such as his encountered resistance from a few pathetic souls. Still, the experience had shaken him.

He would find the identity of the one who got away, and anyone else involved. A stream of names passed through his mind. Brother Steven: loyal. No chance of betrayal, but better to keep an eye on him anyway. Brother Jason: impeccably loyal, but prone to irrational outbursts. Brother Kevin: a history of suspicious behavior. Brother Brian: his most dedicated guard. Brother Willis: weak. Brother David.

Pastor John paused and furrowed his brows. Would his most loyal friend and supporter betray him? It wasn't possible, was it? Unthinkable. He had known David Hatcher since childhood, and had confided so many secrets with him over the years. They had struggled through so much adversity together. Brother David was more than second-in-command with the temple, he was the closest thing he had to a brother.

But sometimes families grew apart. Brother David *had* been distant since Pastor John's return to health.

More names flowed through his head, but they were only guesses. He would need to be diligent in the coming days. He would test each follower's loyalty and watch every move.

But with the assassination attempt came a silver lining. He was awake now. Aware of the evil lurking among his followers. He would find the betrayers and smash them.

He stared into the bathroom mirror at the patches of dark skin over his chest and neck. Areas where he'd been shot days earlier. He ran his fingers over the patch up near his neck. It tingled as if a low voltage battery were arcing between it and his fingers.

What had he just experienced? In an instant he'd been moving out of his body and merging with Brother Andrew. He had stared through Brother Andrew's eyes down at his real body, at Pastor John, as he became Brother Andrew. But he had not only been the body on the bed below him. He had been separate, yet aware of everything Pastor John's body was experiencing. He had inhabited both bodies simultaneously, conscious of both.

Even as he had torn Brother Andrew apart, he had stared up at the carnage and also out through Brother Andrew's eyes. He'd felt all Brother Andrew's pain and anger as his limbs broke apart and burst. And after the destruction of the traitor had been complete, he'd floated in the air, still staring down at Pastor John's body. He hadn't died as Brother Andrew had. He'd felt quite the opposite: exhilarated, yet terrified as he floated in the air sizzling with an amazing energy such as he'd never known in his life.

Then, as easily as it had begun, the consciousness in the air, the black cloud he had become, had been sucked back into Pastor John. He had snapped back into his body with an audible crack like that of a bone breaking. What if he hadn't returned to his body? Would he have floated forever as a ghost?

His own body had cooled during the experience, and he shivered not out of fear. Something inside him moved like hands of ice. His joints ached as he backed away from the bathroom mirror and lumbered down the hall toward the guest room.

It was fortunate that Bertha had not witnessed the gruesome act. It would have upset her greatly. Lucky that she hadn't been in the house, but maybe that had been the intention of the traitor. Only a small group of loyal guards and friends knew she would be staying at the hospital for the evening. He would think it over in the morning, even though he was wide awake now, but his head throbbed.

He debated whether he should try to replicate the experience of separating his consciousness. Maybe it wouldn't be possible again. Or perhaps he would die the next time.

Still, only thirty minutes later as the housekeeper cleaned his bedroom, he lay on the bed in the guest room and closed his eyes. He ran his fingers over the patch of dark skin along his neck, feeling the bristling energy dance below his fingertips. He longed to experience the sensation again.

With his eyes pressed tightly shut, a singularity appeared within the darkness. A point of infinite darkness grew larger and soon enveloped his consciousness. His identity melted away as a creeping sensation flooded in like a swarm of ants, spreading up through his legs and thighs, and across his chest to the top of his head. His body cooled as if he stood in a freezer, even as the creeping feeling poked at his skin like millions of tiny needles.

His stomach churned and nausea passed through him. He resisted every instinct to vomit as the feeling expanded and moved to his throat. He was paralyzed, and he welcomed the creeping.

He cracked his eyes open to see the dark swirling mist rise from the blackness below his chin. As it rose above him, he separated into two again. He stared down at himself and up into the mist. His consciousness moved beyond the constraints of physicality, lifting him like a wisp of smoke, yet he was aware of the weight of his physical body.

Moving down the hall toward his bedroom, he found the housekeeper on her hands and knees scrubbing all the blood and flesh splattered across the floor. He circled around her face and stared into her eyes. She let out a shriek, but he merged with her, floating in through her gaping mouth. She gagged.

As if putting on a new pair of glasses, he stared out through her eyes down at the blood she had been cleaning. The hands below him were of a young woman. He observed her long, slender arms, lifting one briefly in front of his face, and then stood her up. Her strength and youthful energy were invigorating, flowing through him like a cool breeze on a hot summer day. He walked her out into the hallway, relishing the experience as if he were behind the wheel of a new car, and then headed back into the room. He controlled her and became her.

"My name is Sarah Roberts," he said. Her voice was strange, but pleasant. Yet he preferred his own voice to hers. Hers was not the voice of a great leader.

Pastor John separated from the housekeeper's body as easily as he'd merged with it. He willed himself to go into his own body, and his consciousness floated back to the guest room.

Sister Sarah shrieked and ran downstairs after he emerged with his own body again. Four guards rushed upstairs with her moments later. Pastor John sat at the edge of the guest bed when they arrived.

"I've experienced something horrible, Pastor John," Sister Sarah said. "I don't feel like myself."

Pastor John stood and comforted her. "I'm with you. Cast

away your fears. The work of cleaning such an awful mess left by the traitor must be difficult, I know."

She furrowed her brow. "I feel strange." She rubbed her forehead.

"Nothing is more important to me than your welfare," Pastor John said. "You've been working too hard. Take tomorrow off. You've earned it."

Sister Sarah nodded and went back to work.

He reassured his guards that everything was okay.

"These are strange times," Pastor John said. "Keep a vigilant watch over the house. Pray for me."

"We will," said the lead guard.

Fifteen minutes later in the guest room, Pastor John separated again, this time floating out through the open guest room window. Heights normally scared him, but within the consciousness of the black mist he was fearless. The streets were bare, since the night belonged to the phantoms, but he found he could take over any animal, even a phantom.

After several excursions near his home, he returned to his body to get some rest. Each separation sapped a little more energy from his body, as if he had gone on a brisk run. And without more Dunamis, his body would soon break down, just as it had with Bertha.

He needed rest. He lay back in the guest bed and seethed. Brother David should have gotten him some Dunamis by now. Days had passed since the last supply. It was unacceptable that Brother David continued to fail him.

That nagging question hovered in the back of his mind. Would his most loyal friend betray him?

They would have a long talk in the morning.

3

Michael didn't dare go by the windows, much less step outside. The temple vans were parked out in front at all hours of the day and night.

The four of them had spent a great deal of time boarding up everything they could from the inside, although there were small gaps where he might be seen, at a certain angle and the right time of day. All the house lights were on and the only real sunlight came in through the upper section of the kitchen window and some windows upstairs.

They all gathered at the kitchen table for breakfast. Rebecca and Audrey held onto Michael's grandfather as he stepped across the room, although he was looking better than the previous two days. However, his grandfather had still come down with a cough and hunched forward most of the time. He spoke of Grandma Mary a lot. She was on everyone's mind.

"Please go visit Mary for me when you get a chance," his grandfather said to them. "I'm afraid I won't get there anytime soon. She'd love to see you, even if she doesn't always remember you."

"I can do it, Grandpa," Michael said.

"When it's safe," his grandfather said.

Michael smirked. "I need a disguise to go anywhere in this town. Maybe I should throw on a wig too."

"I remember seeing some white clothes in Grandma Mary's room when I was in there," Rebecca said, smiling as she added, "You can look like us."

"Not 'us', honey," Audrey said. "We don't have anything to do with them anymore."

Rebecca looked down. "No, not anymore."

"I'll be right back," Michael said.

He shot up the stairs and entered his grandmother's old painting room with reverence, as if expecting her to be sitting at her painting station. Michael flipped on the light. The sheets on the bed where Rebecca slept were pulled tight. The white dresser next to the bed was clear, except for a few items Rebecca had placed there. Instead of a mirror over the dresser, one of his grandmother's paintings hung there, with several others standing against the side.

The painting over the dresser showed a run-down, abandoned farm with the roof of the barn collapsing on one side. Weeds grew on the driveway and the fields were flowing, grassy plains.

An odd black shadow in the painting caught his eye. On the side of the barn, it spread out like a mangled black starfish. It was like one of the paintings he had seen a few days earlier down in the bedroom. This one did not show the black-shaped thing clearly like the other one had. The shadow looked out of place against the barn, but it resembled a bessie.

Michael lay the painting on the bed. He would bring it with him to show Grandma Mary. Maybe it would cheer her up or spark some memories.

Michael dug through the drawers of the dresser, not expecting to find any white clothes he might wear into town. But Grandma Mary had worn a lot of men's overalls to keep her clothes spatter-free during her painting sessions. He suspected the thickness of the fabric had been appropriate, or maybe Grandpa Artie just had a lot of old, used clothing lying around.

In the third drawer Michael found what he was looking for: a set of white pants and a white suit coat. It reminded him of the suit Pastor John had worn on the stage in the high school auditorium when he'd first arrived in Stone Hill.

Michael took it out of the dresser and tried it on. The suit coat was a little larger than what he felt comfortable wearing, but it was close enough. The pants held up without a belt until he moved. He'd obviously need one.

He searched the room for a white belt to complete his disguise. Not a single one. He had brought along a belt from California in his suitcases, but it was brown. It would stand out against the white outfit. Still, better than nothing.

Now all he needed was a white shirt to go under the suit coat and he was all set. Digging through a few more drawers, he found one.

Another painting, sitting on the floor this time, caught his attention as he closed the dresser and turned to leave the room. It showed a large tree with mostly bare branches beside a stream. The strangest thing he'd ever seen, a winding black and gray mass forming the outline of a human, twisted around the branches as if its bones were missing. Its face was a sprawling web of claws. There were claws where its arms and legs should be, and then another six or eight on top of that. A pair of eyeballs was sunk deep into its head, and its skull was more like the shell of a crab. The eyes, although sunken, were wide and bright yellow, like the yellow in a traffic light.

Where had his grandmother seen such a thing? Maybe in the distorted memories of her dementia she had envisioned those horrible nightmares. Michael broke away from staring at it. How had he not seen that painting before?

Michael removed the white clothes and carried everything to the kitchen, dropping the outfit onto the countertop and the painting beside it.

"I found some, Grandpa. I think I can use these to blend in well enough to go visit Grandma."

His grandfather laughed. "You found your dad's church suit. He was about your age when he wore those."

Michael looked at the clothes again. He imagined his dad wearing them and a wave of sadness passed through him. He would give anything to spend another day with his dad.

"You like that painting?" his grandfather asked.

Michael looked at it. "I was going to bring it with me, to show Grandma. Is that okay?"

"Of course. I think that's a great idea. You'll warm her heart, even if things aren't so clear anymore."

Michael sat at the table with the others and ate breakfast with them. Before he finished, someone pounded at the front door. Nobody ever used that door.

"Downstairs," Michael's grandfather ordered. "Get inside the crawlspace."

Michael shot downstairs with Rebecca at his side, and they whipped across the room to the dark opening he had hoped he would never have to use. They had practiced hiding inside the crawlspace twice, and each time Michael had sworn he would never hide in the ground like that while his grandfather remained vulnerable. He would stay out and fight the temple or the bessies, or anybody who attacked his grandfather. No way would he go in the hole and hide like a scared mouse. He wouldn't fear the temple anymore.

Yet now he crawled inside the hole with Rebecca pushing against him. There was barely enough room for them to get comfortable within the dark cold space. His grandfather and Audrey slid the cement blocks back into place over the hole. All Michael could think, as the light dropped away, was that must be what it felt like to be buried alive.

Their breathing became the only sound as his grandfather moved a wooden bookshelf over the hole, sealing them in so that even if they wanted to get out, they might not be able to. A few minutes later, footsteps thumped above them as Audrey and his grandfather made their way to the front door. The muffled chatter of a conversation seeped through the floor.

"This sucks," Rebecca whispered.

Michael was afraid to respond. The intruders might hear his voice through the boards. He nodded in the darkness and rested his hand on her bare shoulder. Her skin was cold and damp.

Michael clutched the white suit coat in his arms. They had run into the basement and moved into the hiding space with such little notice that Michael hadn't set it down.

He swallowed. His mouth was dry. He wished he had a glass of water.

The footsteps thumped across the floor louder this time. It was difficult to know just how many people were up there. Their movement sounded muffled and spread throughout the house. Soon it became difficult to tell where the sounds were coming from. The floorboards and walls squeaked from every direction.

After several minutes of silence, the sounds became clearer as footsteps thundered down the basement stairs. Michael's heart raced. He wished he had a weapon to defend Rebecca in case the temple found them. But even with a weapon they had no way to escape. They were powerless and Michael hated that feeling.

The voices grew louder and louder as the temple intruders worked their way through the basement clutter. Bumps and crashes filled the air. Something loud and heavy, some metallic object, crashed and clanked against the cement floor.

Audrey let out a brief scream, but not in pain.

"We're not playing around," David yelled, "this is your last chance to cooperate."

"They're not here," his grandfather groaned and then coughed.

"You're lying. They're here somewhere," David said. "They didn't leave the house. We see everything you do. Where are they?"

"They left town," Audrey yelled. "You people are insane. Leave us alone."

More bangs and a crash, followed by a fluttering sound.

"Can't you see he's sick?" Audrey cried. "How can you do this to him?"

"Tell me what I want to know and we'll leave. It's that simple."

Michael's face grew hot, and he inched toward the cement blocks. His muscles tensed and his hands squeezed into fists. He wanted to jump out and strangle David. Put an end to the temple's evil once and for all.

Rebecca must have sensed his desire because she grabbed onto his arm and pulled him back.

"Don't move," she whispered.

Michael took a deep breath of the stale air and the urge to cough rose in his throat. He held it back, breathing in again through his nose and turning his head to the side. No way to avoid the putrid smells.

More banging and clattering around the basement. A thin slice of light had faded around the cement blocks as Michael's eyes became adjusted to the darkness. The light fluttered a few times as the temple guards crossed back and forth through the stacks of accumulated junk.

"No!" Audrey screamed.

"Now put that away," his grandfather yelled.

A gunshot blasted through the room.

"Where are they?" David yelled. "Do you want to die? This is your last warning."

"I'm not afraid of you," Michael's grandfather said.

"No," Audrey added. "Leave him alone. They left town. We keep telling you that. We sent them off to stay at my sister's house in Larston Lake. They left yesterday. How could they stay in town after what happened?"

Silence flooded the place for several seconds, and then footsteps stomped up the stairs again to the kitchen.

"Nobody leaves this house until we find them," David said. "I'm sure they're here and we'll be watching you at all times."

More footsteps stomped through the kitchen toward the front door.

The sound of Audrey helping Michael's grandfather up the stairs came through clearly. He gasped for a breath every couple of steps.

"This nonsense has to end," Michael's grandfather said.

"I know," Audrey said. "It will."

The footsteps stopped near the front door. "We are watching you!" David yelled. "We see everything."

"Not everything," Michael whispered.

❦ 4 ❧

"Where am I supposed to go?"

"I don't know, but as my bartender used to say, you don't have to go home but you can't stay here. You're a big boy, you can take care of yourself. Time to stand up and be a man."

Joey's eyes darted around the room as if he were looking for something that might solve the problem. Looking for a way out of the strange situation he was in. His pet dog Buford lay on the carpet chewing on a bone.

"Who will take care of Buford when you're at work?" he asked.

"Don't you worry about him," his dad said. "I can take care of a dog."

Joey's mouth hung open. "What about all my stuff?"

"Take it with you if you want. Take all of it. But you got one hour."

"How can you do this to me?" Joey's eyes teared up and his body weakened. "This ain't right."

"Cryin' ain't going to help. Get in there and pack up your stuff."

"It ain't right."

Joey lumbered back to his bedroom and started digging

through his drawers, pulling out clothes that he might need over the next few days. No way would his dad not let him come back in to get the rest of his stuff. Just a few days, that was all the time he needed to straighten things out.

His dad appeared in the doorway again with a large suitcase. He tossed it onto the bed. "Put your stuff in there. I ain't helping you either." He walked away, and Joey began stuffing his clothes into the suitcase.

"You can't just throw me out," Joey shouted.

"Hell I can't."

"Those monsters will eat me tonight. Is that what you want?"

No answer from his dad. Whatever was going through his dad's mind would get straightened out in a few days. That was usually how long their fights lasted. Except this time his dad wasn't hitting him. No belt, no back of the hand, no getting pushed around. His dad wasn't yelling either. Give him a few beers and he'd be swinging a bat at Joey.

Maybe his dad had a hangover, but Joey hadn't seen him drinking the previous night. He hadn't said a word from his recliner the previous day day. No yelling at Joey to clean up the living room. No cursing at the dog for whining to be let outside.

His dad hadn't been the same over the last couple of days. The polar opposite of his usual raising hell self. Quiet and sluggish now, just the same rut he'd gotten himself into a few months earlier after his mom had disappeared.

"Where should I go?" Joey asked.

Again, no answer.

Joey kept filling the suitcase with anything he might need. He'd stayed overnight at a friend's house a few times over the past year. Enough times to know the basics of taking care of himself. Bathroom stuff, clothes, food and water. He needed money for that, but he didn't have any money. His dad stashed a little cash in a jar hidden in a kitchen cupboard. No way could he get to that now. His dad would beat him silly if he even tried.

Not a lot of places to go in town. Rebecca's house, Artie's

house, a few classmates might take him in. But his classmates were mostly temple members now. They probably wouldn't talk to him anymore after all that had happened.

He would go to find Rebecca. At least he knew she wouldn't kick him out.

Joey gathered up his bathroom items, threw them in a plastic bag, and into the side pocket of the stuffed suitcase. He zipped up everything and rolled the suitcase out into the living room.

Buford lifted his head as he crossed the room. "See you later, Buford. Make sure you keep the phantoms out."

He went to the front door and reached for the keys to his truck, which he'd left dangling from a nail next to the door. They were gone.

He checked the countertops. Not there. His pockets. No.

He returned to the living room. "I can't find my keys."

"It's my truck," his dad said. "I bought it. You can walk. You got muscles."

"Can you drive me over to Rebecca's house at least?"

His dad shook his head and didn't look at him. "I can't be seen with you no more. That's it."

"How am I supposed to drag this—"

"You'll find a way," his dad said without expression. "You're a big boy. Time to grow up."

Joey took one glance back at the living room and at Buford and then headed out the front door.

His dad's black pickup truck sat in the driveway. The keys were on the hook just inside the door. He could reach in and grab them in a flash. But his dad would fly into a rage and knock him to the floor, if he was lucky.

He scanned the sidewalk and the street. Maybe he would see one of his classmates and they would stop to pick him up.

No way would he be that lucky... He probably looked like a buffoon dragging his big old suitcase along the sidewalk, heading nowhere in particular like a homeless bum.

One of the neighbors was watching him out of her side

window. He wanted to run over and scream at her to stop staring. *You've never seen a boy with a suitcase before? Nosy old bitch.* They'd all be talking soon. Gabbing all their juicy gossip. Joey held his hand to his mouth and imitated their jaws flapping open and shut. The old woman was still staring at him. Joey flipped her off and continued down the sidewalk toward the cemetery.

He estimated it would take him about an hour to get out to Rebecca's house. Maybe longer while dragging the suitcase along the gravel road. That was going to be a real bitch, dragging that through the gravel.

A white van was parked ahead of him on the side of the road. It was facing away, but most likely the driver had seen him approaching. It would be an interesting conversation, if they stopped him. He knew they wouldn't, though. They all knew better than to mess with the son of the captain of the temple guards. He'd gotten away with so much shit over the last couple of years, but there'd be hell to pay now. He had become a troublemaker like Rebecca and Michael. A marked man...well, a marked teenager, anyway.

Just as well. He hated the white shirts. None of it made any sense to him, and he could never go back to the temple, even if he tried. He'd seen too much bad shit.

As he passed the white van, the driver craned his neck around and stared at him. Joey also flipped him off, and the driver sneered. As the front of the van came into view, the guard in the passenger seat joined into the staring contest. Joey kept his chin high and glared straight into their eyes as he flipped off the passenger as well, for good measure.

"You just keep it up," Joey said. "I'll take you down."

Joey walked backwards to keep his eyes on the men in the van, but his suitcase nearly toppled over, so he finally turned around. He kept his middle finger extended as he walked, just to make sure that there was no ambiguity over how he felt about them.

"Dare you to follow me," he mumbled.

By the time he arrived at Rebecca's house, his shirt was drenched in sweat and the crisp morning had given way to humid warm air. There was no breeze to cool him off, and nothing to shelter him from the sun aside from the occasional cluster of trees along the road.

It was impossible to tell if anyone was home or not. Rebecca's car sat in the driveway, but she couldn't drive it anywhere. The temple knew her car and followed her around everywhere. The windows were boarded up from all the shit that had gone down a few days earlier, but the house had electricity.

Joey walked up to her front door and knocked. No answer. He considered stepping inside, if only to get out of the sun for a minute and maybe pour himself a cup of water, but he suspected they'd all gone to Artie's house next door. Audrey and Artie had pooled their resources lately, staying together as much as possible. Safer and easier for everyone.

Joey walked right by the white van outside Michael's house without any obscene gestures. He was too exhausted to bother.

He went around the side of the house to the back door. Three cars filled the driveway. Audrey's white Toyota RAV4, Artie's red Cadillac, and another black truck owned by a guy named Finn, which sat in the same spot they'd left it days earlier. Finn wouldn't ever come back to claim his truck. The temple took him down.

Joey strained to lift the suitcase one step at a time up to the door. It felt as if it had gained an extra fifty pounds since he'd started walking, but at least he was done now.

He caught his breath and put on a smile. Weren't they going to be surprised when they opened it...

Before he could knock, the door opened. It was Audrey.

She looked at his suitcase. "Are you in trouble?"

"You could say that," Joey answered.

Audrey held the door open and gestured for him to come in. "We heard something scraping outside in the driveway."

"I saw the white van out on the road." Joey stepped into the kitchen and set his suitcase right inside the door.

Rebecca walked over with a bright smile on her face and gave him a hug. He pulled back. He was too stinky and sweaty to be that close to her at that moment.

"The temple stopped by this morning," Rebecca said. "We have to leave. Now."

5

M ichael let his suitcase slide down next to him along the edge of the steps as he went downstairs, landing with a thump at the bottom. A lot easier to carry it down than up.

He rolled it into the kitchen and Joey was standing near the back door with a massive suitcase of his own. His underarms and chest were drenched with sweat stains and his forehead glistened.

"What's going on?" Michael asked. "You look like you just got done working out or something? Whose suitcase is that?"

"It's mine. My dad kicked me out of the house," Joey said. "I was hoping I could stay here."

"Why'd he kick you out?" Michael asked.

"Long story," Joey answered. "Can I stay with you guys for a while? I promise I won't be a pain in the ass. I'll help out and everything. Maybe you could use someone to mow the lawn and stuff like that."

"I don't know if you heard, we were on our way out."

Rebecca nodded. "You can come with us. We'll go see if we can stay in Derek Johnson's barn."

Joey cringed. "I don't want to go there. Derek's a dick. That's about as nice a way as I can put it."

Rebecca made a sympathetic face. "He's not the friendliest guy." She looked at Michael. "Don't expect Derek to say much."

"Why would you want to stay in his barn?" Joey asked.

"It's not a regular barn," Rebecca said. "Derek's dad built a little room in the back a long time ago, like a guest house, and since he died Derek uses it to let some kids who don't have parents anymore hide out from the temple. My friend Lucas stays there."

"You mean Lucas Lyon's gang?" Joey asked.

Rebecca nodded knowingly. "He gets into lots of trouble, and he might not trust us, but he's been a friend for a long time in high school."

"I know Lucas," Joey said. "My dad roughed him up a lot over the last year. I feel bad about it now, but I know he gives the temple hell."

"I heard they can get an Internet signal back there and everything," Rebecca said.

Michael perked up. His heart beat faster at the thought of using the Internet again. It would be great to check his email and text messages. Maybe even send a message to his mom. But his cellphone was broken and lost within the maze of tunnels below the church. He'd never get it back.

"Only one problem," Michael said. "If we take the car over there, the temple people will probably follow us. We were planning to walk through the fields behind the house and cut around."

Joey looked down at his shirt. "I just walked almost two miles to get out here."

"You don't have to bring your suitcase right now," Michael said. "We don't know for sure yet if Derek's open to letting us stay there. We'll come back later and get the luggage."

"They'll help us," Rebecca said. "At least Lucas will help us."

"I think I might have a way out for you," Michael's grandfather said as he stood at the edge of the short hallway leading to his room. He was wearing a dark blue robe over his pajamas, and he rubbed his tired eyes and then ran his hand through his messy hair. "You can take the Cadillac out through the back of the garage."

"Your Cadillac's in the driveway, Grandpa," Michael said.

"I have another one in the garage. The back of the garage opens up and we can drive it out through the backyard and the cow pasture. Those vans won't see you leave because of the trees. You can keep driving through Bob Nichols' field around to the main road."

Michael pictured his grandfather's crowded garage. He'd never looked beneath the brown tarp hiding the old car. He'd assumed it was some old junker destined for the junkyard that didn't start anymore.

"So *that's* what's under there," Michael said.

"I've got two of them. I bought the one in the garage when your dad was here about thirty years ago, and I only took it out in the summer back then. It's still in good condition, but I haven't driven it since last summer. If it starts, use it."

"We'll take it," Rebecca said.

His grandfather went to his bedroom and returned a minute later with a single key. "That's the only key. Don't lose it."

"I won't," Michael said.

Michael, Rebecca, and Joey went out to the garage and opened the door. The car took up most of the space with a few rakes and shovels leaning against it. Michael had never noticed a second door, yet there it was. It opened out to the side, like a huge gate door.

"Let's see this beauty," Joey said, ripping the brown tarp off the Cadillac.

Rebecca moved the lawn tools and a few other items. All the time Michael kept an eye out for any sign of the white vans.

Joey helped Michael open the back door. The hinges squeaked as it swung and crashed against the side of the garage, rattling the entire structure. Michael peeked around the garage to the house to see if his grandfather had noticed. No sign of him.

Michael opened the driver's side door as far as it could go and squeezed in behind the steering wheel.

"Fire her up, man," Joey said.

The engine sputtered when Michael turned the key. The smell of gas filled the air. He turned it off.

"Don't flood it!" Joey said. "Want me to start it?"

"I can do it," Michael said. Another try. Nothing.

"I'll do it," Joey said. "Move over."

Michael turned the key again, and the engine burst to life. A puff of dark smoke filled the air. Rebecca fanned the air in front of her face and coughed.

Joey moved out of the way as Michael inched the car forward. Michael focused on the edge of the garage door, steering it only a little to keep the side mirrors from getting broken off. After he cleared the garage, he drove into the back-yard and stopped.

With the engine running, Michael checked the gas tank before getting out of the car. It was three-fourths full. Plenty of fuel for now.

He stepped out of the car and looked back toward the house. The windows were dark, but he was sure his grandfather was watching them. At least Michael hadn't wrecked anything.

It was a clean car, not a scratch on it. A white Cadillac. The same size and style as his grandfather's red Cadillac. Maybe the white would help them blend in with the other temple outfits in town.

"Much better idea than walking," Joey remarked.

"Let's get the suitcases," Michael said, heading toward the house with Joey and Rebecca at his side. The engine rumbled behind them.

❧ 6 ☙

They drove over the grass across the backyard and cut through the cow pasture, passing through a gate at the edge of the yard, just as Michael's grandfather had directed. Years ago, dozens of cows had grazed in that pasture, but now it was nearly empty except for a few hiding in the small barn next to his grandfather's house. His grandfather rented out the barn to a neighbor who took care of the animals, but Michael hadn't seen the neighbor stop by to take care of them since he'd arrived in Stone Hill. Maybe that neighbor had disappeared with the others in town.

Beyond the pasture was a stream that led back into town and flowed further away into the countryside. They followed the edge of the stream for a short distance, the Cadillac bouncing and swaying as if battling through stormy waters. They came to a gravel road after five minutes and turned right, keeping their eyes out for any white vans lurking on the road.

Rebecca directed them along the winding gravel to a small farmhouse with a lawn overgrown with weeds. The farmhouse looked abandoned since someone had boarded up the windows, and no vehicles sat in the driveway.

"Are you sure this is the right place?" Michael asked.

"I'm sure," Rebecca said.

They walked toward the side door, which opened out onto the driveway. Michael checked the roads and fields around the house one more time. No sign of either the temple or anybody else. The nearest farm was across the road, but that appeared abandoned as well.

"We're right at the edge of town," Rebecca said. "If we kept going that way, we would run into the temple's roadblock."

There was a large white painted barn at the back of the yard and a smaller structure next to an open field looking as if it had held farm machinery at some time.

As they stepped up to the side door, a dog ran out from the other side of the house and barked at them. It was small with light brown fur, but its bark was loud, and it didn't look too happy to see them.

"Hey boy," Michael said to the dog as it approached, "we're just looking for help."

Joey reached down to pet the dog, and it snapped at him. "Holy Jesus."

"Is it going to eat us?" Michael asked.

"Maybe," Rebecca said. "I've never been here before, so I guess it might."

"How did you know where to find the house?" Michael asked.

"My school bus drove by here every day. Derek's lived here all his life and it's always looked like this, except for the boarded-up windows."

Michael knocked on the door with Joey and Rebecca beside him. No answer. No sound of anyone approaching the door. Michael waited a minute before knocking again. He was about to give up when the handle jiggled and the door flew open. A dark-haired young man, maybe old enough to buy beer, stood bare chested and partly obscured by the edge of the door. A shotgun stuck out, pointed at their waists.

"Can I help you?" the boy asked sarcastically.

"Derek," Rebecca said. "It's me, Rebecca. Bex. From school."

"I know who you are. What do you want?"

"Is Lucas around?" Rebecca asked. "We need help."

"I don't know where he's at. Go home, Bex."

Derek stood there with the shotgun still aimed at them. He didn't move back into the house, but he didn't offer to help them either.

"We need a place to hide for a few days, maybe longer. We were hoping we could stay in the barn."

"I can't help you. Go back home."

Derek backed away and the door started to close.

"Wait," Rebecca said. She ran both of her hands through her hair. "It's really important that I get in touch with Lucas. I've got an important message to give him."

Derek paused in the doorway, staring at her. "From who?"

She made a sweeping gesture and cupped her hands at her sides. "From a friend of his."

"He doesn't have any other friends."

"I'm serious, Derek. You got to let us talk to him." Her hands clenched into fists as she pleaded. "Something really bad is going to happen if he doesn't get this message."

"Go away." Derek slammed the door. A deadbolt snapped shut.

Rebecca turned to Michael. "Two years in drama. *You* believed me, didn't you?"

"Not really," Michael said, "you overdid it."

"I guess I should have rehearsed something."

She pounded her fist on the door. "Derek, we need your help. I know Lucas is in the barn. If you don't help us, we'll just go walk back there ourselves."

The door swung open again and Derek raised the shotgun to Rebecca's face. She inched back and Michael moved forward. Joey put his hands up as if he were about to grab the barrel of the shotgun.

"You're one of those temple people, aren't you?"

Rebecca shook her head. "No."

"Bullshit, I know you are. You're Maggie's friend."

Again, Derek pointed the shotgun at each of them. "Get out of here. I'm not fucking around. I'll give you three seconds."

"Come on, Michael." Rebecca grabbed Michael's hand and pulled him down the cement steps. Joey followed Rebecca as if shielding her. They circled around to the back of the house toward the barn.

Michael's hair stood on end, and he had the sense that at any moment he would get shot in the back. The small dog barked and growled as they headed toward a door at the side of the barn.

Derek charged up behind them. "You sons-of-bitches better listen to me!"

Glancing back, Michael watched Derek wildly wave the shotgun back and forth at them. A loud blast roared through the air, and Michael and Rebecca froze.

"The next one is going in your brain," Derek said. "Get the hell off my property!"

They turned around and Rebecca took a step toward Derek. "Are you crazy? The temple might have heard that."

"I told you to leave."

"We need your help. I know Lucas is here and if you won't help us, maybe he will." Rebecca grabbed Michael's hand again and continued to the barn.

Derek followed the three of them instead of shooting the gun again, grumbling the rest of the way.

They went inside the barn, and pigeons fluttered in the open air near a vent at the top. Stacks of hay bales lined one side of the barn. At the back was a closed white door, and Rebecca towed Michael toward it.

"Nobody's here," Derek said. "You're all going to end up dead if you keep this up."

Michael got to the door first and turned the handle. The door swung open, and inside was a room that looked lived in, but the wall had collapsed, and the furniture was broken. Sunlight poured in through a massive hole in the ceiling. Bird poop and debris were scattered across the floor, and there were no footprints in the dust and dirt to show anyone had been there recently. It was obvious nobody lived there now.

"I told you," Derek said. "Lucas doesn't live here and I don't know where he is. Get off my property."

A cellphone rang and echoed through the barn. The sound came from everywhere. The pigeons flew closer to the hole at the top. Michael glanced back. Derek was still aiming the shotgun at them.

"Put the gun down, please," Michael said. "Obviously, we're not the only ones here."

"Just get out of here before I kill you," Derek insisted.

A teenage boy a little taller and thinner than Michael stepped out from behind a stack of hay bales. He walked toward them with a slight limp. He wore khaki shorts and a graphic T-shirt that displayed the name of some obscure alcohol brand. His hair was a mess, and when he got closer Michael saw that the rim of his glasses were broken and held together by a piece of white tape. "Nerd" was the first word that came to Michael's mind.

"Lucas!" Rebecca called out. "It's me, Rebecca. Bex. We need to talk with you. It's really important."

"Don't you guys know Derek is *loco?*" Lucas said.

Rebecca held her arms out and walked toward Lucas. "We're so glad to see you. We need your help."

"You're in the temple, Bex. I don't want to talk to you."

Rebecca stopped walking. She shook her head. "No. Not anymore. The temple is after us. We've been down in the tunnels under the church."

"Derek," Lucas said, "put down the gun."

"They're from the temple," Derek said, although he lowered the shotgun. "She's friends with Maggie."

"What were you doing down in the tunnels?" Lucas asked.

"We killed Pastor John," Michael said.

"Bullshit," Derek said.

"Who's your friend?" Lucas asked, gesturing at Michael.

Rebecca grabbed Michael's arm. "This is my friend Michael, from California. He's staying with my neighbor for a few weeks. You don't know what we've been through. All three of us went down into the tunnels a few days ago and we killed Pastor John. The temple is out to get us now. They want to kill us."

Lucas frowned. "What makes you think I can help?"

"We need a place to stay. At least for a few days, until we find somewhere else to go, but I don't know anyone else who can help us right now."

"We didn't hear anything about Pastor John getting killed," Derek said. "I'm still calling bullshit."

Lucas stepped closer to Rebecca. "I know you were in the temple, Bex. Derek's right. You're friends with Maggie. And Joey's in the temple too. His dad is one of their top guards."

❧ 7 ❧

"I'm not in that anymore," Joey said.

Lucas raised his voice. "Joey's asshole dad beat me with a metal pipe once and broke my ankle. It never healed right because they wouldn't take me to the hospital. I couldn't walk for weeks after that, and all I had was a bunch of ibuprofen for the pain." He took a step, demonstrating the limp on his left foot. "Why should we trust you?"

Rebecca sighed. "Because we're telling the truth."

"Prove it."

"What do you want?" Joey asked. "Pastor John's head on a platter?"

Derek nodded. "That'd be awesome."

"How long have you known this guy?" Lucas asked, gesturing at Michael.

"We've been friends since we were kids. He visits in the summer."

"All the way from California!" Derek chuckled. "You're in for a rude awakening here in Minnesota. Better get out before it snows."

"How did you get into the tunnels?" Lucas continued.

"It's a long story," Rebecca said.

"I can prove it," Michael said, digging into his pocket.

Derek raised the shotgun again. Michael pulled out the medallion and held it up so they could see it clearly. "This medallion glows bright red when a bessie is near."

"Bessie? What the hell is a bessie?"

"The phantoms," Rebecca said. "Well, that's what the temple calls them. But they're not really phantoms."

"You mean the squid?" Lucas asked.

Michael, Joey and Rebecca nodded.

"This is from the tunnels. Pastor John wanted this badly before we killed him."

Lucas gestured for the medallion. Michael hesitated, but handing it over was the only way to make Lucas believe them.

"My grandfather and Audrey, Rebecca's mom, were captured by the bessies a few days ago, and we had to go down into the tunnels to rescue them. We got them out, but in the process we killed Pastor John."

"Well, shit," Derek said and walked up to stand next to Michael with the shotgun lowered at his side. "I only know of one other person who got out of the tunnels alive. They said those squid were everywhere, and they had to hide behind some dead people for a whole day before they could sneak out. Is that what you went through?"

"That's what my grandpa and her mom went through, except we had to rescue them."

"Huh," Lucas grunted, "that's an amazing story." Lucas weighed the medallion in his hand and squinted as he studied the markings and symbols on it. "I guess I could help you guys. Do you know what this says on here?"

"No," Michael answered. "Those markings are all over the walls in the temple below the church."

"Maybe we can find out together." Lucas handed the medallion back to Michael.

Shrugging, Derek walked back toward the house as Lucas led them around the bales of hay, squeezing into a narrow gap between two stacks. It would have been easy to miss if someone wasn't really looking.

Joey struggled to get through the opening. He sucked in a deep breath, but even then his large frame scraped against the bales.

They walked over to something like a wooden storm door in the floor. Lucas swung it open, revealing a passageway that led down below the cement floor of the barn.

Michael groaned. "Not more tunnels."

"It's not that deep," Lucas said. "It's not like a bomb shelter or anything. You claustrophobic?"

"No," Michael answered. "Holes in the ground just make me nervous after what we've been through."

"You'll have to tell me all about it," Lucas said.

The passageway opened up to an area the size of a small apartment. Two other boys were playing video games on a massive wall-mounted flat-screen, and a girl watched TV with earbuds on. She was swaying to music the others couldn't hear. The boys and the girl stared at Michael, Joey, and Rebecca when they walked in. One of the boys paused the video game, and the girl pulled out her earbuds.

"This here is Rebecca, Joey, and..." Lucas said. "What's your name again?"

"Michael."

Lucas introduced the three other guests in his place as Twyla, August, and Grim.

"Did you say Grim?" Michael asked.

"Yep, Grim," Twyla said. "His real name's Tim, but he says he hates it, so we call him Grim instead."

"I don't like Grim either," Grim said in a low grumble.

"It's your name," Twyla said. "Get used to it."

"I hate you guys," he said with a scowl.

"Hey, Grim," August said, "I like Grim better than Tim, anyway. Sounds like you're dangerous or something."

"I am dangerous."

August laughed. "Only to yourself."

"You probably can't stay here," Lucas said to Michael, Rebecca, and Joey. "Derek freaks out if anyone else tries to stay overnight, but I'll ask him."

"Thanks, Lucas." Rebecca hugged him.

"Can I change my clothes in your bathroom?" Michael asked Lucas.

Lucas stared at his jeans and t-shirt as if trying to figure out what was wrong with them.

"They're out in the car," Michael explained. "I need to wear something white when I drive into town. I want to fit in when I go visit my grandmother."

"Sure," Lucas said, "no problem. Just know that Derek watches everything that goes on up there, so don't be doing anything suspicious."

"Got it."

Michael went back up to the car alone. He opened the trunk and then his suitcase, pulling out the white outfit he planned to wear into town. His dad's suit looked practically new in the sunlight. His grandparents had taken good care of it.

On the way back to the barn a wasp buzzed his head.

He covered his face and jumped back. "Son of a bitch."

He followed the wasp's flight as it circled up near the top edge of the barn. A softball-sized nest hugged the underside of the roof's overhang. As a child, he was stung by a wasp and had never forgotten the trauma. One of the most painful memories of his childhood. Physically painful, anyway. He never wanted to go through that again.

He crouched forward and cringed as he passed under the nest on his way back into the barn. He expected another encounter with a wasp. No attack. He let out a deep breath after the door closed behind him. The pigeons cooed overhead as he went through the hidden door into the underground hideout.

Once inside, he went straight into their bathroom and slipped on the white suit coat. He stared at himself in the mirror. The off-white shirt beneath the coat didn't match the clean white of the suit, and it had some stains along the collar, but nothing stood out too much. It would be enough to blend in. He doubted anybody would look at his face anyway, and he would keep his baseball cap on and try to stay in the shadows as much as possible.

He walked out into the hangout area, and everyone's expression was the same when they noticed him. Their eyes and eyebrows jumped.

"Look out, temple dude's going to get you!" August jumped to the edge of the couch. Twyla cringed as if she had smelled something awful. Grim reacted as if a spider had jumped at him. Rebecca smiled wildly and held back a laugh.

"That's...uh..." Joey said with his eyebrows squished together. He shook his head. "It doesn't look right on you, but it'll do, I guess."

"What's wrong with it?"

"It just doesn't look good on you. You look like a teenage Pastor John."

"The only white clothes I've got."

"Just don't go near anyone. Someone might ask you to heal them or something."

"Maybe I'll start my own church."

"Oh God, please no," Joey said. "We've got enough shit to deal with. Just avoid getting close to anyone."

"You wearing that?" Rebecca asked, gesturing to his cap.

"I was," Michael said.

"Take it off. A Dodgers baseball cap and that suit don't mix. Maybe if the cap read Minnesota Twins."

Michael removed the cap.

August, Twyla, and Grim went back to their videogame, while Rebecca stood up and went over to Michael. "Be careful. We'll be worrying about you."

"I won't be gone long," Michael said.

"Maybe I should walk you out to the car," August said with a grin, "so Derek doesn't shoot you."

"I appreciate that."

August led him out through the barn and then across the driveway to the white Cadillac. Michael glanced at the house, and although he didn't see anyone peering out the window, he was sure Derek was watching him. The dog that had approached them when they arrived was now gone. Derek must have taken it into the house.

Michael stared down the road in both directions. He really wanted to drive by his grandfather's house again to see if everything was okay, but it would be too risky. The vans would watch everyone who drove by.

"Is there a better way to get into town without going past my grandfather's house?" Michael asked August. "We came in that way." Michael pointed out his route.

"Sure is," August said, "but you'll probably run into some temple vans either way."

Michael bunched up the baseball cap in his hands. "I'll keep my head down."

"Keep your chin up. Less suspicious that way." August pointed to the left. "Follow that road and take the first right. It'll wind around, but you'll get into town. You know where to go after that?"

"Sort of. Does the road come out near the nursing home?"

"The nursing home is way across to the other side of town. Take a right when you get to the first paved street, then the first left. That should get you close to the building."

"Got it."

"Good luck!" August said as Michael climbed into the car.

Michael tossed his baseball cap in the back seat and drove off toward town.

⚝ 8 ⚝

Ten minutes later, Michael parked the car on the street a block away from the nursing home. He sat in the car for a moment before going inside. His heart was racing, although he didn't expect any trouble.

He practiced a wide grin in the rearview mirror before grabbing his grandmother's painting and stepping out.

"I'm just a normal temple nutcase like everyone else," he said with a phony grin.

He strolled toward the front door. Three elderly women sat out front around a small lawn table. A black-haired young nurse stood over them frowning and glaring down with her arms folded over her chest as if they'd done something wrong. Michael eyed each of them, but they didn't seem to notice him.

Michael walked into the nursing home without being stopped or even a suspicious glance from anyone. He passed the nurse's desk and turned down the hall toward his grandmother's room. An elderly man in a white outfit grinned at him from a wheelchair at the doorway to his right. No obstacles this time. The white clothes seemed to make a huge difference.

"Can I help you?" a woman's voice asked behind him only a few yards from his grandmother's room.

"I'm here to visit Mary Halverson," Michael said.

Glancing down at his white clothes and the painting in his hand, the nurse gave a soft smile. "She's right over this way."

The nurse escorted Michael into his grandmother's room, then turned away without saying another word. His grandmother was lying in nearly the same position as a few days earlier. She faced the window but turned and met his eyes when he walked in. She beamed and stretched her arms out toward him. Michael's heart warmed. She had truly recognized him for the first time since he'd arrived in Stone Hill.

"Michael!" she said. "What a surprise! What brings you out here?"

"I came to visit you, Grandma."

She glanced down at his clothes and smirked. "Those are your father's clothes!"

"I had to borrow them."

"That's okay," she said. "You look just as handsome as he did."

Michael lifted the painting, angling it to give her a better view. "I brought you something."

"What's that?"

"One of your paintings."

"Oh," she studied it and frowned, "that's not a good one."

Michael studied it for a moment. It was just as good as any he'd seen in an art store. "I like it."

"I've done better," she said. "Thank you for bringing it. What have you been up to?"

A flood of traumatic images passed through his mind. "Nothing."

She let out the same gentle laugh he remembered from his childhood. "You must have been up to something. I can see it in your eyes."

Michael shrugged and leaned the painting against the wall. A sketchpad sat next to his grandmother's waist, half obscured by the blanket that covered her.

"Have you been drawing?" Michael gestured to the sketchpad.

She glanced in the direction he was pointing, then strained to sit up as she dug her hand on the mattress. A moment later, a grin passed over her face, and she lifted the pad. She studied the drawing on the front page.

Chuckling, she flipped the sketchbook around so he could see what she had drawn. "Oh, I wouldn't call it my best work. Do you like it?"

Michael flipped through the pages of the sketchbook. Some of them were drawings of the forest behind her window, and some were sketches of people who most likely visited her in the nursing home by the way she drew their outfits.

On another page, an odd arrangement of crows circling in the air above a campfire formed a familiar pattern. The fire was surrounded by large stones like the Stonehenge monoliths in England. He recognized the pattern of the crows. It matched one of the symbols from the medallion.

"What is this supposed to be?" Michael showed her the drawing.

His grandmother leaned forward and studied it intensely. She rolled her eyes and shook her head. "I don't even remember drawing that."

On another page was a pencil sketch of a dark landscape littered with pieces of farm machinery beside a dilapidated shed. Clinging to the far edge of the shed was a strange swirling mass of black arms that looked more like claws. The upper section of a torso stuck out above the arms. It was roughly in the shape of a human, but its head was stretched out and misshapen as if his grandmother had bumped the table as she drew it. In the middle of the flowing black arms was the same medallion symbol.

"What is this, Grandma?" Michael asked, pointing to the symbol.

His grandmother looked at it and then looked away, losing her smile. "I don't like that one."

Michael studied it again. "Is this something you saw?"

She tapped the drawing with her finger and furrowed her brows. "Only in my nightmares. The dark horseman."

At that moment, the earth rumbled and his grandmother's hand jumped to the chrome railing at the edge of the bed.

"That's one of them now," she said.

"Do you know about the bessies, Grandma? The phantoms?"

His grandmother stared at him with wide eyes. He'd never seen her so fearful.

"We should run," she said.

"I won't let anything happen to you, Grandma."

His grandmother winced and held her hands over her stomach. "I don't feel so good."

"Should I call the nurse?"

She didn't answer. "That thing,"—she pointed at the drawing again—"I've seen it before." She nodded. "In my window."

"Your bedroom window at the house?"

His grandmother shook her head. "No, that one." She pointed at the window in the room.

The window looked out over the lake, and although there were trees blocking the view, the water was clearly visible between the branches and leaves. Nursing home residents strolled down by the edge of the water, each assisted by a nurse. A group of residents sat in white chairs and stared out over the water. A chain-link fence separated the residents from the lake.

His grandmother coughed again and pointed to the door. "Nurse."

Michael went to the door and called for a nurse. The same woman who had shown him the room entered and helped his grandmother.

"Are you okay, Grandma?" Michael asked.

His grandma shook her head. "No."

Michael wanted to help her, but the nurse laid her back on the bed. He said goodbye, but she began coughing again.

"She needs rest now," the nurse told him.

"I'll come back later, Grandma," Michael said.

She didn't respond. He backed out the door and kept his face down as he left the nursing home.

More residents stared at him on the way out. Their eyes were wide and their mouths hung open as he passed, as if they had witnessed some strange and horrible sight. Had they seen some of the same bizarre things he had seen? He hoped not.

Michael returned to the Cadillac. With his mind swirling about what his grandmother had said, he drove down the street that went past the temple church. As soon as he did, he realized his mistake. A crowd of temple followers were gathered outside the church, and a man stood at the front doors waving his arms as if commanding them to celebrate.

Michael glanced around for a place where he could make a U-turn. The crowd and other cars blocked his escape. A man in military fatigues guided him to park at the side of the road. He had no choice but to do as he was told and keep his face covered. Michael's heart raced. The temple followers soon surrounded his car as they gathered near the church.

A sound system had been set up at the corners of the church, and the same man shouted at the crowd, yelling more and more loudly as if to stir up enthusiasm. Michael made out some of his words, but the crowd's cheers and chants drowned out the man's speech. Michael kept the engine running and rolled down his window to listen.

"He's gonna need more faith than that," the man yelled.

Michael knew that voice. He squinted and stared at the man's face. It was Joey's dad. His focus was on another man near the front of the stage. Two guards stood alongside him, and he was either sitting down or bending forward. The crowd moved in around the man, but more guards stepped in and pushed the crowd away. Maybe somebody had fallen over or gotten hurt. The crowd chanted.

Michael stared down at his white clothes. He had gotten in and out of the nursing home easily wearing them. Just like everyone else in the crowd. It wouldn't be so difficult to move in closer and see what was going on.

Followers dressed in white were running past his car toward the church. He would blend in, no problem.

Michael stepped out of the car and walked toward the church. Hundreds pushed in around him. The only other time he'd been in such chaos was at a rock concert.

Joey's dad stepped forward and moved down into the crowd, lifting the arm of the man below Michael's eyesight. Michael walked closer, catching sight of the top of the man's gray head as he rose within the crowd. The man's face came into view. His neck. His upper chest.

Michael went numb. His jaw dropped open and a wave of panic rushed through him. He gasped in a breath and stumbled back.

Pastor John was waving at the crowd while Joey's dad helped him to stand. Pastor John said nothing, but that made little difference since the crowd was chanting in waves of frenzy from every direction.

Michael took another step back. Pastor John turned his head and stared directly at him. Not near him, not in his direction. Directly into Michael's eyes. They locked stares for a few seconds. Michael's heart pounded, and he spun around toward the car.

Pastor John was alive.

❧ 9 ❧

Pastor John stood out near the edge of the stage. As far out as he could without his followers grabbing at his ankles. The followers crowded in around the church, filling the street in front of the main door and the sidewalks for half a block.

The crowd chanted Pastor John's name, and he held Brother Brian's shoulders out of necessity rather than camaraderie. His legs strained to carry his weight as he stood before the crowd, waving to his supporters. Their eyes were as bright white as their clothes, and each smiled and called out to the pastor in a ceaseless roar of praise. He took a deep breath and basked in their adoration. All the praise was for him, and he deserved it.

Brother Brian leaned into Pastor John as if to whisper in his ear, holding out a microphone just far enough to make it available. "Are you ready to speak, sir?"

"Yes," Pastor John said, grabbing the microphone. The crowd hushed within seconds.

"I am overwhelmed by your love and praise. I am stronger than I have ever been, despite those who seek to hinder my holy temple, and I will never leave you, my dear Risen Temple. You are my people, and I stand here today to tell you that this is just the beginning. We are the light of the world and we will rise to save the earth from the phantoms that plague mankind." Pastor John paused and held back a cough. His body weakened, and he swayed even as Brother Brian stepped in to prop him up.

Pastor John held his head up. "You will get your reward, and together we will be victorious over the evil phantoms that terrorize the faithful of Stone Hill. The power that flows through me will shine and overcome every obstacle in our path. You are my enlightened followers. Are you with me?"

The crowd roared. Pastor John opened his mouth to repeat the words more loudly, but he froze. At the back edge of the crowd, the familiar face of Michael Halverson peered back at him. Michael was dressed in white, as were his followers, and he blended in well with everyone else. If it hadn't been for a beam of light flashing through the branches of the trees to land on his face, he might not have seen the boy. But there he was, staring back at the pastor. Michael turned his face away, but Pastor John kept Michael in his sights, watching him attempt to merge again with the crowd. The boy knew the location of the Dunamis. No escaping now.

Pastor John's followers shouted praises to him during the pause, and their faces remained glowing beacons of elation and pride.

Lowering the microphone, Pastor John turned to Brother Brian. "There is a boy at the back of the crowd. Arrest him."

The crowd's adoration drowned out his words.

Brother Brian moved in closer. "Excuse me, sir? I didn't hear that."

Pastor John spoke into Brother Brian's ear, repeating what he had said. Instead of words, only coughing erupted. He pointed into the crowd where Michael had been standing, but now the boy was moving away, pushing through the throngs of people. Pastor John focused on Michael, tracking his movements with his finger. Michael would not escape.

"That boy," Pastor John said again, raising his voice. "Stop that boy. Michael Halverson."

Brother Brian was looking in the right direction, but he wasn't saying or doing anything.

Pastor John coughed again and turned away from the crowd. Brother Brian stepped in and took the microphone. "Are you okay, sir?"

Pastor John shook his head.

Brother Brian spoke into the microphone. "Pastor John thanks and blesses each of you for being here. He has to get back to his holy work now."

Pastor John didn't wait for Brother Brian to finish talking before he lumbered slowly and agonizingly back toward the church steps.

No one should see him struggle to scale the steps into the church, but there wasn't time to hide. He had to get inside as soon as possible before Michael got away. Brother David had not solved the problem, so he would do it now without fail.

"Pastor John," Brother Brian called out to him, "you don't look well."

Pastor John coughed several times. "Get me inside."

Brother Brian ordered the crowd to disperse and aided Pastor John up the stairs. Guards swarmed around them, blocking the sight of the pastor's physical weakness from his followers. He made it up the stairs, but it took far too much time. Jolts of pain shot up his spine. He was stronger than the previous day, but now his strength had leveled off without the rejuvenation of the Dunamis. If he didn't get more, his body would deteriorate again.

Brother Brian supported Pastor John all the way to his office.

Pastor John shut the door on Brother Brian before either of them had even spoken another word. No time to talk. Michael was getting away.

He dropped into the chair behind his desk. The chatter from the crowd outside faded away as he sat alone in the darkness and closed his eyes. Leaning back in the chair, he focused his mind on the darkness.

His body was weak, but strong enough to deal with the failures of Brother David. In a few moments, he would shed the constraints of his physical self.

And where was Brother David on the day of his first speech after the resurrection? Nowhere to be found. Not a drop of Dunamis either, and the Michael Halverson boy was freely roaming the town. The list of suspected betrayers grew shorter.

He clenched his teeth at the distracting thought and opened his eyes for a moment. He would hold Brother David accountable, but that would need to wait until later.

Folding his arms across his lap, he closed his eyes again and pushed the failures and frustrations of the day aside. The skin of his neck tingled, and within the darkness the familiar singularity appeared. It spread over him, just as it had the night before, and he was eager to use this new ability to his advantage.

The creeping consumed him until his consciousness was drawn out and hung in the air above his physical body. He marveled at the black mist as his temporary body took shape, streaming off the black area of his skin, and swarming as it floated out the open window of his office. The black mist would appear as a wisp of smoke escaping up into the sky to anyone who saw it, but nobody appeared to notice. His guards were too busy clearing all the followers out of the streets and back to their homes.

Pastor John floated above the trees to the spot where Michael Halverson had stood earlier. No sign of him now. In his new shape, the pastor moved down the street, finding that he could do so quite rapidly. Much faster than the speed limit within the city. Perhaps in time he could travel to other towns.

He floated lower, near eye level, and observed each driver whisking past him. Some of his followers pointed him out as they stared up out of their windows. What did they think was floating above them? Maybe a swarm of flies, or just another messenger of evil. Another phantom to be feared.

He raced along each street, weaving in and out between the

trees. The wind had little effect on him, and if he had had more strength in his physical form, he would not have been concerned. But the excursion would take its toll on him, and he needed to hurry.

Out near the edge of town, he spotted a white Cadillac speeding across the country roads. It was instantly familiar. Artie Halverson's prized car rarely saw the light of day. The driver had to be Artie's grandson, Michael. No need to arrest Michael and drag him away with violence. He would merge with the boy and drive the car back into town, straight to the church. Back into his grasp.

Pastor John would have the Dunamis before the end of the day.

❧ 10 ❧

Michael weaved through the crowd toward his car, bumping into a large, red-haired woman.

"Oh, I'm so, so sorry," she said, staring into the sky as if lost in a daydream. Her two young children cuddled in next to her.

He hurried faster as the crowd thinned and more temple followers shot him odd stares. He kept his head down and covered his face by pretending to scratch his forehead.

He arrived at his car with his heart racing and jumped into the driver's seat. Revving the engine earned him more strange glances from a family dressed in white as they walked on the sidewalk next to his car. He inched along with the crowd as they walked back to their cars and homes. A line of vehicles ahead of him prevented a hasty escape.

A group of elderly women crossed the center of the street directly in front of his car. Back in Los Angeles, his friends would have honked and intimidated them, but now he left them plenty of space and even waved them forward with a bright smile when one of the old women looked back at him. Any of those women would have had him arrested if they knew what he had done to Pastor John days earlier.

"I killed him," Michael said to himself. "I know I did. I shot him."

Pastor John was there, up in front of the crowd with no sign of the violence he'd experienced. How was such a thing possible? Michael had shot Pastor John several times at least. How could he have survived? He had to be dead. No doubt about it. Still, there he was.

Michael had only once ever seen a dead body before arriving in Stone Hill. His own dad lying lifeless in his casket. Yet he knew death when he saw it. No way Pastor John could have walked away from those gunshots. Had Pastor John been wearing a bullet-proof vest? His chest had been covered in blood and his face white when they'd left him, and he'd shown no signs of that physical trauma up on the stage.

Michael didn't believe in miracles, but something pretty messed up was going on.

In any case, Pastor John had spotted him from the stage. Their eyes had locked. Pastor John had not only recognized him, but connected with him for a moment. Pastor John's intentions had been clear in his eyes. He wanted Michael dead.

The crowd dispersed and Michael took off through the streets back toward Lucas's farm. He maintained a painfully slow speed to avoid attention, though he longed to floor the accelerator and race away.

He turned down the same gravel road at the edge of town that led past his grandfather's house. A pair of white vans in the distance forced him to make a U-turn and head back into town. He drove ahead anyway, keeping his face in shadow as much as possible as he slowed past a van. From the corner of his eye, the passenger only gave him a brief glance. Maybe the white clothes deflected any suspicions.

He let out a deep breath and continued down the road, passing his grandfather's house without stopping. He needed to warn the others at Lucas's farm about Pastor John.

Something appeared behind him in the rearview mirror. A

black, shifting shape flying through the air several feet above the road. It was closing in on him. At first he thought it was a flock of birds from the way it floated and changed, but its movements were of a single animal. His heart beat harder as it gained on him. He sped faster.

The shape moved like a flying bessie, but that was ridiculous. Bessies were night creatures, and those things definitely couldn't fly, or else everyone would be in big trouble. It was now close enough for him to see it wasn't a bessie but some other strange animal. A swarm of insects? They moved as one swirling mass, expanding and contracting.

Michael's gaze again jumped from the road ahead to the thing in the rearview mirror. It was moving faster than his car. He accelerated, but slammed on the brakes to make the right turn ahead. Going around the corner, he nearly lost control as the car skidded to the edge of the ditch. The driver's side tires rumbled over the weeds and dirt at the edge of the road, threatening to pull the white Cadillac down the embankment, but Michael steered the car back onto the road.

Lucas's farm was only a short distance ahead, but the thing in Michael's mirror was only a car length away now. If he slowed down, it would be on him. His eyes darted from the mirror to the road ahead. The gravel's rumbling below the wheels drowned out the sound of his pounding heart.

The animal morphed into a giant insect with its mouth wide open as if to swallow Michael and his car. Its legs hung low like a giant wasp's with sharp black claws at the end, yet its wings didn't move. Its black torso glistened in the afternoon sun, but something else drew his attention. Several wide-open eyes surrounded the bulbous head, but didn't resemble any animal's eyes. They looked almost human, and they stared as if the thing knew him.

Without blinking, the thing approached his rear window. Its jaw snapped open and shut frantically as its claws clutched the back of the car and cracked against the rear window, fracturing the glass.

A chill swept through Michael's body, and he slammed on the brakes. The back of the Cadillac swung wide and whipped around so he faced the opposite direction. The thing toppled over the entire length of the car, banging against the roof and hood. Michael floored the gas pedal again, now heading in the opposite direction, spewing gravel behind him.

But the thing recovered and flew over the hood, racing out in front of him this time. It stopped a few car lengths ahead of him, and now the insect was gone. In its place stood his dad, hunched to the side and wavering in the middle of the road. Michael slammed on the brakes.

"Oh dear God," Michael cried.

His dad held his arms up over his face, moments before Michael was about to hit him. The car stopped only a few feet in front of him. It wasn't possible. His dad lowered his arms, revealing the blood, the smashed skull, the twisted spine. It was all there in full view. His dad reached toward him with his jaw hanging open, further than it should have, and teetered on the verge of collapse.

"I need help, Michael," his dad said, his voice nearly drowned out by the engine and the glass between them. "Please help me."

I'll save you, Dad. Michael instinctively reached for his cellphone in his pocket. He could call an ambulance. He could do something about it this time.

"Help me." His dad moved around to the driver's side window like a panhandler seeking handouts.

"I don't have my cellphone, Dad," Michael said, staring into his dad's eyes through the glass. "I'm sorry. I don't know what to do."

"Won't you help me?" his dad pleaded.

Something about his dad's eyes were wrong. It was a familiar stare, but the love was gone. Every voice in his head screamed for Michael to get out of there, yet he paused. Everything about the man was his dad, except the eyes.

"I can't," Michael said, locking the doors.

"You...did this to me," his dad growled in a low, guttural sound. "Your selfishness caused this, and you're still selfish. You don't love me. You never loved me, and let me tell you this..." His dad chuckled beneath a sound like someone drowning. "I never loved you. Never."

Michael's eyes watered. He must be dreaming. It couldn't be real. Maybe he had fallen asleep and had driven the car into the ditch. He shook his head, looked away, and back again.

His dad knocked on the glass with his knuckle. "Do you hear me, Michael? I never loved you."

"No," Michael said. "Not real. You're not real."

The face changed sharply, back into the head of the giant wasp. Then the body changed, and the thing lurched onto the hood of the car, slamming its insect claws against the glass. The car shook.

Michael threw the car in reverse, hoping the thing would fly forward so he could run it over this time. He backed away as fast as he could, but the wasp held on. The car weaved from side to side as he struggled to keep the car on the road. He'd only driven backwards once before, and that had ended with the back tires slamming into the curb. He didn't dare speed up.

The steering wheel jerked after hitting a pothole, and he shot off the road into the ditch. Michael slammed on the brakes moments before all four wheels had left the road. The wasp flew into the air and landed in the form of his dad again several feet ahead of him.

Michael threw the gear back into drive. The underside of the car scraped along the edge of the ditch as he broke free and took off straight toward his dad. He would run the thing down no matter what it looked like.

"You're not my dad," Michael said.

It grew a wide grin as he approached. A wide, familiar grin, like the Cheshire Cat.

Michael floored the accelerator. His dad flew upward out of sight.

Everything quieted, except for Michael's racing pulse.

A few seconds later, a black object swooped down in front of him. Not the dark cloud. Something else. No time to react. The windshield exploded, scattering glass over Michael's chest and arms. The sun visor shielded his face.

The black object shot through the car and smashed against the back seat.

Michael let off the gas and craned his head around.

A large dead crow lay behind him mangled and bloody, still fluttering. From the crow's mouth the black cloud streamed out and formed into Michael's dad again.

"I told you to stop!" his dad yelled.

Something burned in Michael's pocket, too hot to ignore. Something was on fire.

The car weaved as he dug out the medallion. There was no red glow, but blue sparks shot up from the medallion's ruby to the dark patch of skin near his shoulder. Electricity arced between them and through the air around his face.

The thing morphed back to its wasp form and tilted forward, sticking its face only inches from his own. All six of its baseball-sized black eyeballs reflected his wide-eyed face. Michael's foot left the accelerator, and the thing moved closer. Its head changed to a particle cloud as it circled his open mouth. He gritted his teeth together, but it moved toward his nostrils.

The medallion arced again, shooting a brilliant blue beam of electricity into his chest.

A cold chill passed through him before the wasp moved any closer. Something bubbled in his chest, almost as if insects were crawling out. A black cloud of jittering particles erupted from the spot on his skin. The cloud streamed out from below his chin and shot at the wasp.

Electricity forked from his black cloud and exploded in the air between it and the wasp. The surging energy reminded him of a thundercloud lightning storm.

The collision of his cloud with the wasp split Michael's awareness between driving and fighting the thing as it struggled to climb over the seat. He wouldn't let that thing get near him, whatever it was, wherever it had come from. Within one consciousness he was facing the wasp, and through his physical eyes he was struggling to keep the car on the road.

Michael's hands clenched the steering wheel as his cloud-self morphed and churned in the air like a phantasm. It flowed over the seats and swirled between his physical self and the wasp, creating a barrier that surged with blue and white veins of energy each time they clashed.

The thing struggled to circle around his cloud-self, buzzing like a thousand wasp nests, and threw itself at him as if testing his defenses. Again and again, it struck with a crack of electricity. It dived and rose, and with each collision it grew weaker. Its power drained a little at a time.

Michael shifted from desperately defending himself to lashing out, forming his cloud into claws that struck and clamped the wasp's limbs. It retreated against the rear seat until he had it pinned under his control. Intense arcs of blue light flashed as he came within inches of it. He stared into the blackness of its six giant eyes.

So familiar. He had seen this thing somewhere before. A nightmare?

Michael pushed through the electricity that sizzled between them, reaching out his consciousness further to know the thing. To know its fears and thoughts and its name. It had a name. Some familiar image dangled at the edge of his awareness. And it knew him.

A little further.

A massive blue arc of electricity flared. The wasp broke away, writhing in his grasp until it broke free and flew out the shattered windshield. It shot off down the road, back toward town.

Michael watched it escape from his rearview mirror, slowing the car and coming to a stop on the side of the road. His hands trembled, and his heart pounded.

His cloud-self calmed and swirled back into his chest, arcing a bolt of blue light one final time before the strange sensation of bugs crawling through his chest tapered off. He wrapped his arms over his chest as chills spread through him. Nausea swelled up in his stomach. He opened the driver's side door and prepared to throw up, but after a few minutes, his stomach settled.

His neck itched. He went to scratch it and pulled back fingertips covered in blood.

Nobody would believe this.

❧ I I ❧

Michael's pulse still raced as he turned into Derek's farm.
He steered the car further into the driveway and parked
the car behind the house, so it wouldn't be seen from the road.
The monster was gone, but he couldn't help peering over his
shoulder every minute. He couldn't shake the sense that it was
still out there watching him from a distance.

The cuts around his neck where the shards of windshield
glass struck him stopped bleeding, but the wounds still stung.

He crossed the lawn toward the barn, clutching the medallion in his hand. Someone watched him from the house.

Before Michael even entered the barn, the side door opened
and Rebecca hurried out with Lucas and Joey. They hurried over
to his side.

"My gosh, Michael," Rebecca asked. "What happened?"

"I'm not sure," Michael said. "Something attacked me."

"A phantom?" Rebecca asked.

"Not a bessie. Something else. It's hard to describe."

"Can we take him inside the house?" Rebecca asked Lucas.

Lucas shook his head. "Derek doesn't let anybody go in
there. Not even for emergencies."

"But he's bleeding," Rebecca said.

"Can't do it," Lucas said. "Get him into the hideout. We have some medicine down there."

Michael followed them into the hideout. Rebecca led him straight to the bathroom. Joey and Lucas watched from the doorway as Rebecca cleaned Michael up.

"You alright, man?" Joey asked.

Michael shook his head. "It was the weirdest thing. A dark creature attacked me. Not a bessie this time."

Michael took off his suit coat. His white shirt was no use anymore, but the blood hadn't touched the coat. He winced when he saw himself in the mirror.

Rebecca helped clean the scratches and cuts with some antiseptic Lucas provided. "It's not as bad as it looks."

"Are you sure it wasn't a wild animal?" Lucas asked. "We got a lot of wild animals here in Minnesota."

"This happened,"—Michael gestured to his neck—"because a crow smashed through my windshield. But the thing that attacked me was something else. Like a swarm of flies. It was like a phantom, but it flew through the air." He looked at Rebecca. "A *real* phantom. It changed shape, starting out as a swarm of particles in the air, but when it got close, it turned into a massive flying bug with big disgusting eyes. For a little while it changed its shape...into my dad. It looked just like him. How would it know what my dad looked like?"

Everyone stared at him in confusion.

"That's not the worst of it," Michael said. "I have some horrible news. Pastor John is still alive. I saw him up on a stage in front of the church."

"Are you kidding me?" Joey asked with wide eyes.

Rebecca's jaw dropped open. "Alive? How?"

"No joke. He's alive, and he appeared to be fine. He even gave a speech to the crowd. I don't know how, after what we did to him."

"Are you sure it was him?" Rebecca stopped cleaning Michael's wounds.

Michael nodded. "Positive."

"That's really messed up," Joey said.

"The thing that attacked me, I don't think it followed me back here. I wouldn't have come back unless I knew for sure."

"Don't you worry about us," Lucas said. "We've got all kinds of weapons here, and we know how to use them."

Michael held up the medallion again and studied it. "The medallion did something to stop the attack. But it wasn't the glow that did it. Something else happened. It's hard to explain. Something like electricity shot out of it into my chest, up where I got injured in the tunnels."

"Cool!" Joey said.

"Did you get electrocuted?" Rebecca asked.

Michael shook his head. "It passed through me. But something else happened. Some kind of dark ghost reached out from my patch of black skin and protected me from the bug thing."

Joey raised his eyebrows. "Yeah, man, that's kind of weird."

"I know," Michael pulled back the corner of his shirt, showing them the edge of the dark spot near his shoulder. "It's spreading. Not a lot, but it didn't go this high before."

"Should we get a doctor to look at it?" Rebecca asked.

"What doctor?" Michael said. "I can't see any doctors in this town. What would he say about it, anyway? He'd think I was crazy if I told him what had happened."

"Can I look at that?" Lucas asked, gesturing at the medallion in Michael's hands.

Michael gave it to him. Lucas studied it, holding it up close to his eyes, flipping it over and concentrating on the markings on the back. "I don't see any kind of energy source. Maybe some electricity passed through your car while you were holding this. A wiring problem with the car."

Michael shook his head. "I don't think the power came from the car. It came from the medallion. I'm sure of it."

"That thing saved our asses in the tunnels," Joey said. "It lights up when bessies are around."

"Interesting." Lucas studied the medallion again. "You know what the symbols on the back mean?"

"Not really," Michael said, "but the markings matched some drawings on the temple walls below the church. My grandfather found this down there years ago. That's where all this began, according to him."

"We should find out what this thing is."

"I wish I could tell you more."

Rebecca finished cleaning Michael's wounds as best she could and applied some bandages over the cuts. "You'll need a new shirt. Give me the keys. I'll run out to the car and grab our suitcases."

"I'll go with you," Joey said.

Michael handed her the keys and she left with Joey a moment later.

"Let me do some investigating," Lucas said, leading Michael back out into the main room.

Michael sat on the couch beside August and Twyla as they played video games while Lucas sat at a small desk in the corner of the room. He started browsing the Internet and typing in various words in the search bar. Some pictures of ancient tools and treasures came up on the screen.

August turned to Michael and held out the game's controller. "You want to play for a while?"

"No, thanks," Michael said. "What's your name again?"

"August," he said. "I bet you can't guess when I was born."

"Um, August?"

"Nope! I was born in October," August laughed. "I was named August because it was my great grandfather's name. Pretty crazy, eh?"

Michael laughed once.

August narrowed his eyes and formed a wide grin, gesturing toward where Rebecca had just left. "She's your girlfriend?"

The question surprised Michael. His face grew warm. "My girl friend," he clarified. "Not my girlfriend."

"Too bad for you," August said. "She's cute."

Michael rolled his eyes. "It's complicated. Where do you live?"

"In the house down the road," August answered. "Not far."

"You just hang out here?"

"Yeah, this place has everything I need. Electricity and internet."

"You don't even have power?"

"Nope. No power. No parents. The house is empty. My parents got arrested by the temple a few months ago. I haven't seen them since then. Lucas and Derek take good care of me. Derek's kind of rough sometimes, but he's awesome to us."

Michael saw the seriousness in the boy's face.

"So you live here with Lucas?"

"No, not enough room down here, otherwise I would. I still sleep at my house, but it gets pretty scary at night. It's so quiet. I can hear everything. I'm not sure what I'll do when it gets cold outside. But we come over to this place a lot and hang out. Lucas lives down here alone. Derek keeps an eye on us from the house. He's twenty-one, and that used to be his parents' house, but they disappeared about a year ago. It's no big deal if we all hang out here. He works in town at the drugstore and pretends to be one of those temple people so they leave him alone."

"So it's like a party house," Michael said.

Grim chuckled. "Sort of, but none of us drink, if you can believe that."

"We find other ways to amuse ourselves," Twyla said. "We've got video games, TVs, access to the Internet, sort of, and the temple doesn't know about any of it. They've searched the place a few times, but it's well hidden and we're able to conceal it fast if we need to. We do all right."

"Where did you get that scar?" Grim asked Michael.

Michael followed Grim's eyes to his arm and the scar from the car accident a year earlier. "I was in an accident with my dad.

I was driving, and I crashed when I looked down at my cell-phone. It was all my fault. I guess, in a way, I killed my dad."

"Whoa," August said. "Sorry to hear that."

"No worries," Michael said. If anyone had asked him about the accident a couple of weeks earlier he wouldn't have said a word to anyone except his closest friends, but the events of the past week had changed him. Still, nothing could change the fact that it was his fault. He was to blame for his dad's death. Even the wasp-thing knew it.

Lucas turned from the computer with a bright expression on his face, as if he had discovered the cure for cancer.

"You said your grandfather found this under the church?" he asked.

"A few years ago," Michael said. "You find something interesting?"

"Very. The symbols indicate this might have had something to do with alchemy. Do you know anything about that?"

"I've heard of it."

"It's an ancient science," Lucas said. "Alchemists tried to turn lead into gold. Like mad scientists of their day. Some called them wizards, or accused them of witchcraft."

"So the medallion is from devil worshippers?"

"Not at all. The church back then accused alchemists of that, but their focus was more science based, although back then science and religion were tied to each other. Alchemists also tried to find a chemical that would eradicate all the world's diseases and stop the aging process. Eternal life."

Michael's breath paused. The Dunamis flashed through his mind. "Why would alchemists be in Stone Hill?"

"Beats me," Lucas said. "They were a secretive group, but it makes sense they worked in underground hidden tunnels. They recorded much of their research using codes and symbols as opposed to regular text, so they could evade detection from religious leaders. All of this was heavy shit back then. It still is, in a way."

Lucas studied the medallion again.

"Did the alchemists create monsters or anything like that?" Michael asked.

Lucas stared with his brows furrowed at Michael. "Not that I know of. Are you talking about the squids? I have my theory about where those come from."

"From the depths of hell!" August mocked Pastor John's screeching voice.

"I think there's a chemical spill or a scientific experiment gone awry below the church," Twyla said. "Maybe the government has something to do with it."

"We didn't see anything like that down there," Michael said. "Nothing to do with the government."

"Don't rule it out," she said. "Our government hides alien bodies at Area 51. You heard about that, right? It's all true."

Michael shrugged. "Maybe."

"You don't believe me," Twyla said, "but it's true. And I think the government's behind everything weird that's happened in this town too. How else can you explain the squids?"

"We saw a lot of awful things," Michael said. "The bessies, you call them squids, take people and animals down to another creature, a Leviathan that I *thought* I killed, but now I'm not so sure. I thought the Leviathan was causing the earthquakes, but they're still happening. There is definitely some weird shit going on down there, but I doubt it's a scientific experiment."

Twyla shook her head. "The government's behind it. Their secret technology is way beyond what they tell us."

"Well, we didn't see anything resembling government property down there."

"Of course, you didn't. They disguise it to look like something else."

"We only found a lot of ancient religious stuff, like the treasures you'd find in an Egyptian tomb."

"Alchemy goes way back to its origin in Egypt with the god Thoth, so maybe there's a connection. It was studied in Greece too, and throughout the centuries. Did you see any Greek statues or symbols?"

"Not that I remember, but I didn't understand most of it. And I was told that Pastor John has most of the artifacts they found in his house. I wish I could take you down into the tunnels and show you all the pictures on the walls. You'd be amazed."

Lucas's eyes sparkled and a wide grin spread across his face. "I'd love to check out the tunnels with you, but I doubt we'll ever get the chance."

Michael winced and he shook his head. "I don't recommend going down there. Ever. At least not without the medallion to protect you," Michael said. "Bessies are everywhere. It's very dangerous."

"We can handle it," Twyla said. "We can handle the squids, and we can handle the cult. Why do you call them bessies, anyway?"

"That's what my grandfather calls them."

"I like that. We call them squids, because they slink around like a giant squid."

"This larger symbol on the back," Lucas said, leaning toward Michael to show him the marking. "I looked it up. It means door or opening."

"We only used the medallion to scare off the bessies. It glows bright red when they're around, and it burns their skin if the light touches them."

Lucas didn't look up from the medallion. "Did you try to use it to open a door down there?"

"I was too scared to try anything," Michael said. "We only wanted to get out of there alive, along with my grandfather and Rebecca's mom. I saw that symbol on a big map on the wall of the temple."

"These smaller symbols represent the different planets. Each planet represents a different metal, like the Sun is gold, Mars is iron, Saturn is lead. There are also references to constellations.

Alchemists used astrology to time their experiments. The main gist of their philosophy was that everything in the universe is connected."

Michael stared at the symbols Lucas had pointed out. "That's amazing."

"I agree," Lucas said. "This thing is priceless. Don't lose it."

"I won't." Michael accepted it back from Lucas.

"If you return to the tunnels," Lucas said, "you should take it to that place on the map and see what it does, if anything."

Michael winced. "I never want to go down there again."

Footsteps stomped down the cement steps into the hideout.

"Michael!" Joey burst in with wide eyes. "Bex took off with the car! There's a fire across the field, over by your house."

❧ 12 ❧

Michael rushed out the door with Joey and August following behind. They passed through the barn and out across the lawn toward the main road. Michael's suitcase lay on the gravel along with Joey's and Rebecca's suitcases. A cloud of dust still hung in the air over the gravel where Rebecca must have taken off. Michael glimpsed the white Cadillac through the dust up the road; the trunk was wide open, bobbing up and down as the car bumped over the dips in the road.

A plume of smoke rose above the trees in the direction of his grandfather's house. It could have been a brush fire, or someone else's house, or a car fire. In his heart, he knew the truth.

Michael looked at Joey. "What the hell happened?"

"She saw the fire and just took off."

"Why didn't you stop her?" Michael asked, taking a step toward Joey.

"Don't get in my face," Joey said. "She just took off all of a sudden."

"Well, what are we going to do now? We don't have a car to go after her."

August took a step forward. "I could drive you. I can drive

the Camaro. It's mine, anyway. Or at least it's my dad's, so I guess that means it's mine now."

Michael stared at August's Pokemon T-shirt. "Are you old enough to drive?"

"Old enough to see over the steering wheel. I'll drive you if you want."

Michael looked back at Joey who was pacing back and forth. "All right, but I should drive."

"No way! I don't let anybody drive the Camaro. Lucas can borrow it, but only in a *real* emergency. That's the rule."

"Fine, let's go. Do you have to let Derek know where you're going?"

August shook his head. "No, he's watching us now. He'll see that I'm taking the Camaro."

Michael looked back at the house as someone pulled a section of blinds covering the window at the far right. He didn't see a face, but the blinds moved slightly.

"Wait here," August said, darting off to the garage.

An engine roared a minute later, followed by an older black Camaro backing out. It stopped at the end of the driveway. It must have been decades old, but it was in great condition.

Michael opened the passenger side and jumped into the back seat, knowing that Joey would moan and groan about having to squeeze in there.

"What's going on?" Joey asked with the door hanging open. "Why aren't you getting in the driver's seat?"

"It's his car," Michael said. "Hop in."

Joey climbed into the passenger seat.

"Hand me that cushion from the back," August said to Michael.

Michael handed it forward.

"How old are you, kid?" Joey asked.

August stuffed the cushion beneath himself, rising another couple of inches, and checked the angle of the mirrors. "Thirteen."

Joey smirked. "Do you know how to drive this thing? Maybe I should sit there."

"Everybody wants to drive my car." August laughed. "*Nobody* drives my Camaro." He took off out of the driveway. "Lead the way."

Michael pointed toward his grandfather's house. "Follow the smoke."

The engine rumbled as August sped down the gravel road. After turning left at the T-junction in the road, they passed a white van and Michael hid his face. His heart raced, and he resisted the urge to glance back after they drove by.

Joey looked in the side mirror from the front seat. "They're not following us. They know better than to mess with me."

A couple of minutes later, his grandparents' house appeared up ahead. The smoke was at least nearby.

"Something bad happened," Michael said.

"Don't jump to conclusions," Joey said. "It's probably not a big fire. The fire trucks haven't even arrived yet."

The house came into view. It was worse than Michael imagined. The flames reached up to the second floor and shot out the windows as something inside ignited. The smoke formed a black tower that stretched to the white clouds above. Joey was right. The fire trucks had not yet arrived, but two white vans were parked near the end of the driveway, and his grandfather's white Cadillac was blocked in.

Michael's pulse pounded in his ears. "Hurry up."

August revved the engine and the car shot faster.

Temple guards dragged Rebecca from the house as she kicked and fought in their arms. They threw her into the back of one van as if they were executing some fancy SWAT team-rescue mission. Audrey ran toward Rebecca, but the guards knocked her back to the ground.

"They got Bex!" Joey shouted.

August raced faster toward the house. As the Camero approached, the white vans sped off toward town.

The house erupted into bigger flames as they approached it. They couldn't let the temple take Rebecca away, but Michael's grandfather might need help too. Michael opened his mouth to tell August to stop the car at the driveway, but then saw his grandfather walk out to Audrey as she stood up. No time to stop now, they had to help Rebecca.

"We can't let them take her," Michael said.

"How are we going to stop them?" August asked as the car thumped hard across a pothole in the road. "We don't have any weapons. They'll just grab us too."

"Fuck those guys!" Joey yelled.

August sped faster and approached the white vans. The car rumbled and weaved near a ditch as August struggled to keep it straight on the road. The boy jerked the steering wheel to the side and Michael was sure they would go off and smash into the field.

The white vans turned right at the end of the road and made a sharp left into the driveway of a scenic farm with a massive white fence surrounding its backyard.

"They're going to The Farm," August said. "I know where they're taking her."

"Michael, we should turn around," Joey said.

The two white vans passed through a gate into The Farm. Further down the road, in the distance, another white van was approaching.

August stared back at Michael with wide eyes. "What should we do?"

"Go back to my grandfather's house," Michael said, "and go as fast as you can."

August spun the car around and once again Michael believed they were about to fly off the road and flip over. But August kept the Camaro out of the ditch and flew back to the house.

They went over a hill and saw that the fire trucks had not yet arrived to put out the flames. At least there weren't any white vans around, and nobody had followed them from town.

August pulled up behind the white Cadillac in the driveway. Michael's grandfather and Audrey stared at the car cautiously as they parked, but they walked over after Joey rolled down the window and waved.

Before the car came to a complete stop, Joey had jumped out of the passenger seat and Michael shot out right behind him. They ran to the two adults. His grandfather was hunched over with a blanket wrapped around him. He was dressed in his pajamas.

"Are you okay?" Michael and Joey asked almost in unison.

His grandfather nodded.

"Yes," Audrey said. "I don't know what's taking the fire trucks so long. We called them over fifteen minutes ago."

"They won't bring out the fire trucks for us," his grandfather said. "Why put out a fire they want to burn?"

Michael hurried around to the back where the smoke and fire weren't as bad and considered running into the house to grab some things. There were some blankets and pillows laying in a pile on the steps. A cardboard box lay on the ground near the bottom step.

Michael opened the back door and was about to go inside, but his grandfather came around the side with Audrey.

"Don't go in there," his grandfather called out, and then coughed.

"It's too late," Audrey said. "We are alive. That's the important thing."

His grandfather nodded.

The door handle was hot to the touch, and Michael let go and backed away. His heart sank as he walked down the steps and held his grandfather in his arms.

"Don't you worry about us," his grandfather said.

"Did you see where they took her?" Audrey asked.

"The kid who drove us here said something about a farm," Michael told her.

Joey nodded. "That's what they call it. The Farm. I've been in there a bunch of times with my dad. It's like a mini concentration camp."

"Well, we've got to get her out of there," Michael said.

"Easier said than done," Joey said. "It's like a little prison. Nobody gets out of there."

"We'll get her out," Michael said.

❦ 13 ❦

Brother Jacob helped Pastor John out of the car and into the house, where his housekeeper had already prepared lunch. Everything was laid out on the table, but Pastor John was still nauseous from the creeping. He turned his face away from the food. Just the sight of it made his stomach churn.

"Help me upstairs," Pastor John groaned.

Brother Jacob helped him climb each step toward his bedroom.

"Is that you?" Bertha asked in a harsh tone from her bedroom's open door. "I need water. Where have you been? I'm withering up in here."

Pastor John grumbled. What was he supposed to do about it? He could barely stand himself.

His legs grew weaker with each step. He was panting by the time he reached the top of the stairs. He passed his bedroom and stepped further down the hall to Bertha's room, across from his own.

Bertha was in bed as always, facing away from the door. A glass jar of black liquid sat on the nightstand next to her. The last of the Dunamis. Pastor John estimated there to be less than one pint left.

It didn't make sense. Brother David should have retrieved gallons of Dunamis from the tunnels by that time. Those three kids knew the location of the source. He would take care of the problem himself if he weren't so weak. Even with the help of his best guards, he didn't think he would make it. Brother David had to come through for him or Pastor John would end up like Bertha, gasping for air and just waiting for death to arrive.

He stood in the doorway of Bertha's bedroom and stared at her. The bed sheets slowly rose and fell with each breath. She coughed and shuddered.

"Leave us," he said to Brother Jacob, waving his hand.

Pastor John stood silently until Brother Jacob had left through the front door.

"I'm dying," Pastor John told Bertha.

"I'm dying too. Don't you see that?" she said. "I need more."

"You have the last of it."

"I'll be dead by morning." Bertha's screechy voice faded off.

Maybe she would be dead by morning, just like she'd said. And she would take every drop of Dunamis with her to the grave. He eyed the black liquid on her nightstand. He could easily take half and the results would be the same.

"You sound better now," he said.

"Bullshit. Do I look better?" she replied. "I have something to tell you. We won't be getting anymore Dunamis from him ever again. Brother David betrayed you. When I saved your life in the gymnasium,—and remember it was *me* who saved you, not that horrible man—he refused to hand over any Dunamis to save you. He's a traitor. He wanted you to die."

"Nonsense," he said without confidence. "Brother David is the most loyal of my followers."

Bertha cackled. "You're a fool. You'd be dead right now if it weren't for me."

Pastor John glanced back at the Dunamis on the nightstand. How much of the precious liquid had she gone through over the last few months? Enough to perform a thousand miracles. Without Bertha consuming every last drop, he'd be a powerful leader at that moment.

"You're mistaken. I've known Brother David since he was a child. He's a disappointment, but he wouldn't betray me. He's like a younger brother."

"You're blind. Brother David wants you dead. I tried to take the Dunamis during your resurrection, but he threatened me. He said he would never waste another drop of Dunamis on me. He wanted it all for himself. Brother David never intended to bring you back to life. He said I would never have another drop of it, and then he pulled the bottle out of my hands like a brute. An awful brute. I'm sure he has grand visions of taking over the temple. I can see it in his eyes. That awful man is a traitor."

"I don't believe you," Pastor John said, but he wasn't so sure. All the circumstantial evidence pointed to Brother David, but it was impossible to accept. How could he believe someone so trusted and loved might betray him? There must be some misunderstanding.

Bertha grunted. "You're a damn fool. You've always disappointed me, you know that?"

Pastor John propped himself up against the wall as his eyesight swirled. He couldn't stand it any longer. He trudged back to his bedroom and dropped into bed. How many more times would he have the strength to get up?

He dug himself in under the blankets without taking off his clothes. Unbuttoning the top of his shirt, he pulled aside his undershirt to reveal the blackness that had grown across his skin. It had spread up to his neck, inching further with each passing hour. By morning it might envelop his face and head. The strange skin was darker than any black he'd ever seen. The color of the Dunamis, and the color of the bessies.

Bertha's faint voice came through the air. "You'll never get another drop."

He sneered. "Maybe not."

Was it realistic to believe Brother David had said that to her? Maybe, but in any case, it didn't matter. The idea of refusing Bertha her life-saving Dunamis intrigued him. She would die no matter what happened. No matter how many gallons of the miracle liquid she absorbed into her wound, she would die. Nobody could save her. The Dunamis on her nightstand would provide two days' strength for him to get things straightened out. If she took it, they were both doomed.

Never get another drop. Smartest thing Brother David had ever said.

Pastor John strained to stand, and he knew he might never have the strength again unless he took care of this one thing. Only one problem stood in his way. *Got to take care of things.*

He opened the drawer in his nightstand and took out the loaded .38 pistol. His head ached, and he wobbled as he clung to the wall, making his way out of his room and over to Bertha's. He should have done this a long time ago. Things would've been much easier.

Bertha was still facing away from him when he walked in.

"I still don't have my water." Bertha said with disdain.

He was silent. It was a matter of mercy, really. Another sacrifice for the temple.

He gripped the side of her nightstand and leaned forward as he raised the gun toward her head and pulled the trigger. The blast toppled him backwards to the ground, knocking his head against the wall. His vision flooded with hundreds of twinkling stars just like in the cartoons of his childhood. Silence filled his ears as pain throbbed in his head.

He crawled forward, leaving the pistol lay on the floor next to him as he stretched his arm toward the glass jar of Dunamis on Bertha's nightstand. With trembling hands he grabbed it and took it to his lips. The smell pushed up his nostrils, and nausea swept over him. He guzzled the black liquid and forced himself not to vomit. After years of using it, the disgusting smell and taste still demanded great control over his senses.

The Dunamis slid down his dry throat as if he were swallowing raw oysters. He tipped the jar upside down and emptied the last of the Dunamis into his gaping mouth.

"Not another drop."

❧ 14 ❧

Michael stood beside his grandfather, helping to prop him up with one arm around his back. Audrey had wrapped him in a bed sheet and leaned into him as she comforted him too. Audrey's eyes, red and wet, reflected the flickering of the fire's rampage.

They watched the fire burn, expecting fire trucks to appear at any moment. The flames and smoke spread from window to window. The smoke was thick and plumed high into the sky. Michael stared into it. His face warmed, and he clenched his teeth as rage swelled inside his chest. They had lost so many things in the fire. Nothing he could do now. His grandmother's paintings were gone. All the family photos were gone. All the memories were burning.

"Where will you stay, Grandpa?" Michael asked.

"You can stay with me," Audrey said, sniffing and wiping her eyes.

"Thank you, Audrey," his grandfather said. "I might have to take you up on that offer. Thank heavens your grandmother is in the nursing home. At least she didn't see this nightmare."

Audrey wept into his grandfather's shoulder. "I can't stand it anymore."

"We'll get through it," his grandfather said.

"You're stronger than I am."

They stood in silence for a minute watching the flames crackle and the smoke billow higher into the sky.

"You boys should get going," his grandfather said. "We can't do anything right now, and I know that you're all here because of what happened to Rebecca. It won't do us any good if you all end up dragged away in a white van."

"I'm sure Derek would let you stay at his place," August said to Michael and Joey. "You can stay at my house too, but there's no water or electricity."

"Get going then," his grandfather said. "Before the white vans come back."

"I know you all care about Rebecca," Audrey said, "but please don't do anything foolish. I mean, don't run in there with your guns blazing or any craziness like that. We'll figure out something."

His grandfather's legs were trembling.

"I don't want to leave you, Grandpa," Michael said.

"I'll take care of him," Audrey said. "Don't you worry about him. Just get to safety now."

They gave a last hug goodbye and took off in August's Camaro, leaving Audrey and his grandfather standing in the driveway.

They took the same road back to Derek's house. It was odd not to see any white vans this time. Maybe they were watching their car from a distance. Michael scanned the horizon, keeping an eye out for spots of white against the thick green trees. The smell of smoke lingered in his nose, and Michael turned around in the backseat as they raced away. The thick black smoke rose far above them, and no doubt everyone in town was aware someone's house was on fire. Fire truck sirens finally blared far in the distance.

"The trucks are running a little late today," Michael said sarcastically. "Why even bother to show up?"

"It's bullshit," Joey said.

"This whole town is evil," August said.

They returned to Derek's farm and August parked the Camaro in the garage. As they crossed the lawn behind Derek's house, the blinds in the corner of one of the back windows rose and fell again.

"Should we talk to Derek?" Michael asked.

"About what?" August asked.

"About staying here," Michael said.

"He won't mind. He hates the temple. But Lucas is the one you should ask. There's not much room down there. Only one extra twin bed, and the couch."

Michael glanced back at the house again. "Why doesn't Derek come out with you guys?"

"He's kind of paranoid," August answered. "I don't blame him. He stays in his house to keep an eye on things. I think he jumps around from room to room and watches out his windows. That's just how he is."

They walked through the barn and into the hideout.

As they were going down the stairs, Joey glanced over at Michael. "I don't know about you, man, but I can't just sit around doing nothing while Bex is in trouble."

"I'm not going to sit around either," Michael said. "Let's think about this for a minute. Audrey is right. We can't run in there and start shooting."

"What's wrong with that?" Joey said with a wild expression on his face. He laughed. "Just kidding, man. My dad is one of them. I'm ashamed to say it."

"Do you think he would help us?"

Joey smirked. "No chance. My dad won't even talk to me anymore. He's hardcore."

Anger welled up inside Michael. He pictured himself charging back into town to rescue Rebecca from wherever they were holding her hostage. He envisioned some wild heroic effort that involved lots of firepower and explosions. But the only weapons he had now were those in his backpack and whatever was left at Audrey's house. And maybe they would burn her house too.

"Do you think they'll kill her?" Michael asked Joey.

Joey shrugged. "Who knows what they'll do? They're kind of whacked out, but I'm betting they took her to The Farm."

"What would they do to her at The Farm?"

"Either brainwash her or sacrifice her. They'd make an example of her."

"What do you mean sacrifice?" Michael asked.

"They'd feed her to the bessies. But they wouldn't do that until it gets dark."

"So we have to get her out today."

"I'll go in there with you and bust some ass, but what's your plan? It ain't easy to get in there, much less getting out. My dad took me there a few times and it's messed up. People screaming, kids crying, and the temple leaders always got a big grin on their face as if everything were sweet and rosy."

"They're probably waiting for us to rush in to get her back so they can get us too."

"Well, we *did* kill their leader. What did Pastor John look like when you saw him?"

"I couldn't see his face very well," Michael said. "He was wearing a hoodie over his head."

"I bet he looks like a zombie now under his clothes. Pastor Undead. That's some twisted shit."

They entered the main living area where Twyla and Grim were playing video games.

"What's going on?" Twyla asked, pausing the video game. Her eyes jumped between their faces.

"They took Rebecca," Michael said.

Twyla's eyes widened. "Why would they take her?"

"They probably want us," Michael said. "Revenge for killing Pastor John. They've been trying to find us for the last couple of days. We were hiding out in my grandfather's basement, but now they burned his house down. If we had been down there today, maybe we wouldn't have gotten out alive."

"I'm not surprised," Grim said without looking away from the video game. "That's how they operate."

"What will you do now?" Twyla asked.

"Well, I don't plan on sitting around playing video games all day," Michael said.

"Harsh," Grim said. "Is that what you think of us? We're just a bunch of lazy kids playing video games? Do you have any idea what we've been through?"

"Do you have any idea what *we've* been through?"

"Settle down, man." Joey rested his hand on Michael's back.

"I can't settle down," Michael said. "Why didn't you stop her from leaving?"

"Whoa, it's not my fault," Joey said as his eyes narrowed. "Be careful what you say now. I want her back as much as you do, probably more."

Lucas, who'd been absent from the room until that moment, walked out from the bedroom. "If the temple took your friend, her mind will be mush when they're done with her. She won't be the same. Maybe it's possible to get her out of there before they do too much damage, but you can't try to get her out alone. You'll need help."

"What are you thinking?" Joey asked.

"Maybe," Lucas said, walking to Michael's side with his cell phone out, "we can get her out, but first I need you to see something I found on the Internet about that medallion of yours."

Michael took a deep breath. "What did you find?"

"Look at this." Lucas held up his phone.

The screen displayed a picture of an ancient stone wall, similar to the construction in the temple below the church. There were designs and symbols, similar to the style of the ones in the temple, but nothing made sense until Michael saw a symbol near the bottom of the screen. It was the same as the one on the back of the medallion.

"Okay," Michael said and glanced back at Lucas.

"Your medallion might keep away the bessies, but maybe it does something else too. Some of those symbols are alchemist symbols," Lucas said pointing to one of the designs on the back of the medallion. "You have the symbol for phosphorus here, which alchemists believed was light trapped inside of matter. They also used it to represent the spirit. And then you have this symbol which seems to be from the old Knights Templar, but the alchemists used it to represent the earth. But I think the symbol in the center is the most important. It's two symbols combined. The inner one is brimstone and the outer one is fire."

"So what does all that mean?" Michael asked.

"You said you saw this symbol on a map under the church, right?" Lucas asked.

"On the temple wall."

"I think if you bring this medallion to the location of the symbol on the map, you will find something. Or at least its purpose will make sense. And if you say this medallion lights up when the squids are around, to me that's represented by the phosphorus symbol, which is smaller than the main symbol. Whatever happens to the squids because of this thing, this main symbol shows that it can do a whole lot more, or lead to something huge. Maybe treasure, or maybe a tomb, or maybe we open Pandora's Box and it ends up killing everybody. But whatever it is, it's big."

❧ 15 ❧

"**I**s she under?" Brother David asked Nurse Betty as she packed up to leave the room.

"She'll be under for the rest of the evening."

Brother David walked over and sat next to Rebecca at the table. "Where are your friends?"

Rebecca groaned. Her eyes were partially open and her eyelids fluttered as if in a dream state. Still, she didn't answer the question. Maybe the nurse had given her too much of the drug.

"Rebecca, do you understand what I'm asking?"

"Yes," she responded.

"Where are your friends? Michael and Joey. Give me their locations."

Rebecca muttered and turned her face away from Brother David.

He reached out and grabbed her jaw, thrusting her face back toward him. "You will answer my questions. Where are your friends?"

"I..." Rebecca shook her head.

Brother David took a deep breath in, releasing the air through clenched teeth. He released her jaw. "Let me start with an easier question. Would you like to see your mother again?"

"Yes," Rebecca answered.

"Good. Would you like to see your father again?"

Rebecca's mouth dropped open and her eyes widened a little. She trembled and looked into his eyes, although her gaze drifted. She nodded.

"That's better," Brother David said. "Now I've got your attention. Answer my questions and all kinds of wonderful things will happen. Where are your friends? I need their help. The temple needs their help. You were such a wonderful helper girl for us before. Pastor John always spoke highly of you. Where are they? I just want to talk with them for a short time. You do trust me, don't you?"

Rebecca shook her head.

Maybe the nurse needed to give her more of the drug. She wasn't complying like the others. Brother David narrowed his eyes and moved in closer to her face.

"Your father disappeared because of you," he said. "It's all your fault. But you can bring him back if you're a nice temple girl. Do you want your father to come back to you?"

"Yes, please." Rebecca's eyes watered up.

"He disappeared because he loved the temple more than you," Brother David said. "He complained that you hid things from the temple, and he didn't like that. Your father wanted you to obey us, just like it says in the Bible. Obey your mother and father. You wouldn't do it. You hid things from us, like the television in the basement, and the music, and the Internet. You must give up your secular ways and devote yourself to the temple, as your father did. He's alive, and he is with us, but he refuses to see you again until you give yourself to the truth."

Tears streamed down Rebecca's cheeks and she shivered with her arms crossed over her chest. She sniffled every few seconds.

"You will help me," Brother David said. "I know you and your friends found Dunamis in the tunnels. I need you to lead me down there to retrieve some. Can you do that?"

Rebecca strained to open her eyes further, and she turned to him. "We'll die."

He shook his head. "You and your friends made it there and back. You didn't die."

Rebecca's pupils grew larger and she spoke slowly. "The medallion...kept us safe."

"What medallion?"

"It keeps the...phantoms away."

"How does it do that?"

"I don't know." Her eyelids closed for several seconds, then she continued. "It turns bright red. It hurts my eyes."

"Where is this medallion?"

She glared at him, then looked down. "Michael has it."

"Where's Michael?"

Rebecca shook her head. Her cheeks flushed and she rubbed her eyes.

"You need to give up your old ways, Rebecca," he said. "It's urgent that we find your friends and get this medallion. You say it will keep us safe. You don't want to die, do you?" He didn't wait for her to respond. "Of course not. We should get this medallion, then, so we don't die. Your mom and dad don't want you to die."

Rebecca looked up at him. "When can I see my dad?"

"One thing at a time. We'll discuss your dad later. For now, you need to help us find them. We need to get this medallion you're talking about, otherwise you'll die in the tunnels alone, and only you can prevent that. You don't want your mom and dad crying for the rest of their lives because you died, do you?"

"No," Rebecca answered weakly.

"No, of course not. Your father told me he wants you to tell us where they are. We need to go get this medallion."

"You're just going to..." she winced, "kill them."

"No, we don't want them dead. I give you my word."

"I didn't mean to hurt my dad," she said.

"Yes, he knows that. He wants you to help us and he wants to see you again, but he can only do that if you talk to us."

"I want to see him."

"Only after you help us. He doesn't want to see you until you turn your back on your secular ways. You need to tell us where your friends are at so we can help them too."

Rebecca cringed. "My head hurts."

You will hurt a lot more if you don't start talking right now. Brother David held back the urge to wrap his fingers around her throat and squeeze. "I'm sorry to hear that. I know your friends haven't left town. Where are they hiding?"

She groaned. "I don't want to say."

"Your dad is waiting. He's waiting for you to tell us the truth."

Rebecca shook her head. "I can't tell."

"Tell me!" Brother David pounded his fist against the table. He stood, slamming his hip against the edge of the table, and cringed from the pain. The guard at the door jumped to attention.

Rebecca covered her face with her hands. "I can't tell."

"I'm tired of this nonsense." Brother David stormed out of the room. His mind exploded with every curse word he'd uttered in his life, but he squeezed his mouth shut. Rage surged through him as he clenched his fists. *Stay in control. No weakness.* He held his chin up and eyed anyone who dared to stare at him.

Within a few minutes Brother David had calmed down. He walked back into the room and sat next to Rebecca, leaning into her as if to whisper a secret.

"Where are your friends?" he asked.

"I can't."

"Bring in her mother if she doesn't want to help us," Brother David said to the guard. "Bring in Audrey."

Rebecca burst out sobbing. "No, no. Mom!"

Brother David grabbed Rebecca's arm and squeezed. "Where are they?"

"I'll...take you there," Rebecca said. "Leave them alone. I can show you where it is."

"You'll bring me to the Dunamis? You said we would die down there without the medallion."

"I'll show you where it is," she repeated.

Brother David stared for a moment. No time to get the medallion, even if it would help. The sooner he took possession of the Dunamis the better. Pastor John might pay an unannounced visit while away, and that would arouse suspicion.

"Good girl. You just lead the way. We'll leave here in a few minutes, and I expect you to obey as instructed. Is that clear? Any attempt to escape or betray my trust will be dealt with severely. You'll never see your dad alive again. Understand?"

Rebecca nodded slowly.

"You will show me *exactly* where you and your friends found the Dunamis you recovered. After you submit to my demands, then we'll discuss your father's whereabouts. Do you understand?"

Rebecca nodded faster. Her hands trembled and she cried.

❧ 16 ❧

"What's The Farm?" Michael asked.

"It's a reeducation center," Lucas said. "They force people to go in, but they don't come out the same. The temple freaks mess with their minds."

"Where is this place?"

"Out behind the cemetery at the edge of town. It doesn't look like a prison camp or anything like that from the outside," Lucas said. "It looks just like any other farm around here, from the front. The main center is behind the farmhouse. They finished building it almost a year ago. The Farm used to be a slaughterhouse for pigs, but they pumped a shit ton of money into it and now it's their headquarters. Don't expect to find Pastor John over there much though. He stays at the church in town a lot, and at home."

"So how can we get in there?"

"It won't be easy, but we've done it twice before. Grim's been in there once, so he provided some valuable information."

"There's another reason they might target us," Michael said, holding up the medallion. "This. Pastor John was furious we had this. He kept yelling at us to give it back."

"See? There you go," Lucas said. "That's what they're really after. Maybe it's more than just Rebecca. Maybe they're planning to get the information out of her."

Michael flipped over the medallion in his hands and studied the symbols again. It made sense, but what could be so special about it? It glowed in the presence of bessies, but the idea that it held some mystical power was hard to believe. He slipped the medallion into his backpack.

"What's the plan, Lucas?" Joey asked. "We got to get Bex out of there."

"You'll need weapons," Lucas said. "And we do have something that might help. But we don't know if it works or not. We haven't tried it."

Lucas walked out of the room and came back a minute later with a thick plastic card the size of a credit card. He held it up and gestured to Joey. "I cloned a guard's key card."

Joey inspected it. "Who's that in the photo?"

"That's Grim."

"Doesn't look like him."

"Go easy on us. It's the best we could do."

"How'd you get it?" Joey asked.

"I swiped it from the guard while he was passed out drunk in his car. Only took a few minutes to clone it, and then I just slipped it back in his pocket."

"When did this happen?" Joey asked.

"About a month ago. We were in town staking out the activity around The Farm. We'd seen him drinking before in his car. He stashes Jim Beam out behind a clump of trees in the cemetery. So we decided to take advantage of the situation that time."

"Is he a little fat?" Joey asked.

"Not a little."

"Yeah, it's Isaac Robertson. My dad's drinking buddy."

"Well, I think we can get in any door he can," Lucas said. "I guess this is our chance to find out if it worked or not."

"We don't have any weapons," Michael said. "I have a pistol in my backpack from my grandfather's house, but that's it."

"Derek has guns and knives and all that shit," Grim said from the couch.

"We can go in there tonight," Michael said, "after the bessies come out. The medallion will keep them away, but the only bad thing is the red glow. That light illuminates us too. They'll see us coming."

"We'll spend some time planning it before we go in," Lucas said. "They won't see us. We'll go over there now and have a look. I'll show you a side door where we can sneak in *if* the cloned key card works. You'll see what I'm talking about. Then we'll come back and put on some black clothes. Break in there like ninjas."

"I don't have any black clothes," Joey said.

Lucas turned to Twyla. "Twyla, find some black clothes for this guy to wear." Lucas eyed Joey's large torso. "I'm guessing extra-large."

She sighed and threw down the game controller as she stood up. "Yeah, I'll find some clothes."

"August," Lucas said. "Can you drive us into town?"

August groaned. "Why do I got to use my car all the time? Grim's got a car too."

"My car is a piece a shit," Grim said.

"It runs as good as mine," August said.

"It doesn't run worth a shit."

August held up his hand. "We're taking Grim's car. We never use his car. It's his turn now." He stepped over to three sets of keys on hooks next to the door leading up to the barn. He picked up the first set. "I'm driving your car, Grim."

"Hell if you are," Grim yelled. He threw his gaming control onto the floor and stormed over to August. "You aren't driving my car. You can't drive worth a shit."

"Then *you* drive," August said. "We're just going into town. Why don't you help us out once in a while?"

"Fine," Grim said. He grumbled as he stormed up the stairs to the barn. "I help you guys out all the time. All the freaking time. I'm sick of everyone taking advantage of me. You guys owe me plenty of favors."

Michael threw his backpack over his shoulder and the five of them headed up to the barn. Twyla stayed behind to find black clothes for everyone.

Grim's car was parked around the backside of the garage, out of sight from the road. Grim was right. It was a piece of shit. A silver Chevy Impala, way past its prime. The rust surrounded the edges of the doors and the wheel wells similar to the amount of rust on Rebecca's car.

Michael crammed into the center in the back with Joey on one side and August on the other. Lucas sat in the passenger seat.

The car sat low to the ground as they took off out of the driveway with Derek watching again from a corner of one window. There wasn't much space to maneuver in the backseat if they would need to slouch down below the windows to stay out of sight.

Grim took the same side road that Michael had earlier, avoiding his grandfather's house and hopefully avoiding the white vans. Within a few minutes they reached the edge of town.

Grim drove the car to the end of the gravel road where the main road crossed in front of them. About a hundred yards to the right were white vans stationed on both sides of the road, each facing into oncoming traffic to stop cars coming in and out of town. Straight ahead of them stood the black iron fence of the cemetery and the main entrance with the words Stone Hill Municipal Cemetery arched in black iron letters over it.

Michael hunkered down in his seat, but raised his head long enough to see that the passenger in the white van facing him up the road was staring at the car through binoculars.

"Think they'll stop us?" Michael asked.

"They stop me sometimes," Grim said. "We won't drive by them."

Grim crossed the road and passed through the entrance to the cemetery, slowly driving the car along the gravel tracks that wound through the sections of gravestones and markers. If anyone were watching them, it wouldn't be difficult to spot the silver car standing out against the dark gravestones and the thick dark green grass.

Sprawling oak trees shadowed many of the gravestones. Michael read some of the names: Mellin. Jones. Anderson. Olson. Lots of Olsons. Some dates went back over a hundred years. The names on those gravestones had worn away after decades of erosion. A newer monument a few feet high and wide sat against the back of the cemetery. The name "Barlow" stood out clearly with four names chiseled in the granite. Three odd circular symbols ran along the bottom below the names. Had an entire family been buried together?

Grim curved around a makeshift roundabout in the center of the cemetery that encompassed a tall, dark gray war memorial featuring a soldier standing on the top with his head bowed. Weeds poked up around its base.

The groundskeeper was doing a shitty job. No flowers either. Anywhere. Many gravestones had toppled over, and patches of grass had swallowed some of them.

Michael glanced back. Nobody had followed them in.

Grim led them along a narrow winding path to the far corner of the cemetery. He stopped beside a massive memorial that somewhat hid them from the entrance view.

Directly behind the cemetery was an open, grassy field, and to the right, about a hundred feet away, a white picket fence surrounded a picture-perfect two-story farmhouse. The porch was fenced in, and an old woman sat rocking and knitting something. Flowers and well-manicured bushes highlighted the landscaping around the front of the house. The scene looked like something straight out of a Disney movie.

Behind the farmhouse stood a solid white fence about eight or ten feet high, separating the backyard from the front section of the property. Above the fence rose the top half of a massive white barn, and beyond that another white brick building.

"That's The Farm," Grim said.

They climbed out of the car and glanced around. Nobody else in sight. Michael slipped on his backpack and walked another twenty feet with the others, hunkering down behind a row of gravestones. A breeze blew across Michael's face and the surrounding leaves rustled.

"That's where they took Rebecca?" Michael asked.

"I'm sure of it," Lucas said.

"It doesn't look like what I thought it would. I thought there'd be a guard tower and barbed wire everywhere. It looks easy to get in."

"That's what they want you to think, so their operation doesn't attract attention. Looks all sweet and cozy now, doesn't it? But don't let that fool you. It's a house of horrors."

"I feel like running in there and kicking their asses right now," Joey said.

"You and me both," Grim said. "My brother went in there a few weeks ago, and I haven't seen him since."

"So how do we get in?" Michael asked.

Lucas pointed to the left side of the complex, where a small door interrupted the perfection of the white fence. "There's a door on the back wall that we can use, if the guard's key card works. Once inside, we'll turn left past the barn and then head to the back building. That's where they keep the prisoners."

"Yep," Joey said, "that's where they keep them."

"It'll be dark when we come back tonight," Lucas said, "so pay attention now to where everything is at."

"What about the squid?" Grim asked Lucas. His face was tight and his eyes wide.

Lucas looked at Michael. "I'm hoping that what this guy says is true. That his medallion keeps them away."

Michael nodded. "It works. I don't know why, but it works."

"Better be right about that," Grim said.

"Nothing to worry about," Joey said. "I seen it. You ain't got nothing to stress about."

"Once we get inside the main building in the back, we'll follow Grim's directions to find her. His prior knowledge of the place should lead us to the prisoner area. We'll find her."

"What if something goes wrong?" August asked.

"If something goes wrong," Lucas said, "we'll meet back here."

Footsteps raced toward them.

Everyone spun around.

"Holy shit!" August yelled.

Two temple guards stood aiming rifles at their heads. A white van was parked halfway along the path through the cemetery, partially hidden by a short, wide memorial. The rustling trees must have disguised the sound of its approach.

"Don't move," the guards yelled as they jumped forward. "Hands up!"

"Jesus Christ!" Grim cried, stumbling backward.

"Freeze!" one guard screamed at Grim.

Grim took off running through the rows of gravestones with his hands behind his head, as if that would do any good. He kept his body low and weaved as he headed toward the open field at the back of the cemetery. One guard chased him, stopped, took careful aim, and fired. A spot of red exploded near Grim's shoulder and he dropped face first into the field. The guard raced over and stood above Grim with the rifle pointed at his head. Grim rolled on the ground, crying out in pain.

"Shit, that hurts!"

Michael's heart pounded. The guard near them was within striking range. Michael's muscles tensed as he considered how long it might take him to knock the rifle out of the guard's hands. His pistol was in his backpack, but it would take too long to dig it out. If he could just grab the rifle, Joey would certainly join in.

The guard who shot Grim ordered the boy to stand up. Grim obeyed, but held his shoulder as they led him back to the group at gunpoint. Blood drenched the left side of Grim's graphic T-shirt. If the shot had hit him a few inches to the right, Grim would have become another corpse below their feet.

With their hands raised, two other white vans charged into the cemetery and stopped behind the first one. Four guards jumped out with weapons raised. They were surrounded. The guards rushed over and ripped off Michael's backpack. They frisked each of them and led them back toward the vans.

A white Cadillac pulled into the cemetery. Michael expected Pastor John or David to step out when the door opened, but it was Joey's dad.

"Dad?" Joey called out.

Brian walked toward them in his military fatigues, shaking his head and mumbling with his chin raised and a big grin smeared across his face.

"Of all the places," Brian said to them, "is this where you've been hiding out?"

"Dad," Joey said, "we don't—"

"Shut up!" Brian yelled.

Joey stopped.

"Michael's backpack, sir." One of the guards handed it to Brian.

Brian grabbed it and immediately began digging through it. "I'm assuming you're here looking for the whereabouts of your female friend. No need to panic yet. She's doing well and will soon aid the temple like all worthwhile Stone Hill citizens should."

Grim whimpered as the guard forced him to stand alongside them without bothering about his wound.

"Who shot this boy?" Brian asked the guards.

"I did, sir," the guard said nervously.

"Why is he still alive?" Brian asked. "You missed! More gun range training for you."

"Yes, sir."

Brian pushed around the items inside Michael's backpack and pulled out the pistol. He glared at Michael. "Why would you have this in here? Planning to use it on someone?"

Brian lifted the pistol and aimed it at Grim's chest.

Grim threw up his hands over his face. "Don't shoot me!"

Brian laughed. "Why shouldn't I?"

"I'm only sixteen."

"You're only a troublemaker."

Brian flipped Michael's backpack upside down and emptied the entire contents onto the grass. "Brother David will be happy to hear I found you."

The medallion dropped and clinked against the edge of a gravestone. Brian picked it up and examined it. He looked back at Michael. "What's this?"

"I found it."

"You probably stole it. Looks like something from an antique store for wizards. Where did you get this?"

Michael was silent.

Brian raised the pistol again to Grim's face, but kept his eyes on Michael. "I asked you a question."

Michael clenched his teeth to stop himself from saying anything that might get Grim shot.

"It keeps the squids away," Grim said as his teeth chattered.

Brian's eyes widened, and he lost his grin. "Do you think I'm joking? What is this?"

"It keeps the phantoms away," Grim said. "At least that's what he told me. And it does a lot more than that too."

"Grim," Lucas cut in, "shut up."

Brian turned to Grim. "Tell me more and I won't shoot you."

"It keeps them away," Grim repeated. "They were trying to break into The Farm."

"Grim!" Lucas yelled.

Brian gestured to the guard. "Put a towel around him and bring him to my vehicle. Don't get blood on my seats. Take the others to The Farm, since they wanted to go in there so badly."

The guard took Grim to the first van.

"Don't say a word, Grim!" August called out.

The same guard who had shot Grim slammed the butt of his rifle into August's chest, knocking the wind out of him. August wheezed and gasped for air.

The guards surrounded them and led them to one of the vans, shoving them inside through the back door. A metal cage encompassed the entire back half of the van. They sat on the floor of the cage after their wrists were zip tied.

"You okay, August?" Lucas asked after they shut the van doors.

"Not really," August said.

"Don't say another word back there," the driver of the van yelled from the front. "Praise be to Pastor John. This is your lucky day! You're on your way to be enlightened."

❧ 17 ❧

Brother David tossed the uniform on the table. Sister Rebecca stared at the white clothes as if she'd never seen such a thing before.

"I'm not sure they'll fit me," Sister Rebecca said.

"They'll do well enough," Brother David said. "You only need to wear them for the short time we'll be down there."

"Brother David, it's too dangerous to go down there without the medallion."

"If you have access to this device," Brother David said, "where is it?"

"I don't know exactly."

"Then stop all your nonsense." He walked in closer to Sister Rebecca's face. "If the Dunamis is where you say it is, it shouldn't take us more than an hour or two. I'm sure we can avoid the phantoms for that short a time."

"Please don't take me down there," Sister Rebecca said. "I'll draw you a map. I'll tell you exactly where to go."

Brother David nodded. "A map will be good, but we need a personal guide. I think you're a perfect fit for the position."

"Please, Brother David, we can't—"

"Stop your pitiful whining," Brother David said. "You should be joyful in helping the temple with such an important task."

Sister Rebecca took a deep breath and rubbed her forehead. "I'm sorry, Brother David. I am joyful."

"Hardly. You're making it quite difficult for us. You *did* agree to help."

Sister Rebecca nodded and then shook her head. "I can't think straight. My head hurts."

Brother David stepped back and gestured to the bathroom. "Put on the uniform."

Sister Rebecca scooped up the pile of clothes and held them for a moment with her head down before walking to the bathroom.

Brother David turned back to his five loyal guards. "This is just the beginning. Once the Dunamis is in our possession, the flawed leadership of Pastor John will fail. You will be my closest allies in the new temple. You will all share in the riches that Pastor John has so selfishly hidden from us. His corruption will end. Be strong down there, and your rewards will wait for you in heaven just as they will on earth."

"What if the girl doesn't lead us to the Dunamis?" asked Brother Matthew.

"She'll do as she's told," Brother David said. "After she comes out of the bathroom, administer another dose of the drug."

"Pastor David, what if—" Brother Christian stopped and his eyes widened. "I'm sorry! I mean, Brother David!"

Brother David grinned. "Soon you will call me by that title."

"What if she reveals the recovery of Dunamis to Pastor John?" Brother Christian finished.

"She'll be under my care," Brother David said. "Pastor John won't get near her. He barely has the strength to walk anymore. The darkness is eating him from the inside. It won't be long." He walked over and put his hand on Brother Matthew's shoulder. "You will be my first in command."

"Thank you, Brother David," Brother Matthew said, coming to attention.

The bathroom door rattled and Sister Rebecca walked out wearing the camouflage uniform. The pant legs flopped over her shoes and the jacket was too large, but they would do.

"They're too big," Sister Rebecca said.

"It's only for a couple of hours." Brother David grabbed a rifle from the table and thrust it into her hands. "Only use this if you need it. We'll take care of the phantoms."

"Do you have machetes?" she asked.

"We don't have any left," Brother David said. "Our rifles will keep us plenty safe."

Brother Zachary approached Sister Rebecca with the needle. "Roll up your sleeve."

"More?" Sister Rebecca asked, wobbling.

"To calm your nerves."

"I don't—"

"You said you would cooperate," said Brother David, raising his voice.

Sister Rebecca relented and rolled up her sleeve. She winced as the needle poked her.

"Good girl," Brother Zachary said.

Brother David led them down the stairs at the back of the kitchen in the church basement. He kept Sister Rebecca at his side, less concerned with her safety than with the risk of her sabotaging their efforts before reaching their destination. The drugs were powerful, but Sister Rebecca was an exceptionally stubborn girl.

After passing through the door leading into the temple, his guards raised their rifles. Each of them wore night-vision goggles. Brother Porter carried the two five-gallon plastic containers and the other necessary tools. Every single item Sister Rebecca had recommended they bring. As long as they dealt with the phantoms, it should prove a momentous day in the history of the new temple.

Sister Rebecca wavered at his side. "I'm dizzy. We shouldn't be down here without the medallion."

"We need to destroy all those relics of witchcraft and wickedness Pastor John found. All of it is devilry. I'll have it melted down when I take possession of the temple."

It didn't matter if Sister Rebecca heard them talking about their plan to remove Pastor John of his duties with the temple. She wouldn't remember anything of their excursion the following day, and within a few days the temple would belong to him.

Brother David raised his own rifle, whipping it from side to side as he advanced. The flashlight attached to the top of the rifle lit his way.

"I'm going to be sick," Sister Rebecca said.

"You'll be home soon," Brother David said. "Focus on what you need to do now. Bring us to the Dunamis. Nothing to worry about. You are well protected."

Sister Rebecca gestured toward the rotating door against the far wall of the temple. It was partly open.

"Through that door, and then take a left up the stairs," Sister Rebecca said.

Brother David went through the door first and followed her directions. A pile of clothes near the bottom of the stairs distracted him. The ragged garments were old and wrapped in a bundle as if a human might be inside.

Brother David trudged up the stairs and turned left with the others closely behind him. No sign of the phantoms anywhere. Why had Pastor John had so much difficulty navigating the tunnels during all his search parties? Not a single excursion had resulted in locating more Dunamis. The result of Pastor John's poor leadership, no doubt. So many loyal followers had died. It wasn't so difficult to navigate the tunnels if one maintained a level head and moved with stealth.

It would be a day to be remembered. So many steps Brother David had taken to secure his grip on the temple. With the

Dunamis in his possession, he'd be unstoppable. It was like playing chess. All the pawns and pieces were in place. Soon he would have the king in check.

They passed through the tunnels without incident and came upon a collapsed section of the wall surrounded by a pile of rubble.

Brother David turned back to Sister Rebecca. "Which way?"

"Through there," she said, pointing at the hole on top of the rubble.

"Brother Zachary, come with me," Brother David said. He led the charge to the mound of rubble and scanned the next room with his flashlight.

Something knocked his rifle to the side. A black tentacle shot through the opening and latched itself to Brother Zachary's arms and head. Brother Zachary cried out as he struggled to back away. He lashed out, but the tentacles had seized him. A moment later, he jerked forward and shot headfirst through the hole, his rifle clacking against the edges of the stone opening as he passed through.

"Fire at it," Brother David yelled, firing his rifle into the darkness ahead. Brother Christian ran up alongside him as Sister Rebecca fell back.

Gunfire exploded behind Brother David as he pushed through the opening. Rebecca screamed. He glanced back.

A tentacle had dropped from the ceiling and latched itself around Sister Rebecca's neck and shoulders. She raised her rifle, but the phantom seized that too. The phantom lifted her into the air a few feet before Brother Porter dropped the plastic jugs and began firing toward the ceiling.

Several more tentacles snaked down and whipped around Brother Porter's torso. The thing clutched him as well, encompassing his entire chest, and hoisted him toward a thick darkness as his legs flailed. He cried out for help, again and again.

Sister Rebecca freed her arms and fired at the phantom.

Brothers Isaac and Matthew joined in. Moments later, the phantom released her and she collapsed onto the ground.

Blood rained down from where Brother Porter had been taken up to the ceiling. His screams ended abruptly.

Brother David continued forward, despite the battles ahead and behind him. He pushed through to the other side, engaging in a full-blown battle with the phantom holding Brother Zachary in its arms. He and Brother Christian fired their rifles as they advanced and circled the creature. The creature lunged forward at them, its tentacles swinging wildly, knocking Brother Christian to the ground.

Brother David aimed for the creature's beak. Its one weakness. He had encountered the beasts before. Blasting at the underside of their beaks while they shrieked always grabbed their attention. He fired with a careful, steady hand.

Flesh exploded from the underside of the beak. The phantom screeched and convulsed, slithering back toward a darkened corner near the room's ceiling, but it dragged Brother Zachary with it. Brother Zachary had stopped crying out. He hung limp as the phantom lifted him higher until he disappeared within the darkness above them.

Moments later Brother Matthew arrived behind them. "Brother Porter's gone, sir."

"Where's the girl?" Brother David asked.

"Brother Isaac is guarding her," Brother Matthew said.

"Bring them through."

Two of his loyal guards had disappeared in a matter of seconds. He wouldn't lose any more. Brother Isaac and Sister Rebecca pushed through the hole, towing with them the supplies Brother Porter had carried along. Sister Rebecca was sobbing into her hands.

"No more of that." Brother David held back a deep desire to slap her. "Which way now?"

"Over there," Sister Rebecca said through her tears, pointing down the hallway to a massive stone archway ahead. A thick wooden door framed in rusty metal strips blocked their path. "It's just through there."

Brother David hurried over to the door. A rope was looped through two metal rings, sealing the gateway shut. He untied the rope and slid the door open sideways along a stone groove.

The sickening stench of Dunamis flooded the air. So strong Brother David gagged and struggled not to vomit. His nausea was quickly replaced with bliss. The keys to taking control of the temple were within his grasp.

They huddled together as they passed into the room, scanning every direction with their rifles.

"It's in here," Sister Rebecca said.

"I don't see it," Brother David said.

"Over there." Sister Rebecca pointed to one side of the room where the floor fell away into darkness.

Brother David followed her gesture and cautiously approached the open pit. The opening was several feet across in both directions, lined with stones as if it held an ancient well.

"This is it," Sister Rebecca said behind him without emotion.

He peered down into the void as he inched to the edge of the pit, using the light from his rifle. About twenty feet below, the surface of the liquid reflected the light like a black mirror. It was the most spectacular thing he'd ever seen in his life. An entire pool of the precious Dunamis.

Brother David vibrated with excitement. "Pastor John is finished."

❧ 18 ❧

Michael sat on a metal bench that was only slightly larger than him. It was bolted to the wall, and he clasped his hands together over his lap. The air was cold and dry, and a muffled conversation in the next room rose and fell, but the tone spoke of desperation and fear. Taunts and commands roared from guards in the hallway, drowning out the weak responses from their submissive captives.

Michael stood up and went to the door. One small window separated him from the outside world. He was alone, and it was a good thing that Grim had not made it in there with him because his anger grew the more he thought about their betrayal.

Michael jiggled the door handle. Locked, of course. He pounded on the door. Nobody in the hallway appeared to notice.

Grim was nowhere in sight. If the ease with which Grim had spilled the info about the medallion to David was any indication, the kid was most likely revealing the hideout's location in the barn as well. The only good thing about what had happened was that he was now inside the same building as Rebecca.

The guards had separated them, putting August and Lucas in a different room somewhere down the hall, but in the same area. They had taken Joey to a completely different section of the building. Michael calculated there were twenty rooms, but it was impossible to tell if they were all occupied. Maybe Rebecca was in one of them. Maybe he was closer to her than he knew.

He stared through the window in the door. The hallway ran left and right, and the walls were painted a dull off-white without windows anywhere in sight. A large mural of Pastor John stared back at him from the wall opposite his room. A guard passed his window and pounded his fist against the glass. Michael recoiled, and the guard laughed.

Why had he trusted Grim, anyway? He'd put his faith in a complete stranger, some homeless kid who at the first sign of trouble wouldn't care less if Rebecca was rescued or not. Michael wouldn't let that happen again.

He dropped onto the metal bench again and tried to get comfortable, although the cold, hard surface provided no relief. The bare concrete walls dulled his senses and drew him back into his mind.

How had the plan fallen apart so easily? He had prepared himself to do whatever it took to rescue Rebecca. He would never put himself in that situation again. *If* he ever had another chance to be in that situation again.

The metal door snapped open after Michael sat down, and a woman wearing white pants and a white shirt walked in. She could have been any doctor from any hospital in the country. She had curly blonde hair and a pleasant smile. Maybe in a different situation she would have sold cosmetics in a department store. She forced a grin at Michael, which didn't help ease his anxiety.

She held a digital tablet and glanced between the data she was entering with a digital pen and Michael's face. She let the door slam shut behind her, and a guard peered in through the glass window at him.

"Why do you want to join the Stone Hill Risen Temple?" the woman asked him.

"What the hell are you talking about?" Michael said. "I don't want to join your shitty temple."

The woman nodded. "Of course. We all have a choice and you are certainly free to leave the temple and Stone Hill if that's what you want. Nobody is holding anybody here against their will."

Michael stood. "Great! Then I'll be going now." He stepped over to the door and cranked the handle down. It was still locked. His attempt to open the door resulted in the guard coming to the window and now glaring at him.

"But we still need to address more important matters at hand here," the woman said in a stern tone. "Possession of a stolen firearm, trespassing, carrying a concealed weapon. All those things are very serious charges. The police certainly would not look favorably on any of this. The city prison cells are only about half the size of this room, by the way. If you'd rather go there, you're welcome."

There wasn't any point to arguing. Michael sat down again and folded his hands across his lap. "Oh, I wasn't aware this was a luxury resort."

"The re-education process is simple," the woman said, reading from her tablet. "The first step in a sinner's journey is to confess your wrongdoings. You can begin now, if you'd like. Once that is accomplished, you move on to step two, which is to submit to the teachings of the temple and Pastor John. We promise to make a new man out of you and to change your life for the better."

Michael groaned. "How long is this going to take?"

The woman smirked and continued reading from the tablet. Michael met the guard's unblinking eyes. Michael considered mouthing the words "fuck you" at the guard, but decided against it. He tried to block everything happening around him.

The woman's voice droned on, and all he could think about was how he would get out of there and find Rebecca.

A small camera stared down at him from the upper corner of the room near the door. Michael stared at it as the woman read paragraph after boring paragraph from the tablet. Most of what she read was sophisticated technical jargon that reminded him of his high school teachers reading the class rules at the start of a new year. The same boring information that only sparked your imagination into coming up with new ways to defeat the system. Oh, he hadn't thought of doing *that* before. *That's a great idea!* When the woman finally stopped talking, Michael rubbed his forehead. He told himself that everything would be just fine. He didn't believe it for a moment.

"Where's Rebecca?" Michael asked the woman. He didn't expect her to answer his question, but he was afraid she would start blabbing again, so he tried to change the subject.

"I assume you're referring to Rebecca Wagner," the woman said. "She's doing well. Is she a friend of yours? You're welcome to spend time with her as soon as the enlightening process is complete."

"I'm feeling better already," Michael said. "You've converted me. I'm enlightened now. Let me go see her."

"I'm afraid it doesn't work like that. It may take only a few weeks. Or, sometimes, months. We'll all be praying for you."

Michael was powerless to do anything. His grandfather could not save him and there wasn't anyone from California looking for him. If he was to survive and succeed at getting Rebecca out of there he would have to do it on his own.

The woman stood in silence for a few more minutes, scribbling notes into her tablet, humming as she input the data, and then went to the door. The guard opened it for her, and she turned back to Michael a moment before she left. "Bible lessons will begin after supper."

The guard escorted her out, throwing Michael one last sharp stare. The metal door latched shut, and Michael was alone again with the camera above the door watching him. The little red light on the side of the camera remained lit all the time.

He sat back on the bench. He had to get out of there. Even if he could get Rebecca out of the building, he couldn't imagine making a run for the front gate without getting shot in the back.

The temple obviously had no problem with eliminating trouble-makers. Not much he could do about that at the moment. He would have to watch carefully for his opportunity to find her. A weapon would help, but there was nowhere to hide it. The room was as bare as a prison cell.

His imagination ran wild with images of rescuing Rebecca. Like a scene in some action movie, she'd wrap her arms around him when he found her. And they'd blast their way out the door.

If he could only know for sure that Rebecca was in the same building... Assuming she was, finding her wouldn't be difficult—but how long would it take for him to get her out? He could be stuck in there for days or weeks before coming up with a solid plan.

In the meantime, they would work hard to fill his brain with temple propaganda. Too much time with them and he might start believing Pastor John was a god.

But he wouldn't let them get to him. No way. He would stay focused on his friends.

Michael imagined all sorts of awful things the temple might be doing to Rebecca. It made his stomach churn. They probably had brainwashed so many people that they were experts by now. He had to act soon. The longer the temple trapped them in there the worse it would be for him. Maybe worse for Rebecca and Joey, since they'd been involved with the temple before.

Michael closed his eyes and focused. "I'm not leaving here without you, Rebecca."

Someone pounded on the door. Michael opened his eyes and looked over. The guard was staring at him again.

❧ 19 ❧

At supper time, they rounded up Michael and a few other prisoners. A group of guards, including the one who'd stared at him through the window in his door, led them into a cafeteria, which consisted of two long, rectangular tables, and directed them through the food line.

The cooks were scrambling to prepare a variety of dishes. Sliced turkey, mashed potatoes, green beans, corn, sweet potatoes, and homemade cookies for dessert. The smells were intoxicating, and he took in a deep breath, remembering he hadn't eaten a home-cooked meal in weeks.

The cooks gave none of it to Michael and the other prisoners. Apparently, it was for someone else, most likely the guards and the other temple workers. Instead, they handed him a tray consisting of a thinly-sliced turkey sandwich, some mixed fruits, and a cup of water.

He sat alongside eleven other prisoners, all of them wearing the same white outfit as him, and most were very old or young. Rebecca was not among them. Neither was Joey. But Lucas and August were there, one at each of the two tables. Michael was directed to sit at the table with Lucas, but at the opposite end. Far beyond whispering range.

The other prisoners didn't look around or even glance at him, but Lucas nodded with a subtle smile. August stared wide-eyed at Michael from the next table with a nervous grin.

Four armed guards stationed at each corner of the room glared at them as they ate. Michael avoided eye contact, but watched them from his peripheral vision.

The food wasn't awful, but hardly enough to call a meal. He devoured everything on his plate, but after finishing, he craved more.

He met Lucas's eyes every minute, and he got the impression that Lucas wanted to tell him something by the way he craned his head and mouthed words. Michael tried to decipher what he was saying, but it was pointless. They were too far apart. He wanted to know if Lucas had seen either Rebecca or Joey. He considered whispering a message to the prisoner sitting next to him, and ask him to pass it along to Lucas, but one of the guards walked over and circled the table.

"Keep your eyes on your food," the guard ordered.

Michael studied the windows and doors. It couldn't be *that* difficult to get out of that place. It wasn't like a real prison or anything. There had to be a way out.

After they finished eating, a different group of guards escorted them down the hall into the chapel. It was nothing more than a small room with a vaulted ceiling. Several rows of foldable chairs awaited them, enough to accommodate thirty or forty people. An assortment of portraits of Pastor John lined the walls. Unlike a regular church, there were no stained-glass windows. No windows at all. Bright lights beamed down from overhead, most likely to help the guards keep an eye on any shenanigans between the prisoners.

Michael got within two seats of Lucas, but still not close enough to exchange whispers with him. The guards directed August to sit two rows behind them.

A short, dumpy man in a flowing white robe got up in front of them and cleared his throat several times before speaking.

"Good evening," the man said in a low, growling voice. "My name is Brother Todd and I am the Chapel Leader for the Enlightenment Center. Some of you are new here. Welcome!"

Brother Todd forced an applause for the new "guests."

"I welcome you all. One of the best ways to cleanse your soul is to sing praises to the temple. For those of you who have been with us for a while, you should know these songs by heart. For those who are new, the words will appear on the screen above you. Please sing along."

A white projector screen overhead displayed the words of the song they were about to sing.

Brother Todd took a sip of water. His eyes were red and his eyelids barely opened as he stared out at the group. "We'll be closing out your day by rejoicing in the Temple Praise Hour."

Music burst out from an unseen source through speakers surrounding the room.

They sang those songs during the Temple Praise Hour for *way* longer than an hour, with only a few seconds of silence between each song. Many of the melodies Michael recognized from his childhood Sunday school days, although the temple had changed some words to suit their needs. They had altered classic songs like Amazing Grace, substituting various words to include Pastor John's name and his "miraculous" healing. Most of the time Michael just mouthed the words, but the guards caught on fast. One of them charged over, his face red and the veins on his neck and forehead appeared ready to burst.

"Everyone's going to sing," the guard said to them. "If I see anyone not singing, they'll regret it."

Michael sang after that and even flashed a smile once in a while to put on a good show. He glanced at Lucas during one of the songs, and Lucas mouthed a few words between one of the verses. Michael understood only one word.

"...Rebecca."

Lucas must have seen her. Maybe while they were eating supper. Michael scanned the room, as if she might be standing in the back somewhere. But he knew what Lucas intended to say. They were in the right place. She was there, and despite getting into the complex in an unplanned way, he had gotten in.

Now they just needed a plan to get her out. Maybe he would get a chance to communicate with Lucas or August in the morning at breakfast, but tomorrow seemed like a distant dream. He dreaded the thought of spending even one night in that cage. He was ready to get the hell out of there right then. Excitement stirred in his chest.

They moved everyone out of the chapel after Brother Todd finished with them. The songs echoed through Michael's mind long after he'd left the chapel. He suspected that had been the point after all. To carry those crappy songs back to their rooms to infest their dreams.

Michael lost sight of Lucas and August as he was herded through the hallway back to his room.

When the door to Michael's room opened, the guard thrust Michael forward, as if he weren't moving fast enough, and slammed the metal door shut behind him.

Michael caught himself singing a line of one song over and over in his head. *"We are safe within the arms, safe within the arms, safe within the arms of Pastor John."* The tune reminded him of something kids might sing at a summer camp sponsored by Disney.

"Shut up. Shut up. Shut up." He shook the words away and stood staring at the wall. If only he had something to read. It could be anything. A phone book would be heaven compared to the maddening void of nothingness within that room.

He visualized the cover from one of the graphic novels he'd brought with him from California. He tried to remember each page from the most recent one he'd read. The pictures came back, but not the words.

He went to the sink and cupped his hands to scoop up drinking water. It tasted good, like the tap water from his grandfather's kitchen sink, although his stomach groaned. He was ready for breakfast.

He walked over to the door to his room and looked out the window. The guard wasn't looking in at him at the moment, but Michael's stomach churned again as Pastor John's smug face beamed at him from the large portrait across the hall.

"I killed you," Michael said, looking into Pastor John's eyes. "I'll do it again if I have to."

Screams erupted from outside the building. A woman's shriek, and it sounded like she was being tortured.

Michael winced and turned toward the window. The sky had darkened to a brilliant blood red. Was it too early for the bessies to be out stalking their prey for the evening? Maybe the temple just tortured prisoners outside their windows to break them down. It was working. Michael ran his fingers through his hair. He had to get out of there soon.

Rebecca.

The guard pounded on the door. Michael jumped.

"Five minutes!" the guard yelled.

Michael assumed that meant the time he would have before they turned off the lights. He used those minutes to piece together the layout of the building, connecting the hallways in his mind, pulling together a mental map that might help their escape.

He stared up at the camera. The red light was on. It was always on. Were they really watching him all that time? He couldn't imagine a guard sitting behind a desk staring at him while he slept and used the toilet. The eye in the sky. Michael considered flipping off the camera, but held back the urge. No sense in stirring up trouble yet. He'd save his energy for finding Rebecca.

Michael paced around the room, inspecting every crack and flaw in the construction. There had to be some points of weakness. It wasn't a real prison, although everything was geared toward that idea. No way the construction was up to the same code as a regular prison. Prisons cost millions to build. The window in his room was just ordinary glass, as far as he could tell. Nothing special about it, and no bars covered it. What was stopping him from throwing something through the glass and making an escape? No way to know for sure without trying, but there wasn't anything in his room to throw.

Maybe if he could rip out the sink or the toilet... The fixtures weren't made of metal, like a prison's, just regular porcelain that you would find in any home. He could break off a piece and smash it through the window. Break it off using what? It made no sense that they'd leave such a glaring mistake in the design. Or maybe they knew anyone foolish enough to attempt such a thing wouldn't get more than five feet away, anyway. It had to be a trick. If the fugitive tried to escape during the day, the guards would arrest them within minutes, or just shoot them dead, and if the escape attempt was at night the bessies would eat them up like a midnight snack.

Michael sat on his bed moments before the lights went out. A cheeseburger with a chocolate shake would have been good about then. His stomach ached as he lay down and drifted off to sleep.

At the edge of his awareness, something thumped against the outside wall of his cell. Another thump against the bottom of the wall, and a rumbling moved up toward his window. A black shape eclipsed the fading deep red sky and climbed to the top of the building. Directly above him, the metal roof squeaked and boomed as the prowler moved away from him.

Definitely bessies out there. Maybe they were as hungry as he was.

He lay awake in bed with his eyes wide open as the noises faded away. The night sky filled his window again.

Michael turned on his side and faced out toward the dark corner of the room below the camera. A ghostly face formed in the shadows. Its lazy eyes stared at him.

Michael recognized his dad right away, even within the shadows. A guttural, raspy voice broke through the air.

"What a fine mess you've gotten yourself into," his dad said. "What would your mother say about you now?"

Michael didn't answer. He was paralyzed. Each shallow breath surged in and out. He stared at his dad, wanting to look away, but his dad's eyes peered into him. His fingers dug into the edge of the sheets. The shadows transformed into his dad's bloody and mangled body, as Michael imagined it must have looked after the car accident. His dad's figure weaved as it shifted in closer toward him.

"What's your plan?" his dad growled as if gurgling through a thick liquid. "You don't have a plan, do you?"

"You are not real," Michael said.

"Oh, is that so? That's no way to treat your dad. Have you forgotten what you've done to me?"

The accident was impossible to forget. Michael had pushed it out of his mind over the last few days, but now the memories flooded back. "You're not real," he said again.

"They're outside waiting for you," his dad said. "You know what happens to murderers. You reap what you sow, and soon you will sow the depths of darkness. They'll find you and feed you to the creatures of hell."

"You're not my dad," Michael said. "Dad was nothing like you. Leave."

The figure stepped in closer. Light from the hallway illuminated its rotting flesh. The sunken, twisted face of his dad attempted to grin.

Michael looked away, then back again as it moved closer. The figure before him couldn't be his dad. His dad never said such awful things to him. His dad had always been kind, always gentle —never judgmental like the horrible fiend standing in front of him.

"Go away," Michael said. "Go away."

Michael broke into tears as he trembled in the cool evening air. His wet palms yanked at the sheet. He tried to sink down into his bed further, but his muscles failed to react. Something brushed against the side of the mattress and scratched along the sheet. Something sharp like a fingernail. The gurgling and gasping for air continued until a fingertip tapped his forehead. Michael shuddered.

"They were right to put you in here," the figure croaked.

"Go away!" Michael screamed. He kicked away the sheets and punched his fists into the air. The figure was gone. Had it dropped below his bed? He couldn't lift himself to check.

From the corner of his eye, a shadow passed over the window in the door to the cell. The guard was watching him again. He heaved in a deep breath and stared at the ceiling. If the guard had entered at that moment, he would have been relieved to have someone else in the room. But the guard only stared.

The red light on the camera in the room's corner caught Michael's eye. If they were watching, they must have seen the thing that had stood in his room. Maybe they had caught the whole thing on video. If it was real, the guards would have rushed in to stop the intruder.

But of course it hadn't been real. It had only been his imagination. Only the bessies were real, and the cage he lay in. Another hallucination caused by the trauma of the accident. Post-traumatic stress disorder. Maybe that's not what he had, but it sure sounded right. His life since the car accident, every single day, was PTSD.

His thoughts drifted to Rebecca. She had to be there, somewhere. He imagined her curled up in bed like him, fearful that everyone had forgotten about her.

"We haven't forgotten," Michael whispered into the darkness. "I'm not afraid."

Rebecca.

𝕏 20 ❧

In the morning, Michael's stomach growled nonstop when they finally opened the door and led him down to the cafeteria. Again, the food they provided was barely enough to survive on. Pancakes without syrup. Scrambled eggs. A child's fruit cup that consisted mostly of syrup. He tried to get an extra fruit cup at the end of the line, but one of the guards pushed him away.

Lucas and August were sitting at the same table this time, although at opposite ends. Michael looked for an open seat next to either of them, but a guard forced him to sit at the other table.

Michael squeezed into the last open seat, surrounded by two large men with scowls on their faces. They didn't look over when he sat down, but grumbled when he bumped into them.

Michael faced Lucas and August, and they exchanged a few quick glances and subtle grins. If he could somehow communicate with them, just get close enough to whisper a few words, maybe they could plan something. But there was no way. Except for standing up and walking over there in full view of the guards, he would have to wait for an opportunity.

A Hispanic man with sad eyes sat in front of Michael muttering to himself.

"Please forgive me, Pastor John," the man said. "I have sinned so much and I deserve only the worst."

A nearby guard took notice of the man's voice and walked over with a billy club ready at his chest. The man whimpered and quieted down as the guard hovered over him.

Michael shot glances at the other prisoners around him. One old man reminded him of his grandfather. What had *he* done to end up trapped in that place? The old man ate his food without so much as a glance to the side. His face was pale, as if he were on the verge of passing out.

Michael caught Lucas's eyes for a moment. Lucas whispered something, this time enunciating the words as he leaned toward Michael, but he still didn't understand most of it. Again, he caught only the last word: Rebecca. A moment later, a guard stormed over, brandishing a billy club near Lucas's face. "Shut up, sinner!"

Everyone at the table froze. Lucas winced and stiffened, hunching forward with one hand over the back of his neck. The guard still hovered over them for a couple of minutes before returning to his place in the corner.

Michael finished his food before the others, so he waited and took the opportunity to make furtive glances at his surroundings. The windows were small and set high, their sills sat a little above eye level. Only the cloudy sky was visible through the uncovered glass. The metal doors led out into the hallway, and they remained closed unless a guard passed through them.

A guard was standing at attention inside the doors, and another stood on the other side. No chance to make a run for it, and no chance to climb out the windows.

Something crashed at a table across the room, and a commotion erupted that spread through the whole space. One of the prisoners, a middle-aged woman dressed in white, screamed and ran into the kitchen, knocking into Michael's table as she darted past them. Her eyes were wide, her face stern, and her long dark hair whipped in every direction as she ran.

"Babylon the great, the mother of the prostitutes and of the abominations of the earth!" she screamed as she entered the kitchen. "Your immoral deeds have given rise to the beast. She will come up out of the abyss and go across the land to destroy your wicked kingdom. The phantoms are coming to purge the unholy. Repent! Repent!"

The guards burst out in cruel laughter as they half-heartedly chased her across the room. The woman grabbed a food tray and used it to deflect the guard grabbing at her. No billy clubs came out, as if she posed no threat.

Most of the prisoners at the tables ignored the commotion. All except Michael, Lucas, and August.

"She's on the loose again," a guard yelled with a wide grin.

"Don't hold me back," the woman screamed. "Fallen is Babylon the great, and she has become a habitation of demons, a prison of every unclean spirit. Come out of her, my people, that you have no participation in her sins, and that you don't receive of her plagues. The phantoms will deliver you to judgment, for in an hour such great riches are made desolate. Do you hear me?"

"All we hear is you yelling, Holy Hannah," another guard said and chuckled.

Michael furrowed his brows as he exchanged glances with Lucas and August. Lucas shrugged. Michael hoped the guards near them might go over to the woman, but they stayed in place and watched the scene with wide grins.

The cooks in the kitchen backed away from the counter and folded their arms, as if the woman were a nuisance.

A guard grabbed the tray out of her hands. "Where's your partner?"

"My partner is the revelation of truth," she said, circling the room with her arms flailing out in front of her. She crouched and hissed as she went around the room as if imitating a bessie. "I got a message for you all."

"Sing it, Holy Hannah!" one guard said. "Tell these seculars what they're up against."

The disruptive woman lashed out at the prisoners with hands curled into claws. "The abomination of desolation is here. The beast and its brood are coming for your souls."

That just made the guards laugh harder.

"Save them seculars, Holy Hannah!" one of them said. "They ain't here 'cause they're angels, don't you know?"

A moment later a short, balding man dressed in gray scrubs hurried into the cafeteria. He glared at Holy Hannah. His face was bright red. "Get back here! You're going to get me in trouble again."

"Better get a grip on your patient," a guard said. "Four days in a row with this stuff. *Four days.*"

"She doesn't listen," the short man said, shaking his head.

"Better get a grip. If you can't handle her, she'll have to go back to the study group."

"No." The short man held up his hand palm out to the guard. "I can do it."

"Aw, Brother Neil," a guard said from across the room, "I like to hear what she got to say."

"We all do, but he's got to get a grip. We can't keep wasting their time." Brother Neil gestured to the cooks who still had their arms folded over their chests. "You know how Brother Harry gets."

The short man in scrubs chased Holy Hannah around the tables. The guards stood back and continued laughing as Holy Hannah evaded capture.

"Help me!" the man in scrubs pleaded to the guards.

"She's your problem," a guard said.

"Preach it, Holy Hannah!" one of them yelled amidst more laughter.

Holy Hannah grabbed a food tray from Michael's table and threw it at the man in scrubs. The fruit cup splashed syrup all over his top.

"Dammit!" the short man yelled, stopping in his tracks.

"Clean up your mess, Brother Cooper," a guard yelled between wild laughter. "You're a disgrace."

"Those phantoms are coming for you too!" The woman pointed and glared at Brother Cooper.

"Knock it off, Hannah," he ordered.

"All right," Brother Neil yelled. "Stop. Ain't funny no more. Get her out of here."

Three guards swarmed in and restrained her. One guard threw his arm around her neck. She flailed within their grasp, but finally submitted when they brandished billy clubs.

Brother Cooper wiped the remaining bits of food from his shirt. A large stain streaked down the front. The food was scattered across the floor in every direction.

"I'm not cleaning that up," Brother Neil said.

"I'll do it," Brother Cooper retorted sharply.

"No place to hide from the eyes of the beast," Holy Hannah called out as she was led out of the cafeteria.

"Would you please shut up?" Brother Cooper yelled.

"They will soon be upon us! Do you hear me?"

"Can't we put a chain on her or something?" a guard asked after she left the room. The other guards laughed.

While the cafeteria door was open, Michael saw a small group of people in the hallway. They turned through a doorway next to the cafeteria. One of the prisoners was a familiar girl dressed in white.

Rebecca. Her face flashed by in a moment, but it was definitely her, and hovering at her side was her friend Maggie. Maggie's face was lit up as she chattered up a storm in Rebecca's ear.

An urge shot through him to jump, run out and grab her. He could be at her side in ten seconds. No problem. But beyond that he had no plan, and it would be a hopeless rescue. It wouldn't do anyone any good if he just ended up an unconscious mess on the floor at the mercy of those guards.

After Rebecca and Maggie had moved out of sight into the side room, the cafeteria door closed again.

Michael looked at Lucas. Lucas was nodding at him with a grin. Yes, Lucas mouthed, I know. They must have seen her too. That's what they had been trying to communicate earlier.

August whispered something to Lucas, and they looked over at Michael. Their eyes went narrow as if some scheme were racing through their heads. Lucas's mouth hung open, a flurry of words that would have to wait sitting in his throat.

Before either of them could break the silence, a guard shouted, "Stand up!"

Everyone stood.

"Move out," another guard near the door commanded them.

The prisoners moved out of the cafeteria in well-ordered lines as they had been instructed earlier, and Michael sank back as far as he could, hoping for the chance to pass by Lucas as they exited the room. No such luck, but he wasn't about to give up.

The door to the room where Rebecca had gone into was open, and as they walked Michael tried to pause and look inside. The room was like a lounge with couches, chairs and tables. A large TV sat at the far side, but Michael recognized the program as religious propaganda. As he stopped, the prisoner behind him pushed him forward. For a moment, he caught sight of Rebecca and Maggie sitting next to each other at a table, but neither of them looked toward him.

The prisoner behind Michael pushed past him with a groan and thrust him to the side. Michael nearly stumbled, but Lucas was now directly behind him.

They moved down the hallway in a single line.

Within seconds, Lucas whispered something behind him. Lucas's words were drowned out in the clomping of their footsteps.

One of the guards must have heard the whisper; he charged over to Michael as he kept walking.

"Keep your mouth shut!" the guard yelled.

He slapped the back of Michael's head so hard that Michael stumbled into the person in front of him, causing them to do the same. Another guard rushed over to them as they walked. The guards slapped their billy clubs against their open palms.

"Better keep your mouth shut," the guard yelled again. "Prisoners who don't learn that lesson end up as food for phantoms. We fix you up one way or another. Either way you belong to the temple now."

Michael's face flushed with rage. He summoned every ounce of strength to keep himself from strangling the guard.

"Fall into line!" the guard ordered.

Michael clenched his teeth so hard he thought they might shatter.

"Time for Bible study," a woman guard shouted from the front of the line. Her face was scarred, as if she'd survived a violent attack.

She directed them to the end of the hallway and right down another hallway. The two guards who had approached Michael now fell back, and their footsteps faded away in the other direction.

Muffled screams and crying echoed faintly through the walls. The source appeared to be behind one of the doors without a window. It was a young girl's voice, and a man yelled at her even as she wept.

"All alone," the man mocked. "Crying like a baby and never going home."

What had she done to deserve that?

At the end of the hall, the guards directed them into a small room. On the door was a large portrait of Pastor John reading the Bible. They joined several other prisoners already inside.

A circle of folding chairs surrounded a blue and white plastic chest cooler. Michael couldn't help but wonder what was inside. Beer?

Banners hung from the ceiling against opposite walls, displaying the circle and cross symbol he'd seen around town. A few more images of Pastor John's beaming face filled in any remaining wall space.

They filed into the ring of chairs and sat. When the guard nearest to him glanced away, Michael squeezed in next to Lucas and August. They sat down together and Lucas nudged Michael's leg.

"Hey," Lucas whispered without turning his head. "Look." Lucas pointed from behind folded arms to the open door of a bathroom across the room.

Brother Cooper stepped out in dark green scrubs. His soiled gray scrubs lay in a heap on the floor behind him. He shut off the bathroom light with the door open and left.

Michael glanced back at Lucas, who was grinning at August.

"Holy Hannah," Michael whispered under his breath.

Pastor John stood next to the bed where Bertha had spent most of the time in recent months. Bertha's form remained sunken into the mattress, and although the housekeeper had put on fresh sheets, the cold emptiness of her absence was striking.

Bertha's medications were gone, yet the smell of disinfectant and Bertha's distinct body odor hung in the air. One of the windows in the room was open and a faint breeze blew in, but it did nothing to erase her presence from the room. The breeze fluttered the dull pink curtains that she had received as a birthday present years earlier. He would tear those down as soon as he had the strength.

The silence embraced Pastor John as he dropped onto the edge of the bed and hunched forward. He took a deep breath and coughed. His chest ached, and a sharp pain sliced up his back. Nothing had functioned well since his recovery from the gunshot wounds days earlier. He had gotten better for a while, but now his body was breaking down again. The Dunamis had not worked well with Bertha's cancer, and it was not working well with him either. He needed more of the substance.

Pastor John ran his hand up the front of his shirt and poked a finger into one of the gunshot wounds that had healed. He undid the three top buttons of his shirt and looked at the black mass that had spread across his chest. Smooth black flesh that wrinkled and moved with his body like a living organism.

The black flesh felt no different from his own skin. At the same time, it was separate from himself. It was swallowing up his natural skin, and he was transforming. It was rising further up his chest every day, every hour, and soon it would be visible on his neck and face. He could close the top button of his shirt, but soon the blackness would be difficult to hide. If it continued to progress further, his followers would start asking questions. Something would have to be done.

Sister Laura could apply makeup to his face. He cringed. This wasn't the theater, and the makeup would ruin his perfectly white outfits. He could wear turtleneck shirts, but they'd be extraordinarily uncomfortable in the heat and humidity of a Minnesota summer.

He clawed at the black skin, nearly drawing blood. The punk kid responsible for doing that to him had to die. No, worse. He needed to suffer.

Michael Halverson.

Pastor John scowled, remembering the name clearly. And he clearly recalled the sensation of being shot.

He'd gone numb instantly, but sharp pain had flashed through him. Pain like he'd never felt before. Not since the days of undergoing grueling dental work had the agony been so overwhelming. He would cause Michael to suffer and all his friends too. Not one of them would survive.

Death had overwhelmed Pastor John, but he'd conquered it. God had been merciful, dropping him away into a dark, safe place, far from the basement of the church where his enemies had shot him down. But then the devil's hands had taken him, dragging him out of that safe darkness toward a mob of devils who surrounded him and taunted him.

Hundreds, even thousands, of devils preyed upon his weakness and vulnerability. They ripped and clawed at every part of his body. Every piercing fingernail and intrusion sent torrents of pain rushing through him. They tore away his eyes, his throat, his intestines, his groin. And after they tore him apart, he became whole again, and they repeated the process over and over. They humiliated him. Violated him and laughed like schoolyard bullies.

"You won't be needing this where you're going," one of them screamed in his ear as it tore out his stomach.

"What are you hiding here?" another demon shrieked as it tore a gash through his chest and ripped out his liver.

Even amidst all the pain and agony of the demons, Pastor John screamed at them and cursed those who had put him there. He would get revenge. He would make sure his enemies ended up in the same place and endured the same torments he had suffered.

Pastor John fought the devils that swarmed around him, knowing that they were just getting warmed up. Ahead of him was an eternity of torture as they dragged him deeper into the darkness. They yanked at his hair and stretched his jaw to the breaking point. Biting down on their fingers made no difference. They delighted in his agony. They rejoiced in his anguish and fed off the pain he inflicted back on them.

He couldn't escape their clutches. He accepted his fate. His new reality of darkness would be upon him forever.

But a miracle happened. A bright light broke through the darkness. The roaring applause of a high school auditorium drew him back into the world of the living. The surrounding devils faded away as the light transformed into spotlights that illuminated him as he lay on a table in front of his followers.

His insides burned, and he screamed as loud as he could, a shriek that echoed like the horrible devils that had screamed at him in his hell. The devils no longer held him, but a million tiny phantoms swarmed in his chest as if eating their way out.

Bertha stood over him beaming with wide eyes, as if she were delighted and terrified at the same time.

Brother David also stared down at him, his face flushed with sheer terror.

Pastor John had awakened from a nightmare. Worse than any horror he could imagine.

❧ 2 2 ❧

"Where's the Dunamis?" Pastor John grumbled into the handset.

"Glad to hear from you," Brother David said.

"Cut the bullshit. Where is it?"

"We're working on it."

"I'm dying," Pastor John said, pressing his hand to his chest.

"We are continuing our search for it," Brother David said. "As you know, it's very difficult to find it, much less retrieve it. There are so many factors involved, the most difficult being to find its location."

"I told you to get one of those kids. Michael Halverson, or Rebecca Wagner, or even Brother Brian's worthless boy, Joey Lynch. They know where to find it."

"I've got three vans assigned to that task," Brother David said. "As soon as we find them, we'll definitely inform you."

Pastor John focused on the odd background noises coming through the phone. Something heavy banged against the floor. Muffled, broken conversations of Brother David's guards.

"I can't lift it," one guard said. *"Where is Brother Zachary?"*

"Brother Zachary didn't make it," another guard replied.

"...smells so bad," a different guard said.

"I'm sorry," Brother David spoke more loudly. "We're putting together another search party now to find the troublemakers you mentioned. Get some rest, sir. I'm sure you'll feel better in a few days."

"She is recovering," another guard said.

"Where are you?" Pastor John asked.

Brother David paused. "The Farm," he said. "We're discussing the best way to proceed."

"Who is with you?"

Another pause. "Of course my guards are with me. Brother Matthew is planning to head up a party to enter the tunnels by the end of the week."

"Did you hear me?" Pastor John raised his voice. His throat burned. "I need it today. Today!"

"We are doing our best, sir," Brother David said.

Pastor John switched off the receiver and slammed it down onto the nightstand. "Worthless."

He sat hunched forward at the edge of Bertha's bed. If his legs worked properly, he would take care of the problem himself. Something wasn't right.

He's a traitor, Bertha had said. *You're a damn fool.*

He stared at the indentation in the mattress left by his wife. She couldn't have been right about such a thing. She had no true understanding of the temple's inner workings. Brother David would never dare challenge his leadership.

If things continued on the path they were on, he wouldn't last another week. He needed to pay a visit to Brother David. A surprise visit, just to make sure everyone's loyalties were genuine. But arriving by car would be less than ideal. He could ask one of his guards at The Farm for inside information, but it was better to see things for himself. Only one way to make a true surprise, stealth visit. He would separate again, traveling there by way of his shadow self.

He lay back on the bed and sank into the indentation left by Bertha. If he had withheld the Dunamis from her sooner, he wouldn't be in such a weakened state. Never again would he put anyone above the interests of the temple. Never again.

He lowered his eyelids, staring up at the ceiling, and opened himself to the darkness within his body. It stirred in his chest like a mound of maggots.

He rested his hand over his chest. The black patch of skin warmed and then burned. The fire inside energized him. His jaw dropped open as nausea churned his stomach. Something pushed against his ribcage as if a thousand swarming insects sought to escape.

There it was. His personal phantom. Moving over his collar and between the gaps where his shirt buttoned together. It flowed out like thick smoke and merged above him. The form swirled and twisted into a vague silhouette of his own body.

His consciousness split.

He stared through his own eyes, watching the dark shape float up, but at the same time his consciousness stared down on his body. The particles vibrated within his new form, expanding and contracting at will.

Go, he willed, and he floated out the bedroom window, rising into the afternoon sky. He observed the trees and houses below as he traveled across town to The Farm.

The lightness was exhilarating, and the wind had no effect on him, yet he discovered he traveled in a form with definite rules. He needed to circle around the trees and buildings. He couldn't pass through physical objects. The birds raced away from him. He soared astonishingly fast until he reached a point of maximum speed. He moved far above the treetops, still bound by a vague sense of gravity. The higher he ascended, the greater the effort.

Within minutes, he was at The Farm. He floated along the side of the main complex behind the farmhouse and entered through an air vent on the roof. Within the aluminum ducts he wound in many directions to Brother David's office.

Pastor John came out of the duct in the upper corner of the

office. The room was empty except for one guard standing alone beside a large plastic tank of black liquid. The guard's name was Brother Kevin. He'd been a loyal guard for the past year, recruited after many weeks of indoctrination and had proven himself to be a powerful asset for the temple.

Pastor John raced across the room and entered Brother Kevin's nostrils, consuming his consciousness and taking control of his body. Brother Kevin shuddered and flailed from side to side as if warding off a swarm of bees. He clawed at his hair as Pastor John flowed into his brain.

Pastor John's consciousness merged with the guard's and they became one.

The smell hit Pastor John first. The familiar stench of Dunamis.

What's in the plastic container? Pastor John asked by way of a forced thought. Pastor John directed Brother Kevin to stare down at the container, sensing his terror at being controlled.

"Dunamis," Brother Kevin said.

Pastor John had known it to be true. The stench was overwhelming. Pastor John seethed, and a bitter fury rose inside Brother Kevin's body. Perspiration formed across his host's face, although Pastor John didn't allow him to wipe it off.

Where is Brother David? Pastor John thought-projected.

"He's down the hall checking on the prisoners," Brother Kevin said.

How did you get it? Pastor John thought-projected. No need to be specific. The thought's intention was clearly understood.

"The girl took them there," Brother Kevin said.

When?

"Yesterday."

Brother Kevin's body trembled as Pastor John contemplated the situation. Brother David had lied to him. Bertha had been right. Brother David had betrayed him.

Pastor John's rage flooded through his host's body. He desired to rip Brother Kevin apart like he had done to Brother

Andrew, but he restrained himself. He scanned the room. A second jug of Dunamis sat atop a plastic tarp strewn across the tiled floor.

Brother David had denied its existence.

A liar. A traitor.

And Brother Kevin had also taken part in the betrayal, even if he hadn't helped retrieve the Dunamis.

Who else has betrayed me?

"Brothers Matthew, Isaac, Zachary, Christian, Porter, Nathan, and Paul. Brothers Zachary and Porter are dead. The phantoms devoured them in the tunnels."

All of them had been loyal guards to the temple, but Brother David had authority over them. Their minds and souls were twisted and corrupt now. He would destroy the coup members without mercy.

Is that all of them?

"Yes."

He pulled the gun from Brother Kevin's holster at his hip and thrust the barrel into his open mouth. Brother Kevin resisted the control, and even briefly lowered the gun a few inches as Pastor John pushed the barrel up against the roof of his mouth.

Don't bother fighting me. I have become death, the black horse.

Pastor John pulled the trigger. Pain exploded through Pastor John's face, but it faded away a moment later. He released himself from Brother Kevin's body, and it crumpled to the floor as Pastor John's consciousness gathered near the vent opening where he had entered the room. Blood flowed out and pooled in a wide oval around the body.

The connection to the black swarm had weakened. Pastor John willed the black ghost to return. It traveled slower on the way back to his own body. It demanded intense concentration and strength, mental and physical, to continue. Better to save his remaining strength to return to The Farm and take care of things in person. He looked forward to claiming the Dunamis and separating the faithful from the traitors. He would divide the righteous from the unholy. Cut down and destroy the enemies of the temple. Stone Hill would soon be cleansed.

Pastor John floated out into the afternoon sky. His consciousness moved over the trees, flying lower now, back to merge again with his body.

He entered his house through the open window and sank his ghost into his chest, completing the merge at last with a loud snap.

Turning over in his deceased wife's bed, he again sensed the cold emptiness of her absence. "You were right. I should have listened to you, my sweetheart."

His body chilled after his consciousness returned, and the weakness weighed heavy on every part of his body. He reached for the phone and started to call Brother Jacob, his limo driver. He switched off the phone and set it down.

Brother David's attempted coup called for something special. Something memorable.

❧ 23 ❧

A flurry of questions flooded Michael's mind. How to use those scrubs for Rebecca's escape. How to slip away to the bathroom to put them on. Would they even fit?

Two of the four guards had left with Brother Cooper. The remaining two guards stood over by the door, leaning against the wall facing each other. Under their breath, they chuckled and grunted as if sharing an obscene joke.

Lucas leaned into Michael like he would whisper something, but before he spoke, a muscular, elderly man walked between the chairs and stood in front of them, next to the cooler. Behind the lenses of his thick glasses, his eyes bulged as he stared at his captive students. His face was red and weathered, as if he'd just escaped an argument. A hunting knife sheath hung at his waist.

"Good evening, my recruits," the man said, his eyes darting back and forth at the faces around him. "God bless Pastor John! Welcome to our new members. So happy that you've chosen to be here with us."

Something inside the cooler thumped against its side, and it shifted slightly.

The man ignored the disturbance. His voice was harsh, almost grating. Michael winced as the man spoke.

"We'll get your mental frequencies to the correct pitch," the man said. "Yes, we will. One way or another. Pastor John needs you to be strong in mind if you're to be accepted as a member of the temple. Let's hear some applause for our great leader!"

Michael pretended to clap with the others.

"My name is Brother Frank, your spiritual guide through this enlightening process. Did you all hear that Pastor John is risen from the dead? Praise the temple!"

More forced applause.

"Got any ideas?" Michael whispered to Lucas beneath the clapping.

"Not yet," Lucas said.

"You're all in for a treat today," Brother Frank said. His wide grin exposed unnaturally white teeth. Probably dentures.

The prisoners who'd been in the room before Michael's group arrived hunched forward, staring at the floor. Their eyes were dull and expressionless as Brother Frank circled the space in front of them.

"Some of you have been through this before, but failed. You *will* learn what it means to have faith. Faith in the power of the temple and Pastor John. You *will* gain that faith or die. It's as simple as that. Let's begin."

Brother Frank hunkered down in front of the cooler and lifted the lid. The cooler moved on its own again before he opened it. Once the lid was removed, something sloshed inside as if a group of fish were slapping together. Brother Frank stared down into the cooler's contents and his grin grew even larger.

"Who wants to be the first?" Brother Frank asked.

"The first for what?" August asked.

Brother Frank's eyes burst open and he jumped over to August. "We have a winner. Congratulations! Stand up."

August remained seated. "I'd rather just watch, thank you."

"This is not a game. The demons that surround this town are powerful, but you can be saved through the power of Pastor John. Stand up."

"I don't need to be saved," August said.

"I should say you do. Do you think you can defeat the phantoms on your own? Is your faith so strong that you don't need Pastor John?"

August shook his head. "I don't need anyone. I can take care of myself."

"Show me. Come over here."

August shook his head and glanced over at Lucas.

"You're afraid," Brother Frank said.

"What's in the box?" August asked.

"You said you can take care of yourself. Stand up and come over here."

August glanced over at the guards near the door, then stood up. "All right, fine. Whatever crazy shit you got in there, I guess I'll find out anyway."

"Wise choice. You took your first step toward faith in the temple."

August stood up with a groan and glanced again at Lucas as he lumbered over to Brother Frank's side. He smirked before peering down into the cooler. His face turned white. His eyes widened as his mouth dropped open. "Holy shit! What the hell is that?"

"Pick it up," Brother Frank commanded. "It can't hurt you if you have faith. Lift it out and show everyone how well you can take care of yourself. Let your faith shine."

"I'm not touching that shit," August said.

The two guards near the door walked over and stood on either side of the circle of chairs. They moved into an attack stance, a hand on their billy clubs.

"You will pick it up," Brother Frank said. "You have three seconds. Three..."

"What are you, my mom?" August asked.

"...two..."

August winced. "Why do I got to touch that crappy thing?"

The two guards stepped into the circle and stood behind August.

"...one..."

"Fuck this," August said leaning forward and reaching into the cooler.

A black tentacle lashed out and gripped his arm, the teeth along its underside scratching across August's skin. It was a severed bessie tentacle roughly the size of a baseball bat. It writhed as it slithered up his arm toward his neck. August cried out and yanked at it. He strained to pull it away, but it twisted around his arm and shoulder. August's eyes darted between Michael and Lucas. He twisted around, clenching his teeth as he fought to remove the thing.

Michael stood and lurched forward. One of the guards swung around and brandished his billy club.

"Sit down," Brother Frank ordered, "unless you want to be next."

A guard pushed into Michael, knocking him back into his chair.

"You can't do that to him," Lucas said. "He's just a kid."

Brother Frank ignored Lucas and yelled as he clutched the sides of August's face, "Do you have faith?"

August pulled and clawed at the tentacle as it slinked its way around his neck. "Get it off me!"

"Do you have faith?"

"Yes, whatever," August cried as he gasped for breath, "just get this thing off me."

The tentacle snaked around August's neck like a thick black noose and squeezed. His face turned red as he choked.

"I can't take it off you," Brother Frank said. "If you have faith, you will be protected by the power of the temple."

"This is bullshit," Lucas shouted. He lurched forward, but one of the guards swung his billy club inches from Lucas's neck.

"Your friend will die without faith," Brother Frank observed. "He said he didn't need anyone." He turned to August. "You did say that, didn't you?" August's face was purple, and the air wheezed into his lungs as he desperately pulled at the flesh. He shook his head.

"You have no faith?" Brother Frank asked. "You lied to me. Liar!" He drew a deep breath, taking his time to continue. "But I will show you the power of the temple." He turned to one of the guards. "Brother Killian, the UV lights, please."

The guard went over to a switch near the door and turned them on. The room was bathed in bright daylight.

The tentacle convulsed as its skin sizzled. A fine mist of smoke poured from any area exposed to the overhead UV lights.

August gasped and pulled at the tentacle again as it loosened its grip. It fought to hold on, but he wrestled it away from his neck and slammed it to the tile floor, where it continued to writhe like fish out of water.

August backed away, bending forward with his hands over his neck, gasping and coughing. He stumbled into the prisoners behind him, finally finding his chair and sitting down. Lucas put his arm around his friend.

"Light has power over the darkness. The temple's light has power over this phantom as long as you have faith that the temple will protect you," Brother Frank said. "Were you scared? Of course. But I have no fear. Your fear is your weakness, and your lack of faith in the temple will kill you. We will protect you. Do you see?"

A guard walked off to the side of the room and returned with a stack of disposable plastic plates, forks, and knives.

Brother Frank picked up the squirming tentacle and dropped it back into the cooler. The thing thumped against the walls of the cooler, shifting it back and forth. The fine smoke still drifted up from its burning skin.

"I'm aware that all of you have just eaten," Brother Frank said. "But we must consume our enemy now to prove our faith in the temple."

Brother Frank reached into the cooler again, this time

pulling out a small chunk of black meat the size of a fist. The flesh still writhed as he gripped it, holding it out so everyone could see. He pulled the knife from the sheath at his waist and sliced it up, with each plate the guard held out receiving a single truffle-sized piece. The flesh squirmed even as the guard handed the plates to the prisoners.

"You must eat all of it, if you are to pass this test of your faith," Brother Frank said. "Don't leave even a single, tiny scrap. All the evil must be devoured. If you have faith, you will succeed. If you don't, as I said in the beginning, you will die. Those who fail this test, as some of you have discovered, will not receive food or water until it's completed. The test will be given once per day until you either have faith, or you perish. Bon appétit."

Brother Frank stood and watched them holding their writhing meals. The prisoners who were in the room before Michael's group began eating the squirming mass even before Brother Frank had finished speaking.

"I'm not going to eat this," Michael said.

"Then you will die." Brother Frank reached into the cooler and pulled out the tentacle, moving it toward Michael's face. "Do you say you have no faith?"

Michael glanced at Lucas and grimaced before biting into the meat. How bad could it be? Rebecca's image passed through his mind. He would do this for her. The bitter flesh was more awful than anything he could have imagined. His gag reflex kicked in and he struggled to keep from vomiting. The coarse skin of the flesh scraped against his tongue until the slimy muscles burst through and slid to the back of his throat. Its black blood squirted over his lips.

Brother Frank turned to the other prisoners. "Everyone will learn their place here at the temple. You belong to Pastor John now. You will do what we say. And in return, you will live with open eyes and hearts that rejoice in Pastor John's name."

Michael vomited.

Brother Frank groaned and shook his head. "That's unfortunate. You will return tomorrow for another chance to prove yourself. No food or water until then."

Without asking permission, Michael jumped out of his seat and rushed to the bathroom. The guards didn't stop him or go after him.

Michael shut the bathroom door and started removing his white prisoner's uniform, staring down at Brother Cooper's gray scrubs. Maybe they would fit, maybe not. He wouldn't know until he tried.

He stopped. Something bulged within one of the pockets of the scrubs. He scooped up the scrub top and reached his hand in. He pulled out a Taser.

Michael's heart beat faster. *That* would help them more than the uniform.

A guard cracked his billy club against the door. Michael scrambled to find a place to hide the Taser.

"You can't be in there," the guard said.

"Yes, sir," Michael said, stuffing the Taser within a fold of his uniform. He pushed the scrubs into the corner and flushed the toilet even though he hadn't used it.

Opening the door, he clutched his stomach and winced as if he'd spent his bathroom break in great pain. He adjusted his clothes as the guard followed him back to his seat. Michael stared at Lucas with a subtle grin.

Lucas studied his expression and then formed a grin of his own with narrow eyes.

Two more prisoners vomited after Michael sat down. The distraction gave him a chance to whisper to Lucas.

"I got you a present," Michael said.

"What?" Lucas asked.

Michael pulled back a corner of his prisoner's uniform, revealing the Taser underneath.

Lucas's eyebrows shot up. "Holy Hannah."

A rush of excitement passed through Michael, mixed with the nausea. At least they had a chance now.

❧ 24 ❧

Joey sat alone in his room. A camera in the room's corner near the door stared down at him. A red light glowed below the camera. They were watching him. What for? What were they expecting he'd do? He was a rat in a cage, on display for everyone to see. No better than a damn lab rat waiting his turn for medical experiments.

His dad had dropped him in that cage like a sack of cow manure. His own dad. Nothing Joey could do about it, except do what he was told. He had no choice.

He'd tried explaining that his friends needed help, but his dad couldn't understand that. His dad didn't have friends. Not human friends. His friends were bottles. Lots of bottles of every color and size, stashed in cupboards and drawers and behind piles of clothes scattered around the house. His friends liked to chat too. After emptying the contents of those bottles, his dad talked to them at night, sometimes answering silent questions with confessions Joey would just as soon forget. Not even the temple could break the friendship between his dad and those bottles.

But his old man had left him there.

"Rot in hell," his dad had said before slamming the door.

So he sat there and rotted, unable to think of anything that might make the situation better. He'd really messed up this time, and maybe he'd never get another chance to be somebody in his dad's eyes.

"Never amount to a bucket of shit," his dad had said after arresting him and his friends.

So what was the point of arguing anymore? His dad never listened to him, anyway. Joey just wanted to get his friends out of there and get things back to normal. He missed his bedroom and his dog Buford. And his mom. At least she would have stood up for him.

"Mom," he said to the bare tile floor. "Where are you?"

The door to his room opened, and Joey didn't bother to look up. It would just be some stupid temple guard to harass him, or some clever temple doctor to help *enlighten* him.

"You really did it this time," his dad's voice bellowed after the door latched shut. "As soon as I came around that corner and saw that pack of shit kids, I knew I'd find you stuck in the middle somewhere."

Joey twisted around and stared up into his dad's eyes. His dad's arms were crossed over his chest and the usual scowl on his face was gone. He stared at the floor with dull eyes.

"I told you what would happen if you kept hanging out with those shitty kids," his dad said in a softer, monotone voice. "I've done everything I can to get you to wise up and follow Pastor John, but you just keep crawling deeper into your hole, don't you? What the hell happened to you over the last couple of weeks? You been a real pain in the ass."

"You got to help get us out of here," Joey said.

"Shut your big trap," his dad said, raising his voice. He shut his eyes while taking in a deep breath, continuing in a softer tone. "Things are looking bad. Ain't nothing going to get you out of here this time. I got all my buddies laughing at me, saying I don't know how to raise a kid."

"I'm sorry," Joey said.

His dad stared into Joey's eyes. "Look what you've done to me. The whole temple thinks I'm in on your little scheme too."

"We just came in here to get Rebecca out. That's all we wanted. I didn't mean to cause you any trouble."

"Well, look where that got you."

"We just wanted to help Rebecca. That's all."

"Now it's a real mess, isn't it? Got all your shit friends in here too. What the hell are you going to do about it?"

"I don't know." Joey hunched forward and looked at the floor while running his fingers through his hair.

"It's a real mess."

"We still got to get Rebecca out of here." Joey met his dad's eyes. "We can't let them hurt her. Maybe they'll even try to kill her."

"That's none of your business. You sow what you reap. She'll get what she deserves."

"But I care about her."

"Rebecca's gone." His dad raised his voice again. "She ain't your girlfriend no more. I jumped for joy when you two broke up. I always knew she wasn't right in the brain. Always singing and dancing like she just got out of the nuthouse. She's one of those wacky drama students too. None of them ain't right. She's one of those secular rebels."

"She's not like that."

His dad jumped forward, displaying the back of his hand. Joey winced and his muscles tightened, preparing to be smacked across the face, but his dad backed down.

"Just a smart ass know-it-all. You don't have any idea what you're in for. They won't just have a little talk with you. *Little Joey, you been a bad boy. Please be good now,*" his dad mocked. "They will process you today and run you through the whole program. You ain't coming back the same, I promise you. But that ain't such a bad thing, seeing as though you was needing an attitude adjustment for years. Probably just as well you went through the program, anyway. You've been needing a real kick in the ass. So who will help you now?"

Joey stared at the floor. "I don't know, but I have to help Rebecca."

"There ain't no more Rebecca! They'll show her the light just the same as you."

His dad turned his back on him and stepped toward the door.

"You can't just leave me in here."

"Hell if I can't. You got a lot of growing up to do. It's time you took care of yourself."

"I'm only seventeen."

"Old enough to know better than to hang around with a bunch of loser kids. I thought I raised you better than that."

"They're not losers."

"No?" His dad glanced back at him. "So where are they? Huh? You tell me where they're at right now. They're sitting in the other rooms rotting away just like you'll do. I can't get nothing through your head. Looks like you need to learn things the hard way."

Joey's dad took another step toward the door. "That's all I got to say about it. Time to grow up. Welcome to life."

"You got to help us."

His dad groaned and shook his head. "I don't know what you're going to do now. Things are bad."

"Help me, Dad."

"I may not see you again," his dad said softly. "What a waste."

He swiped his key card against the key pad next to the door, and the lock clicked open. He walked out into the hallway without looking back. The door slammed shut behind him.

Joey stood up and hurried over to the small window in the door. His dad walked away and never looked back. Was that it? His dad really would not help him?

Joey tried to turn the door handle. Locked as expected.

A guard marched by the room and sneered as he passed. That

same guard had worked with his dad during the construction stages of The Farm. Joey had spent many hours hanging out at the construction site as it was being built and remembered laughing with that guard after he'd shared some particularly disgusting jokes.

Now Joey was appalled that he'd laughed with the guard about anything. A bitterness passed through his chest. None of the temple folk were good people. All of them, just a bunch of phonies.

The guard would probably run back to all his friends and have a laugh. *Brian Lynch's kid got himself stuck in The Farm.*

"Ha-ha," Joey muttered to himself. "Have a good laugh, you shitheads."

"Never amount to a bucket of shit," his dad had said. Maybe his dad was right. Maybe he was just a waste.

Joey sat back down on the metal bench and punched his fist into his open hand. He would break out of there one way or another. Nobody could keep him down. If he could just get his hands on a good weapon, he'd bust right out of that room.

Something slid under his door. He stared at the object for a moment. It appeared to be a credit card at first, but then he recognized it. A key card for the door lock.

Joey eyed the window in the door, expecting someone's face to stare in at him. It couldn't possibly be a key card. The guards were pulling a joke on him. Maybe the same guard who had just walked by. They were setting him up, but he would not fall for it. His eyes narrowed as he kept staring at the window for a few minutes, waiting for someone to peek in to see if he was falling for the bait.

A few more minutes passed, and he still hadn't seen anyone in the window. Not even the guards walked by. Maybe one of the guards had dropped it by accident and had kicked it into his room. If so, they'd be looking for it soon.

Standing, Joey sauntered over to the key card and snatched it up from the ground. He kept his eyes on the window, still expecting the joker guard's wide grin to appear. He pressed his forehead against the glass and looked out in both directions. Nobody in sight. If it was a joke, they were doing a good job of playing him. It had to be a decoy card. They'd wait until he swiped it, then have a good laugh when the light flashed red.

Okay, he'd play along. Joey stretched the card out and swiped it against the key pad beside his door. The green light appeared and the door latch clicked. He pulled on the handle. The door opened.

Joey shot a glance up at the camera in the corner of his room. The red light was off. They wouldn't have shut it off if it was a joke. Maybe the light had malfunctioned. Either way, joke or not, he was getting out.

Heading out the door, he glanced in both directions before moving forward. The guard had passed by fifteen minutes earlier. They'd be checking on him again soon.

He scanned his memory of the corridors and rooms near him. He'd explored every foot of the place while it was being built. The whole concept of architecture fascinated him. He'd studied the blueprints with his dad at his side, asking questions about every phase of the construction. The plumbing, the electrical system, the heating and ventilation system, the purpose of each wall, door, and window. Not many places to hide, but there were a few. Some maintenance closets, a storage closet, a utility shed out back. But within those rooms, he'd be trapped.

He needed to get as close to Rebecca as possible, but also find Michael and Lucas. He needed a way to get around The Farm unnoticed.

Only one way to do that. Pastor John's passageways under the building. Joey had raced through them, chasing squirrels with a .22 caliber rifle two years earlier while they were being built. Only a select few high-ranking temple leaders knew about them —including his dad, who'd explained they existed so Pastor John could get in and out without being seen. One of the entrances was only a short distance away, hidden behind a door at the end of the hallway.

Joey's heart pounded as he hurried down the hallway. Maybe his keycard wouldn't work for that door. Footsteps echoed in the distance. He arrived at the door and swiped his key card against the pad. The light turned green. A name also appeared on the key pad. *Lynch, Brian.*

🙏 25 🙏

M ichael surveyed the room. Only two guards to deal with at the moment. With a good plan and a little luck, it might be their best chance to rescue Rebecca. Lucas whispered something to August as another prisoner regurgitated his bessie meal.

Brother Frank shut the cooler lid and slipped his knife back into its sheath. Brother Killian flipped off the UV lights.

"Looks like most of you failed the test," Brother Frank said. "You'll be good and hungry by tomorrow, and that hunk of meat will taste like a fine delicacy."

The floor was littered with pools of vomit. Everyone except for one prisoner had contributed to the mess. The other guard brought over a mop and a bucket of water, setting it down in front of Michael.

"You started this," the guard said. "You clean it up."

Michael groaned and folded forward holding his stomach. His arm lay over the Taser beneath the white clothing.

"I don't feel so good," Michael said.

"I don't care," the guard said. "Stand up. This is your mess."

Lucas stood suddenly and grabbed the mop. "I'll do it."

The guard jerked back, resting a hand on his billy club and unlatching his Taser. Brother Killian remained by the door.

"I don't mind," Lucas said. "We need to help each other, right?"

The guard glared at Lucas and stepped back. "I don't care who cleans this mess, but the floor better shine when you're done."

Lucas started mopping it up.

August looked at Michael. As the guard stepped away, Michael revealed the Taser, and August's eyes went wide.

"Brother Frank?" August said, standing up. "I can do it this time."

Brother Frank eyed him suspiciously. "Sit down. One chance per day. No food until tomorrow, *if* you succeed."

"I don't care about the food," August said, pointing at the cooler. "I have faith. It won't attack me. I'm sure of it."

Brother Frank chuckled. "You have a long way to go before you can claim to have faith in our temple."

"Please give me another chance. I'll do it this time."

Brother Frank's eyebrows jumped up and he smirked. "Fine. Let's see if you're right. Except I won't be stepping in to save you. You're on your own."

August took a deep breath. "I understand."

Brother Frank moved over to the cooler with the guard at his side. "Get in close," Brother Frank said with a wide grin. "Give it all the faith you got."

The guard chuckled and stood between Michael and August with his hands on his billy club and Taser.

In an instant, Michael understood what August was doing. It would be a simple matter for Michael to reach out and tase the guard. Lucas was still mopping, but watching the events from the corner of his eye. If they all struck at once, they could do it.

August stood directly in front of the cooler as Brother Frank leaned down to open it.

"I got a good feeling about this," August said, rubbing his hands together with enthusiasm.

"Wonderful." Brother Frank's grin widened as he lifted the cooler lid.

August lurched sideways and spun around. He grabbed onto the back of Brother Frank's head and thrust him down into the open cooler. The tentacle latched onto Brother Frank's face and he stumbled back, clawing at it as he screamed.

Lucas swung the mop handle around, cracking it into the guard's neck. The impact knocked him to the side, but he grabbed the mop handle on the rebound and yanked it away.

The guard regained his balance for a moment before Michael jumped forward and tased him. The guard cried out and dropped to the floor convulsing.

"Stop where you are!" Brother Killian yelled, flipping on the UV lights and jumping toward them with his Taser and billy club out.

A few prisoners scrambled back against the wall. Some froze in their chairs. None of them moved to help them.

The bessie tentacle writhed and smoked, as Brother Frank struggled to rip himself free.

"Get on the ground!" Brother Killian yelled as he approached them.

A woman appeared in the doorway. Holy Hannah stood alone with wide eyes as she gasped and pointed at the ghastly scene in the center of the room.

"What have you done?" she shrieked.

Brother Killian jumped when her voice pierced the air.

"You've butchered its offspring," Holy Hannah cried out. "Such evil. The beast will demand retribution."

Brother Killian shot a glance over his shoulder. "For God's sake, Hannah, get the hell out of here."

Holy Hannah screamed, "Pastor John has committed fornication with the great harlot!"

"Any more of that nonsense and you'll go back into solitary."

Michael, Lucas, and August lurched toward Brother Killian. Michael lifted the Taser again as he ran. A surge of energy pulsed through him. The moment had come and he wouldn't stop for anything.

"Freeze," Brother Killian shouted.

Moments before they collided, Holy Hannah jumped onto Brother Killian's back and yelled, "You butchers!"

"Knock it off!"

"You've desecrated the children of the beast."

"Goddammit, Hannah." Brother Killian stumbled forward.

Holy Hannah's arms were wrapped around his neck and face. "The beast will make the harlot desolate. Pride goes before destruction!"

Michael brought the Taser in to Brother Killian's chest and fired. The guard collapsed with Holy Hannah still riding him.

"Beg the beast for forgiveness," Holy Hannah yelled. "Plead for mercy!"

Michael, Lucas, and August charged out the door and down the hallway.

The guards were slow to react at first. Maybe they assumed Holy Hannah was behind the commotion. But despite the distraction she provided, the guards soon closed in on them.

With his heart racing, Michael led Lucas and August toward the door where he had seen Rebecca earlier.

After turning a corner and entering the room, echoes of shouting guards filled the hallway behind them. They wouldn't have much time to get Rebecca out of there.

Rebecca was still sitting at the same table, with Maggie next to her. Her eyes were wide and dazed.

Michael charged over and threw an arm around her. "Rebecca, let's get out of here."

She met his eyes and her face lit up. "Oh, Michael!"

She jumped out of her seat and wrapped her arms around him. The warmth of her body melted his heart, and he never wanted to let her go.

"No, no," Maggie said. "Go away! Guards! Guards, help!" Maggie wedged her fist between them.

Michael pulled Rebecca toward the door, but not only did Maggie tug at her, Rebecca also resisted him.

"What's going on?" she asked with glassy eyes.

"Rebecca, let's go. Now," Michael said.

Lucas and August pulled at Maggie's waist and arms, slowly ripping her away from Rebecca, but Maggie held on and wrapped her body around Rebecca's as if to shelter her from an attack.

"Why?" Rebecca asked.

"We're getting you out," Michael said.

Maggie slammed her fists into Lucas and August. "Leave her alone."

Rebecca stared into Michael's eyes and turned back toward Maggie.

"You can't take her!" Maggie screamed.

A guard appeared in the doorway to the room.

"We have to go," Lucas said, pulling at Michael's arm.

He clung to Rebecca for as long as he could. Maggie yanked Rebecca back, putting her in the middle of a tug-of-war for a moment, before she slipped from his grasp.

"Time's up," Lucas said to Michael. "We'll come back."

"I'm sorry," Michael said to her.

Rebecca stared wide-eyed at Michael as the boys fled through a door across the room.

They burst into a short hallway with closed offices on both sides. Small dark windows in the center of each door revealed that the rooms were empty. They tried each door, but all were locked. Ahead of them, the hallway ended. No way out.

❦ 26 ❦

"What do we do now?" August asked. "I don't want to go back in there."

Michael rattled the door handle to the room closest to him, even though August had already done the same. "There's got to be a way out."

A face appeared in the darkened window on the door furthest away. It was Joey. Michael was stunned as the door opened.

"Get in here," Joey urged, gesturing them to come in. He held a broom handle like a sword. "I thought I heard your voice."

"What the hell?" Lucas asked.

"Just get in," Joey said pushing them in as they hurried past him. "Go to the back."

They rushed in, and Joey shut the door behind them. By the light coming in through the small window in the door, Michael saw they were in a storage room full of towels, clothing, bed sheets, and many other supplies. Boxes of toilet paper stacked to the ceiling filled in the back wall. He scanned the room for anything he might use as a weapon. A toilet plunger. A toilet brush. Nothing more than that.

They crowded in behind the stack of toilet paper where

some boxes had been pushed aside. An air intake vent cover hung partially open.

"Keep going," Joey said. "Through the air vent." Joey lifted the metal cover revealing a dark passageway roughly two square feet wide.

Lucas and August crawled in first. Michael followed, then Joey closed the grate behind them. The metal walls of the duct rattled and banged as they entered. August's shoes squeaked as he pushed forward.

"How did you get in here?" Michael asked.

"Shh," Joey said. "Stop."

They all froze. The door to the storage room had opened, and the light was flipped on, throwing a row of fine beams on the bottom of the air duct behind them. Someone entered the room, knocked against some of the boxes and left.

They started moving again, slowly at first.

"Where does this go?" Michael asked. "I hope not to the incinerator."

"It's the fresh air intake," Joey said. "It goes far enough to get us out of here. I guess you didn't get Rebecca yet, huh?"

"We couldn't get her out." Michael couldn't believe he was saying that. "We were right there with her, but she refused to leave. I even tried to pull her away."

"The temple's already clouded her mind," Lucas said.

"Don't you worry about it," Joey said. "I got it all taken care of. Keep going forward, but go slow or someone might hear us."

They shuffled through the ducts, crawling along on their hands and knees, until Joey instructed them to turn right.

"Just a little further," Joey said.

The darkness of the shaft gave way to light peering through a metal grate ahead.

Lucas whispered back to Joey. "Out this way?"

"Yes," Joey answered. "Twist the two metal tabs near the top to open it. Don't let it fall open. It'll bang really loud, so make sure—"

Lucas stopped moving. Voices erupted on the other side. A group of people walked by, throwing a strobe of shadows across Lucas's body. Lucas peered out and waited until after they had passed to speak.

"Four guards," Lucas whispered. "Some prisoners too."

"What do we do?" August asked.

"Wait," Lucas said.

"They go back to their rooms after supper," Joey whispered. "Rebecca's room is just down the hall."

"How do you know?" Michael asked.

"The computer told me," Joey said.

"What computer?"

"My dad's computer," Joey said. "I snuck into his office with his key card and located her room. We're only about twenty feet away."

"How'd you get his key card?"

"Someone slipped it under my door."

"Why would someone do that?"

Joey paused. "I don't know."

"Maybe that was her walking past just now."

"Maybe," Joey said.

They sat in silence for a long time until Lucas confirmed that all four guards had left the area and flipped off the main hallway light. Lucas opened the grate, and they climbed out into a small area like a waiting room. They scanned the area for any signs of guards, but everything was quiet. They stepped lightly through the open room toward a hallway.

Joey stared at the Taser in Michael's hand. "Where the hell did you get that?"

"Someone left it behind. I snagged it."

"A gun would have been better."

"He didn't have a gun."

"That's your only weapon?"

"Well, my Taser beats your broom stick."

Joey looked at the broom handle in his hands. "It might come in handy. Better than nothing, man."

"Lead the way," Lucas said.

"Where are we going?" Michael asked.

"Not far," Joey said. "Bex is down this way."

They hurried down the short dead end hallway to a single door, passing an empty guard station, a swivel chair, and a desk with a small lamp lighting a mess of papers.

Joey stepped ahead of them and pulled a key card from his pocket, swiping it along a magnetic strip at the side of a door at the back of the waiting room. The door latch snapped open. "She should be in here."

They entered the room and Michael flipped on the light switch. Rebecca lay on her bed in the corner. Her hair poured off the edge of her pillow and a white sheet draped over her figure.

Rebecca moaned and covered her eyes when the light came on.

"Just like Sleeping Beauty," August said.

"Wake her up," Michael said. "I'll watch the door."

Joey walked over and crouched down next to her.

"Bex," Joey said.

Her eyes sprang open, and she gasped as she raised herself onto her elbows. She peered around the room with her jaw hanging open. She looked at Michael and then back to Joey. "What are you doing here?"

"We're getting you out," Joey said.

She looked at the broom handle in Joey's hand. "What are you going to do with that?"

"Oh," Joey said, swinging the pole from side to side, "I just brought it in case."

She squinted. "What time is it?"

"Beats me," Joey said. "But we better get our butts moving."

"How did you get in?" She sat up even further and brushed the hair out of her eyes. "You shouldn't be in here."

"We broke in to rescue you," Lucas said.

"What for?"

"Like I said," Joey said, "to get you out of here."

Rebecca's white pajamas contrasted with a patch of cuts and bruises running down the left side of her neck as if someone had tried to strangle her. Her eyes were bloodshot, and she raised her arm to block out the light.

Joey moved in a little closer to her. "What happened to you?"

"It doesn't matter." She forced a grin. "We got more Dunamis."

"What do you mean? We don't need any of that crap."

"For Pastor John. Brother David led us into the tunnels yesterday. I took him over to the place where we found that pond of the Dunamis. We got some out for him, a lot more than last time. Brother David said that Pastor John will be very happy."

"What are you talking about? Why did you do that?"

Rebecca nodded slowly. "All for the temple. I was doing my duty."

"She's been drugged, guys," Lucas said. "She's not thinking straight. Let's get her and go."

"Who did that to your face?" Joey asked in a harsh tone. "Jesus Christ, Bex, you're a mess. Did David do that?"

Rebecca gently touched her swollen eye and the cuts across her cheek. "No, not Brother David. The phantoms got too close. It's my fault, really. I should have been more careful. If Brother David hadn't protected me, the phantoms would have taken me away too."

"David doesn't protect anybody." Michael said. "Why did you help them get more of that black crud?"

"The temple needed it. I wanted to do my part."

"Why would you help them?" Joey asked. "You can't trust them."

"They're not so bad. I was wrong not to trust them. I see now that everything we did before to stop them was wrong. We have to help them."

Joey moved in close to Rebecca and rested his hand on the back of her hair. "Oh, Rebecca, did they mess with your mind?"

Rebecca pulled away. "Nobody's messing with my mind, Joey." She pursed her lips and stared at the floor. "And I don't need anybody to get me out. I want to be here. And now I just need to rest, so you guys can leave."

Joey looked back at Michael. "They either drugged her or brainwashed her. Or both."

"You can't stay here," August said to Rebecca. "You'll die."

"I won't die. That's ridiculous."

"No, Rebecca, we're taking you out of here tonight. Get out of bed." Michael pulled her by the arm, and for the second time she resisted him.

"You can't make me," she said. "Michael, I don't want to be saved. Some of us don't want to be rescued. This is what I need. They really understand me now, and I want to help them. I'm fine."

"You're not fine," Michael said. "You just told me that Pastor John is not such a bad guy. That's nuts. That just screams 'I'm not fine.'"

"We've been wrong about him," Rebecca said. "We never took enough time to really listen to what he has to say. You know, before you came here, I finally saw the reality that Pastor John has so much to offer the world. I see the big picture now. I don't think you should have come. You shouldn't be in Stone Hill."

Rebecca's words pierced Michael's heart. He never imagined she would say such a thing. *You shouldn't be in Stone Hill.* The words echoed in his mind.

It made no sense that she should want to stay. It had to be the temple talking through her. Those words hadn't come from her heart. Her mind was polluted now.

Her words hurt his heart anyway. He glanced at Joey.

"Huh?" Joey's brow furrowed, and he scratched his head.

Michael shook away his feelings. "After we get you out of

here, you'll get better."

"I don't want to be better, except through the temple." Rebecca crawled out of bed and stood staring at Joey. "You understand, right? I mean, you were in the temple. Maybe you'll come back with me?"

Joey raised his brows and looked at Michael. Then back at her. "After our last run-in with Pastor John, I don't see how I could ever go back."

She turned her face down. "Oh, I thought we were so close."

Stepping in, Joey put his arm around her shoulder. "We are close, Bex, and we'll always stay close. You're just not thinking straight right now. They did something to you. Please trust us. We're doing what's best for you."

Michael wanted to put his arm around her too. Rebecca leaned into Joey and Michael wanted her to lean into him. He wanted to comfort and support her, but reality seized him. No time for feelings. They had to get out of there. Take her home so she could clear her mind again, like opening a window in a smoke-filled room. By the sound of it, she would need time to get back to normal. It was appalling how much damage the temple had done in such a short while.

"Rebecca, you need to get out of bed. We're not leaving without you."

"I don't want to go," she said.

"What should we do?" Joey asked.

"Drag her out of here if we have to." Michael stepped toward Rebecca. She folded her arms over her chest.

Joey tugged at her arm, but she resisted.

"I'll scream," Rebecca said.

"Bex, you're being ridiculous," Joey said.

"Rebecca! My name is Rebecca!"

"Keep your voice down," Joey said.

"Don't tell me what to do."

"Your mom misses you," Michael said. "She's in a lot of pain without you."

"I'll see her in a few weeks when I leave here."

"They'll never let you out of here alive," Michael said. "Just look at yourself in the mirror. They'll keep taking advantage of you until you're dead."

A voice echoed down the hallway. They all went silent. Michael and Joey looked at Rebecca.

"Rebecca," Michael pleaded, "just come with us now. Your mom is worried about you. Trust me."

Michael took her arm and she sighed, allowing herself to be pulled toward them. He held one arm, while Joey held her other side. She wobbled forward as if a little drunk.

Michael stared at her bare feet. "Where are your shoes?"

"I don't need any secular possessions. The temple serves all my needs."

Joey rolled his eyes and moved her forward slowly. She limped and winced when she stepped onto her right foot.

"I can't walk quickly," she said. "My legs are pretty banged up too."

"What did they do to you?" Joey asked.

"They didn't do anything," Rebecca said. "It's my fault."

"You'll feel better at home with your mom," Michael said.

"I don't want to go home. I'm happy here."

Rebecca's bare feet slapped down against the tiled floor as she lumbered forward.

"I found her shoes," August said, holding up a pair of white tennis shoes.

Lucas and August slipped them on her feet as Michael and Joey held her up.

"I don't feel so good," she said, resting her hand on her forehead.

Michael examined the cuts on her neck. "We'll get you to a doctor."

"Pray for me."

They moved her over to the door and stopped. The echo of men's voices in the hallway grew louder.

"Stay back," Michael said, flipping off the lights. He pushed the door closed and slid against the side of the wall next to the door.

Joey handed the broom handle to Lucas and led Rebecca toward the back of the room.

"You hit him first," Michael said, "then I'll zap him. Same as before."

"Got it," Lucas said.

Michael's heart pounded as he raised the Taser to chest level and stayed motionless, watching the door. Lucas lifted the broom handle over his head, standing opposite Michael. August crouched down with his hands forming claws as if ready to pounce on the guards like a tiger.

Joey and Rebecca stood in the darkest corner of the room, yet their silhouettes were still visible within the ambient light. Maybe the guards would pass by without looking in.

The door lock clicked, and the door swung open toward Lucas and August. The first guard entered the room with his billy club out and ready. Footsteps from another guard rustled further back; only the front edge of his figure was visible.

The first guard flipped on the light and drew a pistol from his holster. "What are you doing in here?"

Joey's eyes were wide, and he moved in front of Rebecca. "Ah..."

"Get on the ground," the first guard yelled at Joey, aiming the pistol at his chest.

The second guard moved forward, brandishing a club. Lucas swung the broom handle down on the first guard's pistol. The handle cracked against the barrel of the weapon, breaking the handle in half, but it served its purpose. The pistol flew from the guard's grasp and cracked down against the tiled floor.

Both Lucas and the first guard lurched for the pistol at the same time. Lucas grabbed it first and fired it into the guard's chest. Rebecca shrieked as the guard reeled backwards and collapsed to the floor.

Joey growled as he charged at the second guard.

At the same time, Michael thrust the Taser forward and zapped the second guard in the chest.

When Joey slammed into the man, he was already convulsing from the shock, and both toppled onto the cement floor. Joey wrestled with him for a few seconds before slamming his fist across the guard's jaw, knocking him out.

Joey was gasping as he stood, keeping an eye on his victim. "We should get out of here."

Michael turned to Rebecca. "Where's the Dunamis?"

Rebecca frowned and looked at the floor.

He repeated, "Rebecca, where is the Dunamis?"

"In Brother David's office," she answered. "We went through so much to get it. Two men died."

"A lot more than that will die if we don't get rid of it. Where's his office?"

Rebecca stared into Michael's eyes and nodded. "Down the hall. I'll show you."

Joey retrieved one of the splintered ends of the broom handle. "See? I told you it would come in handy."

The five of them rushed down the hall with Rebecca leading the way. Lucas gripped the pistol at his side. Joey held the broken broom handle, and Michael carried the Taser.

Joey moved with a limp.

"You all right?" Michael asked.

"I jammed my knee on the floor," Joey answered. "I'll be fine. Better than those guys we left back there."

"It's not too far," Rebecca said, her voice wavering and cracking with the tears that dripped into her mouth. "This is all so wrong."

"That's the temple talking," Michael said.

"Did they give you any drugs, Bex?" Joey asked.

"They gave me some shots of medicine," she answered. "To clear my mind."

"It wasn't medicine," Joey said.

They only walked a short distance and turned a corner to face a closed door.

Rebecca had stopped crying, but her eyes were red and watering. She gestured to a door ahead. "It's through there."

Joey dug out his key card again. If it didn't work, they could use the pistol to blow off the lock.

Joey swiped the card along the strip at the side of the door. The light turned green, and a latch clicked. Joey held the door open as they all ran in.

Within the darkened room, a giant face stared back at them. A poster-sized portrait of Pastor John hung on a wall between two rows of metal lockers.

Michael stared into Pastor John's eyes, and a chill passed through his body. His heart raced. He'd seen those eyes in his nightmares. They looked familiar, as if he were experiencing a déjà vu. He'd been there before, up close to that phony smile.

The connection hit him like a blaring horn. He shuddered. Those were the eyes of the thing that had attacked him on the road the previous day. The eyes of the black cloud that had swarmed in on him. That thing had come from Pastor John. It *was* Pastor John.

Rebecca broke the connection when she flipped on the light. The feeling of déjà vu drifted away.

"This doesn't look like his office," Joey said.

"It's part of it," she said. "His desk is in the next room through that door." She motioned to the right. "Over there."

Against the wall to the left was a row of lockers stacked two units high and ten units across. A name was displayed on the front of each locker. Maybe Teacher Tony or one of those asshole guards kept their stuff there. Along the wall to the right a set of metal shelves reached the ceiling. Each shelf was packed with large plastic buckets without labels. Through the clear plastic Michael saw they were filled with odds and ends, like things you'd find in a person's pocket. Cell phones, wallets, jewelry, watches, coins, and other paper items.

Michael spotted his backpack on one of the shelves. He grabbed and unzipped it. Empty. The medallion was missing, along with the pistol. He searched the shelves for any sign of the items, but they were gone.

August dug through one of the plastic buckets and pulled out a handful of cellphones. "I'm taking these!"

"Grab a bunch," Lucas said. "We can use them."

"Throw them in here," Michael said, opening his backpack as if it were a Halloween bag accepting candy. August dropped several phones inside, and Michael slipped on the backpack.

Next to the shelves, another pair of lockers were painted orange. A metal mesh revealed their contents, a row of eight assault rifles. A large, thick padlock secured the door.

Michael moved to the entrance of David's office. "Joey, get your key card over here."

Joey walked to the door and swiped the key card. The light on the magnetic strip flashed red and Michael's heart skipped a beat.

"Again," Michael said.

Joey swiped it a second time, and that time it worked. The light flashed green, and they pushed into the next room. A horrible smell filled the air. A nauseating, familiar stench that made his stomach churn, but he couldn't escape it. He breathed in the disgusting air of Dunamis.

August groaned. "What's that stink?"

"The stuff we're looking for," Michael answered.

"Smells like dead animals."

Michael flipped on the light as they all entered. He spotted the Dunamis right away. Two large, clear, five-gallon plastic jugs sat in the center of the room on a large plastic tarp. The black liquid filled both jugs, and traces of it had spilled over the top edge, leaving streaks down the sides. An assault rifle lay on a small table to the side of the room. Another smaller portrait of Pastor John stared down at them from above the desk in the corner. Pastor John's eyes watched them as they moved further into the room.

"Over there," Rebecca said, pointing to the desk. "That's Brother David's desk."

"He had you bring all this back?" Michael asked, gesturing to the two plastic jugs.

"Yes."

"From that same pit where Michael got his?" Joey asked.

"Yes," Rebecca said. "I'm sorry."

"You don't have to be sorry," Michael said. "They're using you."

Michael jumped over to one of the two jugs. He unscrewed the cap and scanned the surrounding area.

"How can we destroy this?" Michael asked.

"There's a drain in the locker room," Lucas said.

"Perfect." Michael set down his Taser on the floor and struggled to lift the first jug. Lucas set down his pistol next to the Taser and helped him. Together they carried the jug back to the locker room and toppled it onto its side near the drain. The Dunamis chugged out and disappeared into the hole.

Rebecca cringed. "Pastor John needs that to help people."

Michael shook his head. "We have to get rid of it, Rebecca. He's not using it to help people."

"If you get rid of it," Rebecca said, "he'll just force us to go back down there and get more. Better to just let them have it now."

"We won't let them kidnap you again," Michael said.

Joey wrapped his arm around her. "That's the temple talking. They really messed with your mind."

Michael and Lucas returned to David's office to get the second jug. A few steps into the room, Lucas stopped them.

"Look what I found," Lucas said. He snatched up an object from David's desk and held it up. The medallion. He handed it to Michael.

"I thought I'd never see this again," Michael said, running his fingers along the gem in the center for a moment before glancing around the room.

What other things would he find if he snooped through David's office? What other items was David hiding in there? Drawers and cabinets sat behind the desk. He would search through every one if he had more time.

Michael slipped the medallion into his backpack and pointed to a door in the corner of David's office. "Rebecca, does that door lead outside?"

"I'm not sure," she said in a broken voice.

Michael hurried to the door and jiggled the handle, but it was locked. Joey walked over with his key card and swiped it. The light turned red. He tried it again with the same result.

The pistol was on the floor near the second jug of Dunamis. Michael could shoot the lock off, but the blast would attract attention. He glanced back at David's desk. A black stone, about the size of a softball, sat below the computer monitor. He picked it up and was surprised by its weight. It should have only weighed five or ten pounds by its size, but it was thirty or forty pounds.

"Someone could use this as a cannonball," Michael said, carrying it over to the door.

"Let's do it," Joey said. "Find me a cannon."

Michael smashed the black stone down onto the door handle, shattering it on the first try, but the latch inside the door remained locked. A few swings later, the latch cracked, and the door swung open.

August moved forward, but Michael stopped him.

"Just a minute." Michael set the black stone on the floor and returned to David's desk. This time he picked up the assault rifle and checked the magazine. Fully loaded.

Joey walked ahead this time and flipped on the lights. The room inside was cold and sterile. It resembled an operating room at a hospital. The walls were lined with metal cabinets and countertops they might find in a restaurant. A large metal table sat in the center of the room like a kitchen island, with drawers on each side. Against one wall, a plastic red canister had the words "Hazardous Waste" written across the front in large yellow letters.

Michael looked at the others. Their faces reflected his own feelings of confusion and amazement.

"It looks like a doctor's office," Lucas said.

"Dr. David," Joey said.

They stepped further into the room. Another door on the far side of the room had metal bars and a small circular window in the center. The window was dark.

Lucas and August peered into some cabinets and drawers. August pulled out some knives and medical tools. One device was a freakishly long silver corkscrew. Another was a hacksaw with teeth like razors. He lifted out a massive metal syringe, holding the needle-less tip against his upper arm.

"I'd hate to be the one getting my flu shot with this thing," August said.

"That looks like something a veterinarian might use," Lucas said.

"I'm afraid to ask," August said, "but who are the patients?"

Nobody answered him.

Michael walked over to the door with bars and looked through the small window. The only visible shapes inside were countertops along the walls, and something else against the far back wall.

"I hear someone coming," Rebecca said.

"Keep going," Michael gestured toward the barred door. "Joey."

Joey ran up and swiped his key card again. The light turned green, and they hurried forward.

Before the metal door slammed shut behind them, a greater stench flooded Michael's nose. The Dunamis had nauseated him, but this room smelled worse. So much worse. It was the smell of rotting flesh and disease. Michael found the light switch and hesitated to flip it on. The light would reveal something awful. He turned it on anyway.

His jaw dropped open at the sight of what was inside. He gagged as he tasted the air.

"Holy shit," Joey said next to him. "There's got to be another way out of here."

❦ 28 ❦

Pastor John fumed as he stepped out into the backyard of his house. He strained with each step, clenching his fists as he trudged toward the gate.

He had switched off the backyard light. The darkness soothed his eyes. Bright lights had become irritating recently, and his eyesight worked best after the sun went down. Better in the darkness than in the daytime.

He swiped his keycard across the pad to open the gate and slipped into the small stretch of lawn that divided his gate from the edge of the trees ahead. The phantoms would arrive soon. The sound of the gate cracking shut would draw their attention.

Pastor John kneeled in the middle of the cement path leading out to a small gazebo on the lawn. He closed his eyes and let the energy of the darkness within spread through his body. The blackened skin across his chest swarmed as it had earlier. The familiar crawling sensation began and filled his chest. It radiated out until his entire body vibrated. A fullness washed over him and flowed outward into the night air.

The dark ghost snaked out of him and formed a misshapen, swirling mass. His consciousness split, seeing through human eyes and also through the eyes of his shadow ghost. The churning cloud stretched out and hovered near him.

The trees cracked and rustled as branches broke and fell. It wouldn't take the phantoms long to reach him. Their familiar clacking gave away their location as they approached.

Pastor John moved his shadow form out toward the approaching phantoms. One stalked him straight ahead, and another maneuvered around to the side. Through the dark ghost's eyes he spotted the nearest phantom, the one straight ahead, and raced toward it. He reached it in seconds.

Its beak snapped open and shut as he swarmed around its torso, its tentacle unable to swat his fluid form away. As its mouth gaped wide, he flew in and merged with its flesh. He took control of its limbs within moments. It reacted as expected, with thrashing and violent convulsions. Controlling so many limbs was a strange sensation, yet empowering. Easier than "driving" a human, but required more concentration with so many processes happening at once.

He circled the beast to protect his physical self from the other phantom who had moved in closer, but it stopped when he lifted and cradled his physical body. The other phantom backed away and disappeared into the darkness at the edge of his yard.

The phantom belonged to him.

Exhilarated, he headed toward his first target. Brother Matthew would pay the price first. The house was only a short distance away, and since Brother Matthew was the highest in command under Brother David, it would be best to remove him first. He would save Brother David for last.

He moved between the trees, sensing the lightness of his being as he floated through the night. The occasional sound of a phantom broke the silence and the gentle breeze of the night air, but no fear touched his mind.

Brother Matthew's house was easy to enter. The phantom smashed through the front door with ease and moved swiftly, plucking the man from the kitchen table as he sat with his wife.

Brother Matthew's abduction would no doubt raise great fear among the community. But it would serve as an example to his family and everyone else of what happened to those who betrayed the temple.

The brethren of Stone Hill would come running to Pastor John the next day, begging him to locate their lost Brother and protect them from the phantoms. Brother Matthew would be long dead by then. Pastor John would comfort and pray for them.

"The wages of sin is death," he would say. No greater sin than betraying the temple.

Brother Matthew had betrayed him and had paid the price. Now each traitor would receive the same judgment. They had betrayed him just as Judas had betrayed Jesus. There could be no mercy.

The phantom dragged Brother Matthew screaming and writhing from the house in one swift motion. A beautiful arc of black flesh. One coordinated fluid motion that came as naturally as riding a bicycle. The phantom was a stunningly perfect vessel through which to build his temple.

He quieted Brother Matthew's screams by covering the phantom's flesh over his mouth, nearly suffocating him. He let Brother Matthew breathe through his nose. It wouldn't serve his purpose to kill him immediately. He would bring each of them to Brother David alive, strung up like fish on hooks. He would exhibit the fruit of the insurrection for all to see. Brother David would see his coup crumble and fail before him.

Brother Christian's house was only a few blocks further up the road.

The phantom arrived there within minutes. The lights were on upstairs and shadows moved within the room. He scrambled along the side of the house toward his target, pausing outside the bedroom window before smashing through. Brother Christian and his wife had been preparing for bed. Her screams pierced the air. The neighbors would be alarmed, but it made no difference.

Brother Christian had jumped for a gun, but the phantom's tentacles whipped across and clutched him faster than he could move.

The phantom added Brother Christian to his collection, now composed of Brother Matthew and his own physical body.

Brother Christian struggled within the phantom's grasp and called out to Pastor John. "They have you too!"

Pastor John laughed.

The phantom muffled Brother Christian's cries for help the same way it had silenced Brother Matthew.

Brother Isaac lived alone in a small house only three blocks from The Farm. His house was full of weapons, and the blinds over the windows hid his whereabouts. But not even the fear of Brother Isaac's weapons slowed the phantom's rage. Brother Isaac wouldn't be expecting him.

The phantom crashed through the back door, dangling the other two traitors before it to use as human shields. It rushed through the kitchen and paused, listening to footsteps clomp across the floor overhead.

A door slammed at the top of the stairs. The phantom flew up the steps and smashed through the first door. A barrage of bullets hit the phantom, some of them striking Brother Christian.

"Don't shoot me!" Brother Christian screamed between the cries of pain.

Another flurry of shots, and Brother Christian shrieked and twisted. All in vain. The phantom would never let Brother Isaac escape.

The rounds slammed against the phantom, and Pastor John felt each blast as only a pinch—a brief sting of a doctor's syringe. The phantom lurched forward and knocked Brother Isaac's weapon from his hands.

He plucked Brother Isaac from his house kicking and screaming. Brother Christian continued to whimper, but soon all three had submitted and became powerless within the phantom's grasp. He choked off their attempts to speak or cry out as he moved out through the streets toward his final target at The Farm.

❧ 29 ❧

Joey never imagined he would see something so horrendous. This room was a mirror of the doctor's room, except some horrible creature occupied a massive cage at the far side. It was a bessie, and it hissed and snapped its beak at them as they entered the room. The metal door slammed shut behind them, and the bessie retreated further into the cage. The hisses were deafening. Rebecca covered her ears as the bessie charged forward and slammed its body against the cage. The walls of the room shook.

"Oh my God," Rebecca shrieked.

Lucas moved toward the cage, and the creature hissed louder as he approached the bars. "I can't believe what I'm seeing. Is this the monster that's been killing everyone?"

"There's more than one," Michael said.

Medical instruments lay strewn across the countertops next to massive chunks of black flesh. Sections of the creature's body were stacked in plastic bags and hung from hooks; the lower half of the bags were filled with black blood that had drained from its flesh.

Rebecca turned back to Joey, and he put his arm around her. "I don't want to be here," she said.

"We'll all get out of here now," Joey said.

He spotted two large utility doors against the side wall. They had to lead out into the courtyard, but a chain was strung between the two crash bars with a hefty padlock linking them together. They would need something like a bolt cutter to cut through the chains.

Michael ran over to the exit doors and pulled on the chain. Lucas and August scavenged through the drawers and cabinets.

August pulled out a hatchet. "This might help."

"Perfect," Michael said, gesturing for him to bring it over to the door.

"We forgot to pour out the other jug of Dunamis," Lucas said.

"I'll take care of it," Joey said, hurrying through the medical room to David's office.

Joey pushed the container across the floor into the locker room. He strained to tip it over, and it slammed onto its side near the floor drain. The black ooze flowed out like chocolate syrup and disappeared into the drain.

Before the container had emptied, voices echoed from the hallway. One voice caught Joey's ears. His dad's voice. His dad would be armed and angry if he came through the door. Not the best conditions for a confrontation with him.

The door to the locker room swung open a moment later and his dad charged inside, followed by three guards. All of them had their pistols drawn.

"Dad, it's me," Joey said. "Don't shoot."

His dad's eyes went wide and his mouth dropped open. The three guards paused to aim at Joey.

"Hold your fire," Joey's dad said with a scowl on his face. "Hold your fire!"

Joey raised his hands and stood. The container of Dunamis continued to empty beside him. He stepped back and blocked the doorway leading into the medical office.

"I thought you might be involved in this. Get out of the way," Joey's dad commanded.

"Don't go in, Dad," Joey said. "One of those things is in there."

"It's none of your business what's in there. You're trespassing. Get out of the way."

"Please listen to me. This place is evil. Pure evil."

"It's God's will."

"Why did you give me your key card if you didn't want to help us?"

His dad's scowl melted away. "Get out of the way, Joey. I got a job to do."

"Are you going to shoot them?"

His dad didn't answer. "Step aside, son."

"You can't shoot them. I won't let you."

"I wanted you to get the hell out of here," his dad said. "I gave you a chance. I didn't think you'd break into Brother David's office and start raising hell. Get out of the damn way."

Something crashed, and the bessie screeched. Rebecca cried out.

"Are those your *friends* in there?" Joey's dad asked, pushing forward. "They aren't doing you any favors, you know. Your *friends* will dump your ass right after they get what they want. They're just using you."

"It's not like that."

"Why the hell didn't you run when you had the chance?" His dad's eyes watered up. "Damn, you're stupid."

"I ain't stupid," Joey said. "Stop calling me that."

"Look what you've done," his dad said. "Everything's messed up. What can I do now? How will you get out of this one? You got yourself stuck again."

David rushed in with a guard at his side. He glared at Joey and then back at Joey's dad.

"Brother Brian," David said. "What's the holdup? Those kids in the next room are getting away."

"Move out of the way," Joey's dad yelled, raising his own rifle toward Joey's face. "I'll shoot you myself. Move!"

David's face flushed red, and he jolted toward the jug of Dunamis, which was now only a quarter full. "Mine!"

Joey grabbed the jug before David got to it and took off through the medical office with the remaining liquid splashing against the sides of the container as he ran.

"Shoot him!" David ordered.

Gunfire blasted holes in the medical office's walls around Joey as he scrambled into David's office. The metal door leading into the room with the monster was shut.

He could buy his friends some time for their escape if he had a weapon. The pistol was on the floor, where Michael had left it. Joey snatched it up and took a position behind David's desk. Joey ducked down. The metal desk rang as rounds exploded against it. A couple of framed pictures on the walls, including the one of Pastor John, shattered and collapsed to the floor.

"God dammit!" David yelled. "Hold your fire!"

The guards stopped firing.

"Stay away from me!" Joey yelled. "Dad, don't shoot me."

He was only a few feet from the door leading to the room with the bessie. He couldn't let David and his guards get past him. If they shot him, he vowed to drop dead in front of the door to block it. Good luck moving all two hundred pounds of his dead-ass weight.

"Get away from there," David ordered. "Step out and we'll talk about this." He turned to Joey's dad and screamed. "Get your brat son under control!"

His dad's voice wavered. "Joey, get the hell out of there."

"You'll shoot me," Joey said.

"They won't shoot you."

Joey doubted he could stall much longer.

"Throw your gun away," David said.

"Joey, throw your damn gun out before I blast a cap in you myself," Joey's dad said.

Joey pushed the gun away and it slid a couple of feet on the floor. "I'll pour the rest of this crap out on your computer if you try to shoot me."

"We won't shoot you," David said. "Lower your weapons. Now, stand up and come out of there."

Joey poked his head over the edge of the desk. The guards had lowered their weapons, but their arms were stiff, as if ready to pounce.

Taking a step to the side, Joey held the Dunamis container in front of his chest. "Dad, don't let them shoot me."

David formed a ghoulish grin. "You know, there is plenty more Dunamis in the tunnels, and thanks to Sister Rebecca, I know where it is. I don't need you or your friends anymore." David raised his pistol and took a step toward Joey. "You are expendable."

Joey's dad stared at Joey with wide eyes.

"No!" Joey's dad lurched toward David, knocking his arm to the side as the pistol fired. The blast exploded into the wall, and David stumbled forward.

"Joey," his dad grumbled as the guards tackled him, "get out of here. I'm sorry."

Joey spun around and jumped toward the metal door, flinging the jug of Dunamis to the side. A gunshot rang out behind him. He glanced back at his dad before escaping through the door. Blood streamed across his dad's face as he lay limp on the ground.

Joey went numb. His mind reeled as a torrent of ear-piercing blasts banged around him. He ran toward his friends, letting the door slam shut behind him.

He let out a guttural scream that carried with it the pain of what he had just witnessed. His eyes watered up, but he held back the tears. "Guys!" Joey yelled. "They're coming!"

His friends stood near the two exit doors at the far side of the room. Lucas hacked at the chains with the hatchet August had found earlier. Michael stood ready with the rifle.

"Break it open!" Joey yelled.

"I can't," Lucas said.

"Stand back," Michael ordered. He swung the rifle around and fired it at the chain.

The chain rattled wildly as each round struck it. Many shots missed their mark, blowing holes through the door, and some rounds clinked against the metal and ricocheted into the air, zipping past Michael's head. Neither the padlock nor the chain broke.

"Dammit!" Lucas yelled, hammering the hatchet against the chain and door.

David and the guards rushed in, and Joey stood defiantly in front of his friends, as if his size would somehow shield them from the barrage of bullets that would soon come their way. He scanned the room for a weapon. Nothing that might make a difference. Michael came up beside him and raised the assault rifle toward the guards.

"Blast them all!" Joey said.

❦ 30 ❦

Michael fired, but the rifle clicked empty after two rounds. Those two rounds blasted through a small refrigerator on one of the counters near the door. The guards hunched down and then rose with their rifles pointed at them. David strutted through the door with a wide grin.

Michael's heart raced as the bessie screeched and rustled within its cage behind them. It was clear they would all die. David would never let them leave, and Lucas had stopped hammering the hatchet against the chains.

"Drop your weapons and raise your hands," David yelled.

A guard circled around them toward Lucas and August. "Drop your weapon!"

The hatchet slammed into the floor as they obeyed. They gathered between the exit doors and the cage.

Michael stood his ground, with his rifle still aimed at David.

David walked straight forward, aiming his pistol at Michael's head. "You're out of ammo. Lower your weapon."

Michael pulled the trigger. It clicked, and he expected David to shoot him at that moment, but instead David laughed. Michael lowered the rifle.

"I win," David said. "Why shouldn't I kill you all right now?

Because I will not waste this blessed opportunity you've given me. All of you will retrieve another batch of Dunamis tonight to replace what you've destroyed."

David moved toward Rebecca. He got within a few feet of her. Michael and Joey stayed at her side, but the bessie's cage was directly behind them.

She stepped back. "Stay away from me."

David's eyes narrowed, and he inched forward. "What's this, Sister Rebecca? I thought we were on better terms."

"I'm—" Rebecca said, pushing one hand onto her forehead. "I'm confused."

"I see that," David said. "You caused yourself a lot of trouble by wasting the Dunamis."

Rebecca shook her head and stared at the floor. "I can't think straight. I just want to go home. We all do."

"I know, Sister Rebecca. You will go home. But first you and your friends will retrieve another supply of Dunamis later this evening."

Rebecca shook her head and crossed her arms. "I can't go down there again. I won't go."

David took another step. "The temptation to return to your old ways and old friends is always there. Remember that you're part of the temple now. You need to stand against your secular friends and obey the temple."

"I don't want to hurt anyone," she said.

"I know," David said, "and I don't either. So let's do this peacefully, shall we?"

The edge of the cage was only a few feet away, and the bessie's mid-section smashed against the bars. A hiss burst from the creature's mouth and blew against Michael's hair. He turned his head to the side. From the corner of his eye, he could see the bessie's limbs protruding between the bars, slowly snaking out along the ground. The guards and David continued moving toward them.

Michael glanced at the door on the cage. A metal rod sealed

the door shut, but the padlock holding the rod in place was not of the same high grade as the one holding the exit door chains together.

The hatchet Lucas had used earlier was lying on the floor only a couple of feet away. Michael calculated how long it would take him to grab it.

Something tugged at Michael's backpack. He didn't glance back. Maybe Lucas or August were trying to get his attention.

"Oh, Jesus!" August yelled behind him.

Michael turned, but something held him.

"Michael!" Lucas yelled. "Look out!"

Michael twisted around. The bessie's tentacle grabbed hold of his backpack and yanked him toward the cage. Another tentacle snaked around his right leg, and he nearly flipped forward onto his face.

Lucas, August, and Joey fought the creature as it whipped another limb around his chest. He was pulled back and pinned against the bars, his arms caught in the straps of his backpack. The creature's beak poked out, and the razor-like tip cut across the back of his neck. His pulse pounded in his ears as he struggled to keep his head and body as far away from the cage as possible, but he couldn't break free. He gripped the bars of the cage to keep from being pulled further inside.

Rebecca cried out and jumped toward Michael, but the guards took hold of her arms.

David stepped closer to Michael's face. "Our resident phantom is hungry. You will make a delicious meal for him tonight, if you're not careful."

"Please Brother David," Rebecca pleaded, "help him!"

David drew his fist back to knock Rebecca down. Joey groaned and grabbed hold of the barrel of a guard's rifle. With teeth clenched and eyes crazed, he yanked the weapon away from the man, and almost brought it up to David's face before the guard threw him back to the ground, taking control of his rifle again. The guard kicked Joey in the side, then moved away.

When Joey fell, something bumped into Michael's shoe. The hatchet was lying at his feet. Joey nodded at him.

Michael struggled as he slid down the bars, acting as if the bessie were forcing his actions.

"Brother Henry," David said to one of the guards, "transport them to the church where we can begin another retrieval party. No need to send guards with them this time. Rebecca will stay with us. If they don't come back with the Dunamis, she will pay the price."

When a tentacle whipped up and lashed out at one of the guards, Michael pulled far enough away from the bessie's grasp to pick up the hatchet. He only had a moment to act. Joey had stirred up trouble again, fighting with the guards after he got to his feet. Once more, the guard knocked him to the ground.

"Tase him," David commanded.

"No!" Rebecca screamed. "Don't hurt him!"

Joey lumbered to his feet as one guard prepared the Taser.

Michael shifted around and moved closer to the cage door. He pressed the hatchet to his leg as he strained against the force of the creature. The bessie's tentacles ripped at his muscles, and pain shot through his arms. He winced and clenched his teeth. One guard sneered at him as he struggled.

The lock on the cage door was within striking range. He took a deep breath and turned toward it. In one flowing stroke, he raised the hatchet over his head and slammed it down on the padlock. It broke apart on the first hit, the pieces clanking against the bars of the cage before hitting the floor. Michael pushed forward with all his strength and thrust the metal rod out of the latch holding the door shut.

The bessie exploded from the cage. The guards scrambled and shot their rifles as the bessie whipped its tentacles wildly in every direction.

Michael jumped out of the way with everyone else, but the bessie ripped his backpack away as it sprawled its tentacles across the room. The guards blasted at the limbs snaking toward them.

David stumbled back and retreated to the door with his guards following closely.

The creature turned toward Michael, Joey and Rebecca as they hurried toward the exit door. Michael held up the hatchet, ready to strike at the creature's limbs, although one hatchet was not nearly enough to battle such a thing. He eyed the room for more weapons.

"Grab weapons!" Michael yelled at Joey and Rebecca.

The bessie captured one of the retreating guards and pulled him away from David's side. It dragged the guard by the feet toward the cage as the guard blasted a barrage of rounds at the creature's face and head. Each bullet exploded across the bessie's flesh. Its gaping mouth hung open, revealing rows of razor-like teeth.

The guard lost control of his weapon as the bessie yanked him closer and closer. Tossed upward, the guard's head cracked against the monster's beak. The bessie clamped down. The guard shrieked. Blood flowed from his face across the creature's body and dripped to the ground. His white shirt splattered red and his arms flailed even as the creature's beak tightened around his face. The guard cried out once more, then fell silent as another guard near David shot him inside the creature's mouth. The victim's body went limp.

The guard's rifle clacked and slid across the floor. August lurched toward it.

"August!" Michael yelled. "Get back!"

Only a few yards from the creature, August attempted to grab the rifle but slipped on the guard's blood and tumbled flat against the ground. He squirmed to get back to his feet. His sneakers squeaked across the wet floor.

Joey grabbed the rifle and helped August back up.

"Head for the exit," Michael commanded.

He glanced back as he rushed to the exit with the others.

David and the guards were cornering the bessie, blasting it limb from limb. Black mangled chunks of flesh flew in every direction. Some pieces slapped and slid across the floor. Rounds from the gunfire clanged against the metal bars of the cage and blew holes in the wall and ceiling.

Michael reached the exit door first, throwing it open and ushering everyone outside. Joey came out last, firing the rifle back toward David one last time.

A stray round exploded against the doorframe beside Michael's head as he jumped outside with the others. Joey huffed beside him and the metal door slammed shut. They paused for a moment in the darkness and relative quiet. Thumps and gunshots echoed through the door.

"Which way?" August asked Michael.

"Follow me," Joey said, gesturing toward a barn across the courtyard.

They moved in that direction, just as overhead lights burst on, illuminating the entire area, including them. Several guards charged out the back doors of the complex with rifles raised.

"Don't move!" one guard yelled to them. "Drop your weapons!"

With the building behind them, the white fence on one side, and the guards approaching, they raised their hands. Joey dropped the rifle and Michael dropped his hatchet.

The door where they had just exited opened again, and the guards who had fought the bessie with David rushed out with their rifles raised. The guards closest to them aimed directly at their heads.

Michael closed his eyes. They would be shot now. He accepted that, but he regretted that he hadn't gotten Rebecca out safely.

One guard thrust the butt of his rifle into Joey's chest, knocking him onto the grass.

"Not so tough now without your daddy, are you?" he yelled at

Joey. "I have no problem killing seculars. Make one move and you'll end up in hell like your daddy back there."

David came through the door a moment later, panting and wiping some bessie flesh from his hands onto his shirt. His hair was a mess, as if something had thrown him around.

"I should have my guards mow you down like dogs right now," David told them. "But that would be merciful. You deserve pain. I'll make an example of you."

David turned to the guard standing at his side. "Tie them to the tree."

"I'm so sorry, Brother David," Rebecca whimpered with her hands folded over her heart. "Please forgive me. I didn't want to hurt you or cause the temple any problems."

David stared at her. "It's too late for mercy."

"Please give me another chance," she said, running her fingers through her hair and shaking her head. "I just want to do the will of the temple. I never fired a weapon against you. Not once."

"What are you saying, Bex?" Joey blurted out.

"I didn't want to leave anyway," she said. "*They* made me go along with them." Rebecca made a wide, sweeping gesture toward her friends. "I was fine before they showed up." Rebecca stepped toward David. The guard next to David pushed her back.

David paused, then sneered. "You can stay with the temple." He turned to the guard holding her. "But search her."

The guard patted Rebecca down, and she stepped over next to David with her hands still clasped together as if in prayer. She stood with her shoulders hunched forward and her eyes staring down.

Michael was exhausted and silent. It was better that Rebecca should take her chances and stay with the temple if they would be executed, anyway.

"Now," David said to them, "pray for your souls. Your day of judgment has arrived."

❧ 31 ❧

Overhead lights cast a harsh shadow over everything as the guards led them out into the middle of the courtyard. The noxious stench of Dunamis and sweat on Michael's clothes slowly drifted away. The fresh evening air flowed into his lungs and sparked him back to life. He took a deep breath and held it for a moment before one of the temple guards jabbed him in the side with a rifle.

"Get moving, and keep your eyes forward," the guard commanded.

An enormous tree stood at the top of a small mound in the center of the courtyard, as if something from deep inside the earth had pushed it toward the sky. The tree was a thick oak, trimmed of its thinnest branches so that only two large ones and the main trunk remained, forming a giant wooden cross. Its two arm branches supported several long ropes hanging down on either side of the base. The bark of the tree had been stripped off, exposing bare wood, and something had spattered dark stains around the lower half. A ring of torn grass circled the base of the tree, and another ring of dark brown grass spread out until it blended in with the rest of the manicured lawn.

The temple guards led the four of them across the grass. Joey mumbled something, and the nearest guard kicked him on the side of the leg.

"Touch me with that again," Joey said.

"And what?" the guard asked.

"I'll kick your ass."

The guard eyed Joey and chuckled nervously.

Voices chattered from the back door of the complex. Several people came outside and stood watching them from the shadows. They murmured and stared as if attending a spectator sport. Dark silhouettes lined the windows facing the courtyard. Whatever was about to happen, there would be witnesses.

The guards positioned each of them below the thick branches of the tree facing the building.

"If you try to escape," an older dark-haired guard said while tying a rope around Michael's wrist, "I'll shoot you."

After tying Michael's other wrist, he motioned for another guard behind them to pull on the rope. Michael's arms shot up above his head. The ropes were stained with blood and streaks of a black residue. The source of the black stains was unmistakable. They were being offered as prey for the bessies.

Several feet in front of them was the circular brick structure of an old well. A thick, rusted metal cover lay over the opening. Chains snaked through rings attached to the cover and were anchored to the lower sector of the stone well.

Two guards pulled the chains from the rings and dropped them into the grass nearby. Then they pulled open the metal doors using ropes attached to the handles. A large, gaping black hole stared up into the evening sky. Michael had been in Stone Hill long enough to know what came out of holes like that. After the sun went down, the bessies would come and rip them from the tree as if picking apples.

"You'll make a tasty treat for the phantoms tonight," one guard said. He made chomping noises and the other guard laughed.

"You're funny, Brother Rodney," the second guard said.

The guards headed back to the building's doorway and stood beside David. Rebecca stood at his side.

"Rebecca, get help!" Joey yelled.

"Fight back!" Lucas yelled. "They are lying to you."

None of the spectators reacted. If anyone heard them, nothing would be done about it, anyway. Their show was about to begin.

A spotlight switched on above the building, illuminating the four victims more clearly, as if the perimeter lights weren't bright enough. David would have no problem seeing all the gore and blood as they died.

"If you've got any ideas for escaping, feel free to share them," August told Michael.

"I wish I had," Lucas said, his head hanging forward. "I'm sorry, August."

"Just fight like hell when the bessies grab you," Joey said.

The image of his grandparents and his mom popped into Michael's mind. He had let them down. He had failed Rebecca too. How would she get out of the temple now?

At least they had emptied the Dunamis. That would slow them for a while, but Rebecca was right. They would only force her down in the tunnels to get more. They had the entire pond at their disposal now. It would last them a lifetime. They didn't really need her anymore, since they knew where to find it, but they would force her down there again and again until some horrible tragedy removed her from the game.

Michael noticed how thin August's wrist was. "August, can you slide your hand out?"

August tugged and groaned. "It's too tight."

"They'll just walk back out here and tie it again," Joey said.

"No, they won't," Michael said. "They won't come near us because of the bessies."

August squirmed and pulled harder. He twisted his wrists back and forth. His skin was red where the rope scraped him.

August snarled. "Almost."

The rope slipped away from his wrist. He used his free hand to pull on the rope around his other wrist.

Someone fired a gunshot from the building. The bullet whizzed past them and struck the tree.

August froze. "They're shooting at us."

"Hurry," Michael said. "You can do it."

Michael stared up at the darkened faces of those watching them from the building. If Rebecca was watching, he hoped she would look away. He didn't want the last thing she remembered of him to be so horrible.

A clicking sound echoed from deep within the well. The familiar sound that marked the arrival of the bessies.

Everyone standing outside clapped and shouted "Praise the temple! Praise Pastor John!"

Michael's heart raced, and he fixed his eyes on the well opening.

August continued struggling with the rope, crying out now as he pulled, "I can't get it off!"

Michael struggled too, the rope burning against his skin as it cut into his wrist.

"I'll beat the shit out of Pastor John when I see him again," Joey said. "This is bullshit."

"He's here," Lucas said.

"Who's here?" Michael asked, a moment before seeing him.

Pastor John.

❧ 32 ❧

The icy fingers of Pastor John's "better half" wrapped around the faces of the three traitors, leaving their noses uncovered. Just enough air to keep them alive. The gasps of their stilted breaths caught his attention every few moments, but like a fish out of water their lives served no purpose now except to set an example to the others.

Brothers Matthew, Christian, and Isaac had given up the struggle long ago. Their near-lifeless bodies hung inches above the ground as Pastor John's phantom dangled them along beside him. The desire was strong to drag them through the mud and the dirt, and scrape their faces along the asphalt, but to do so meant they would most likely bleed to death before reaching Brother David. No satisfaction in that. He wanted so much to hear each of them cry out and beg for mercy. He would crush them all at once.

Pastor John grinned and savored the control his phantom provided him. The degree of strength and flexibility was exhilarating, but at the same time the creature was weakening, as was his own body.

He would need more Dunamis soon. If what he had seen in

his ghost form earlier were accurate, he would find plenty of the black substance in Brother David's office.

He licked his lips. "I will quench my thirst on Dunamis and the blood of my enemies," Pastor John mumbled within the arms of his phantom.

Pastor John arrived at the end of the driveway leading up to the picturesque white house that served only as a façade for outsiders. An ideal situation. The Farm resembled most Midwest farms, except for the tall white fence that separated the main house from the larger complex in the back. Any visitor who stopped by would go to the front house first, then be instructed, cordially or not, to meet with a temple representative and begin the initiation process. They would welcome troublemakers within the gates of the complex to have their minds cleansed of any doubts or hostilities.

He had accomplished so much in the last three years. His successes were miraculous, to say the least. He truly was a man of God. A man-god.

The phantom lowered Pastor John's physical body to the gravel. He walked the length of the short driveway to the gate, leading the phantom toward the two guards who stood to attention with wide eyes. Their faces were white with terror within the pale moonlight, as if they'd seen the devil himself.

"Open the gate," Pastor John ordered.

The guards scrambled to obey. They moved off to the side with their weapons ready, as if debating whether to shoot the phantom behind Pastor John or protect it.

Pastor John smirked as a guard fell to his knees and bowed before him.

"Welcome back, Pastor John," the guard said. "Thank you for saving us!"

Pastor John raised his chin as he walked by. They would all bow to him now.

He circled around the house to the main gates leading into the complex. The guards thrust the doors open well before his arrival. They stared at his "catch" behind him. Let them stare. They would see what happened to those who disobeyed him. Let them tell all their friends he was their leader. He was the voice of God.

Pastor John moved through the complex quickly, intoxicated by the promise of revenge. The phantom scraped along the sides of the doors as it pushed through, the traitors wrapped firmly within its tentacles.

He hurried into the locker room. An empty container of Dunamis sat near the drain. The stench was strong, despite it being empty. Black residue hung near the edges of the drain.

A small amount remained at the bottom of the plastic jug. He picked up the jug and drained the final drops. When the black liquid touched his tongue, he gagged for a moment, but it revitalized him at the same time. A tinge of energy spread through his throat and down to his stomach. He sensed it trickling down inside, and he licked his lips as if he hadn't drunk water in days.

Tossing the plastic jug aside, he continued into Brother David's office. The second jug sat on the floor next to Brother David's desk, flipped over on its side. It, too, was nearly empty, but at least enough remained to satisfy his thirst for another day or two. He guzzled the leftover contents and leaned against the edge of the desk. The Dunamis would take time to re-energize him, but he had no time to wait.

He held back the urge to vomit and nodded. "Nectar of the gods."

Pastor John steadied himself and hurried through the experimentation lab to the room where they kept the captive phantom. Its cage had been opened and its mangled flesh lay everywhere. Chunks had splashed against the walls, and its black blood had splattered in every direction. The creature's massive torso lay in a heap. Medical equipment, supplies, and books were strewn across the floor. Some cabinets bolted to the walls had collapsed, with splintered chunks of wood everywhere. Many weeks of experiments had likely been destroyed. The chain securing the exit doors leading into the courtyard was dangling loose over the metal crash bar on the door.

"Your friend has passed away, it seems," Pastor John said to the phantom behind him with a sneer.

Pastor John moved across the room and went outside. A broad smirk spread across his face. All his enemies were there. The three remaining traitors surrounded Brother David, who stood near the back door to the complex. The troublemaker girl was standing with him as well. Four other troublemakers were strung up below the arms of the redemption tree. Brother David had been preparing for their execution. At least he'd gotten something right.

Brother David and the guards were obviously stunned to see him. The overhead floodlights reflected against their wide eyes. Their mouths dropped open. They didn't move as he approached them.

With a wide gesture of his arms, the phantom's tentacles mirrored his own actions, raising the three traitors high into the air behind him.

"Brother David," Pastor John called out. "This is what happens to those who betray me." He waved their bodies in his phantom arms.

Brother David's eyes narrowed as Pastor John moved toward him.

"What is all this?" Brother David asked.

"It is in dying that we are born to eternal life!" Pastor John yelled, staring into Brother David's eyes. Watching the frozen terror on his face sent waves of joy through him. So much pleasure in watching him squirm.

Brother David eyed the complex doors behind him.

No, Brother David wouldn't escape so easily.

Brother David stepped forward with his chin raised. Pastor John resisted the urge to strike him down in that moment. He would let everyone hear Brother David's pleas for mercy.

"Pastor John," Brother David stammered, "what a pleasant surprise. I have good news."

Pastor John stretched out a phantom tentacle toward Brother David. It whipped through the air and clutched Brother David's throat. Pastor John clenched his fist, and the tentacle clamped off Brother David's air.

"We are through with you," Pastor John said. "Witness my glory."

While Brother David stared, Pastor John willed his phantom to raise Brother Matthew into the air. It dangled him like a rag doll between them. The traitor's body writhed as the phantom's arm squeezed. The teeth lining the underside of the tentacle dug into Brother Matthew's neck and blood sprayed across the surrounding grass.

Pastor John tightened his grasp, the rage boiling through his mind, and twisted his wrist. Brother Matthew's spine cracked and his head was ripped away, crashing down only feet from Brother David. Pastor John let the traitor's body drop.

He raised Brother Christian and Brother Isaac next.

"Your insurrection has ended." Pastor John snapped off their heads, making sure their remains landed at Brother David's feet.

"This is all a horrible misunderstanding," Brother David pleaded between gasps of breath. "I've been loyal. Your enemies are here on the redemption tree, and I have Dunamis for you."

"You betrayed my trust," Pastor John said. "There will be no forgiveness."

The phantom moved in and captured the remaining three guards loyal to Brother David. He lifted them into the air like the others, but this time higher, so everyone watching from the windows of the complex could see them clearly.

The traitors screamed and prayed, but judgment was upon them. No mercy now. The gates of hell awaited them.

Pastor John snapped off their heads, all three at the same time. Blood sprayed over Brother David's face and clothes. He gasped, spitting out the blood that had sprayed into his mouth.

"You're wrong!" Brother David cried out.

Pastor John slammed the bodies to the ground and moved in closer to Brother David, who defiantly stood his ground. "I would have you die a thousand deaths if it were my choice."

"I am your loyal servant," Brother David said.

"Liar!" Pastor John yelled. "I know everything. I see everything. I know you hid the Dunamis from me. I know it was Bertha who resurrected me, not you. I trusted you more than my own family, and you betrayed me."

Brother David wiped the blood from his eyes and struggled with the phantom's arm clutching his throat.

Pastor John inched forward. He lifted Brother David off the ground and moved further out into the light where everyone in the complex could see them. He would burn the spectacle of the traitor's death into the minds of his followers. A legendary display of Pastor John's power to crush all opposition.

"Fear me!" Pastor John called out. "I am the judgment. I am the black horse of death!"

From the corner of his eye, he could see the creeping shadows of a phantom slinking from the well in front of the redemption tree. It would claim the troublemakers soon. The phantoms could have their prizes.

The girl troublemaker, Rebecca Wagner, sprinted from behind Brother David and ran toward the redemption tree holding a backpack. They wouldn't escape. The phantoms would only have a fifth meal for the evening.

He turned his attention back to Brother David. His phantom sliced a tentacle across Brother David's neck. Another tentacle slashed across his body. The blood spattered and splashed as the phantom snapped muscles from his bones. Brother David screamed and his shrieks became a joyful chorus within Pastor John's mind. The most beautiful music. Heavenly songs that lifted his spirit and raised him to a bright and beautiful glory. He had never experienced such elation.

The floodlights overhead went dark.

✤ 33 ✤

The courtyard went dark, except for smaller lights illuminating the doorways of the complex. The floodlights had been like the sun compared to the moonlight that now lit their surroundings.

"Oh shit," Joey said.

"What happened?" August asked.

"I'm not sure," Michael said. "Keep trying to slip out of the ropes."

Rebecca had disappeared from the front of the complex for a short time, then reappeared near the door carrying Michael's backpack. She maneuvered between the commotion, pushing aside the crowd as Pastor John lifted the guards surrounding David and then finally David himself.

Michael's eyes adjusted to the faint light to witness a tentacle rising from the well.

Rebecca sprinted away from the complex toward them. She hunched forward as if that might somehow help her not be seen. She ran in an arc around the well toward the tree, staying clear of the opening. The darkness within the well opening burst to life as a massive black tentacle snaked out along the side of the hole and moved through the grass toward them.

Michael gestured for Rebecca to go back. "Stay away! The bessies are here!"

The top of the bessie's head rose, followed by its gaping beak revealing the rows of razor teeth. Another tentacle spilled out and clung to the outside edge of the well. More tentacles flowed out, then another and another. Its torso poured over the side and moved toward Rebecca.

"I got the medallion!" she called to them joyfully, holding up the backpack.

She stumbled on something in the grass and flopped forward onto her chest. The backpack dropped a few feet in front of her, closer to the bessie.

"Get out of there!" Michael yelled.

Rebecca moaned as she pulled herself onto her hands and knees.

Michael's breath stopped. His mouth dropped open, but no air rushed in. His heart stopped along with his mind, and everything faded away as if he were watching some crime drama on television. Nothing was real. The world swayed around him and he bolted toward her. He only made it a few inches before the ropes tightened around his wrists, yanking him back, and pain shot up his arms.

"Bex," Michael said, his mouth dry and scratchy. "Bex! Run!" He strained against the ropes to reach her.

All four of them called out her name.

"Take the medallion!" Michael yelled.

The bessie shifted across the grass toward Rebecca. The tip of one tentacle slinked closer to her leg. She scrambled toward the backpack.

"Rebecca, get up!" Michael yelled at her.

Her feet slipped on the wet grass. *Oh God, oh God, oh God. Please breathe. Please get up and run.*

Joey was near tears as he called out to her. His voice wavered and faded off. Michael glanced over at Joey; his eyes were pressed shut.

August railed against the ropes around his wrist. "Damn it!"

A tentacle wrapped around the backpack as another lashed out at Rebecca's face. The bessie crept faster toward her. Another tentacle whipped across her arms and up her shoulder. It latched on and yanked her closer to the bessie's snapping beak.

"Bex!" Joey called out. "Get out of there!"

Rebecca screamed, but her voice cracked. She groaned and twisted within the bessie's grasp.

Michael strained with every ounce of strength against the ropes. His arms bowed backwards as pain shot through his shoulders. He pulled harder and was sure his arms would break. His muscles burned and fell numb.

Rebecca got her arms around the backpack and scooped it up. She opened it as the bessie tumbled her around.

The medallion flew out and slid onto the grass, throwing a radiant red light over the bessie and the surrounding area. The bessie convulsed and hissed like a thousand angry cats.

Michael winced and turned his head away. No way to cover his ears.

The bessie screeched and scrambled back toward the well opening, leaving Rebecca behind. Smoke rose from the bessie's skin as it retreated.

It wouldn't be long before Pastor John and the silhouetted figures watching them from the complex figured out what had happened. The red glow that saved them also provided the temple a clear target.

"What happened to the lights?" Lucas asked.

"I did it," Rebecca said, grabbing the medallion. She snatched up the backpack and pulled out the hatchet.

"Perfect," Lucas said.

Rebecca hurried over to Lucas, the first in the line of captives. She sliced at his rope. Lucas pulled the rope tight and soon it frayed enough for him to snap his wrist loose.

"It's taking too long!" August said. "They're watching us."

Rebecca hurried, cutting through each rope in seconds. Joey was the last to be freed. A moment after she cut his rope, the main complex door opened, and shots exploded against the tree and grass around them.

They huddled behind the tree. To one side was the barn. A smaller white shed stood in the other direction. All around them, the massive white fence made it impossible to escape.

Within the medallion's glow, Michael looked at each of them. "We don't have much time. Can we get over that fence?"

Joey shook his head. "How?"

More gunfire cracked against the tree.

Michael scanned the fence for anything that might help propel them over the top. There had to be a way out. Lucas crowded in next to him and followed Michael's gaze.

"Holy shit," Lucas said. "He's going to kill that David guy."

They all peered around the tree as Pastor John and some other shadowy creature lifted David high into the air. A cry of pain, a crack, and David's head separated from his body. Blood sprayed everywhere as the head and body dropped to the ground.

"Good riddance," Lucas said.

Rebecca gasped.

That could have been their fate. Michael shivered.

A gunshot slammed against the tree and they all recoiled.

"Why would he kill David?" Rebecca asked.

"What difference does it make?" Michael said. "We can't just sit here waiting for our turn."

"That's messed up," Joey said.

Michael returned the medallion to the backpack and again peered around the edge of the tree. Without the red glow to stop them, the bessies rose again from the well, and tentacles fanned out over the edge toward them.

"Don't put that thing away," Joey said. "Get the medallion out. They're coming back."

"I've got an idea," Michael said. "There's only one way out."

"How?" Lucas asked.

"Down."

"What do you mean, down?" Lucas asked.

"Into the well."

"Are you nuts?"

"It's the only way out," Michael said. "They'd be fools to follow us."

"We'd be trapped down there," Rebecca said. "We don't know where it goes."

"We *do* know where it goes," Michael said.

"The bottom of a well," Lucas said.

"Into the tunnels," Michael said. "After we get down there, I'll take out the medallion. We can find our way out. We did it before. At least we know our way around. Sort of."

"We can't climb down there, anyway," Rebecca said. "We don't have any rope."

"We don't need rope. The bessies will take us down there."

"What, we jump on their backs?" Joey asked.

"Trust me."

"Absolutely nuts," Lucas said.

"What if it kills us?" August asked.

"It won't," Michael said. "It'll bring us to the Leviathan, if it's still alive."

"How are we supposed to defend ourselves?" Joey asked.

"We've got a hatchet," Michael said. "We're dead if we stay here, anyway." He gestured to the hatchet in Rebecca's hands. "Hold that close."

"The squid's over here!" Lucas yelled as he scrambled to stay away from the tentacles.

"I'll go first," Michael said. "Try to stay together. Don't fight when it takes you. Don't make it angry."

"I don't want to go down there," August said.

"I've got you," Rebecca said, putting an arm around him. "I won't let go."

Michael trembled as the bessie's arms latched onto his legs.

Another arm wrapped around Joey. "I'm really not liking this."

"It'll work," Michael said without conviction.

Another Bessie emerged from the other side of the tree and scrambled toward the others. The monster shrieked and hissed as it approached.

August crouched next to Rebecca. She whispered in his ear. "Do you trust me?"

The boy nodded in the tree's shadow.

Tentacles flooded around them and cloaked them. "It's going to get a little bumpy," she warned.

❧ 34 ❧

I t pulled Michael away from the group first. Joey followed
right behind him. Two bessies emerged. The one on the right
took Michael and Joey. The one on the left grabbed Rebecca.

She shrieked as it overtook her. "I don't think this is a good
idea!"

It took August next, then Lucas, who burst into a flurry of
cursing.

"It'll be okay," Michael said.

"We're definitely not okay, man," Joey said.

"I can't breathe," Lucas yelled. "Son of a bitch!"

"Rebecca, you okay?" August asked.

"Right here," Rebecca said.

"Take a deep breath," Michael said. "It won't kill you."

"How do you know?" Lucas said, his breath blowing in
and out.

"I know," Michael said. "It wants us alive."

"For what?"

"It's best you don't know," Joey said.

Michael glanced at Joey. "It won't get that far. Just trust me."

"I'm trusting you," Lucas muttered.

"The guards are watching us," Joey said.

"Pretend you're going against your will," Michael said. "Pretend you're suffering."

"Fuck this!" Joey said. "Who's pretending? I'm suffering. Look at me!"

A tree-sized tentacle bound Joey's mid-section. If it had wanted to kill him, it could have done so in an instant.

"You can breathe, right?" Michael asked.

"I guess," Joey said and moaned. "This is disgusting."

Michael watched them as long as he could to make sure they were safe, but eventually he lost sight of them as the bessie's slick damp texture covered his face. The bones on the inside of its tentacles scraped across his cheek and chin, and he winced in pain.

Michael clutched the backpack tightly against his chest and unzipped it, stuffing one arm inside. He gripped a hand around the medallion and pushed it down as far as he could to keep the red glow from seeping out through the openings. Everything else Michael had stowed in the backpack was gone, including the cellphones August had grabbed from the locker room. They couldn't have used them to make phone calls, but if they still held power they might have worked as flashlights.

The bessie squeezed, pulled, and scraped its teeth along his skin, but he held onto the medallion through it all. If they ran into trouble, all he had to do was pull his arm out and the bessie would scramble away. At least, that was the idea. As long as they made it down out of the complex, he was sure they'd be safe. The temple would assume they'd died a horrible death and wouldn't come looking for them.

The bessie took hold of Michael's body and lifted him like a toddler carrying a doll. Strange bellows rose from below its skin. Growling and rumbles shook the creature as if another animal were trying to claw its way out of it. Were the sounds coming from another victim? He pushed the thought away.

As it towed Michael along the grass and up the embankment to the well, the creature's beak clacked at him and nearly ripped off his face when he struggled. Michael surrendered. *Go with the flow.*

Rebecca shrieked. Everyone cursed and groaned. Maybe this wasn't the best idea. Too late to change his mind. The bessie lifted Michael over the edge of the well and he sank into a thick darkness.

They had no choice. The temple would have shot them if they'd escaped. Or worse. The vision of David's head flying off flashed through his mind. If they only had more weapons, he wouldn't feel so vulnerable. At least Rebecca had gotten the medallion. Thank God for that.

It was clear now that she had been putting on a show earlier, with the crazy waving of her arms and the odd antics. Her days in high school drama had paid off.

Before Michael descended into the well, Pastor John shouted at his followers. His words were muffled by the bessie's grasp, but Michael understood the tone. Anger and bitterness.

Joey cursed repeatedly as the monster lowered them into the well. Lucas and Rebecca attempted to keep August calm, but it was Lucas who became agitated on the way down.

"I'm claustrophobic," Lucas said. "I don't like this at all."

"Just close your eyes," Michael said.

"What if it drops us into water?" August asked.

"I'll hang on to you," Rebecca answered.

"I can't swim," Lucas said.

"Neither can Michael," Rebecca said.

"Thanks for reminding me," Michael said.

With the bessie still grasping them, they splashed down into water and Michael prepared to hold his breath, but the water was only a few inches deep. Only the edge of his clothes got wet. His left foot slipped through the tentacles and touched a lumpy, squishy surface. He forced himself not to think about what he might be stepping into.

The bessies moved them swiftly through a narrow hole in the side of the well until finally descending to a solid floor. The bessies moved them at a brisk pace, about as fast as he could run. Maybe the bessies were in a hurry to get their food to the supper table for the Leviathan.

Michael clutched the backpack as he was carried along, curled up into a ball. The bessie's flesh slapped against the stone floor at times and dragged through the gravel and dirt at other times.

A brief flash of red glow escaped from a narrow opening in the backpack. The bessie shuddered, loosening its grip around him, and convulsed as if someone had jabbed it with a knife. He was sure it would drop him into the darkness and scurry away, but it continued after hesitating for a moment.

Sometimes the bessie hissed into the darkness as if warding off unseen predators, but what could threaten a bessie down there? Its limbs tightened around Michael, nearly suffocating him, and it dragged him across the ground only for a few moments. Apparently, the Leviathan didn't like its dinner scratched up.

The muffled clacking and squirming of other bessies grew and faded around him. The bessies had definitely not died. Or maybe there were simply way more than he ever imagined. Had the Leviathan really died in the crash? Maybe it had only been injured. He suspected he would find out soon.

Michael shifted so he could breathe through the swaying limbs of the creature. His muscles tensed defensively, resisting the crushing arms that clutched him. The darkness was thick, but his heart rate had slowed after the initial descent. He strained his eyes to pick out any piece of information from the surroundings. Pitch black. Only the echoes of the bessies scraping across the rocks gave any clues of their location. Maybe he could make out a familiar sound. A familiar pattern. The distance from one room to the next.

"Do you know where we are?" Joey asked in a strained voice.

"I can't see shit," Michael replied.

"It smells like we're in it," Joey said.

Joey was right. The air around them stank of human sewage.

"Oh, God," Michael said wincing in the darkness. He sucked in a deep breath and held it as long as he could. Maybe the odors would pass. But between each gasp of air, the stench only grew stronger. He could taste the air, and it nauseated him. He resisted the urge to vomit. Holding his breath was making him dizzy, so he tried burying his nose and mouth into his shirtsleeve, but it made little difference.

A short distance further, the bessies slowed and stopped. By the surrounding echoes it was obvious they had moved out into a larger hallway. The bessies slinked across the stone floor and entered a room.

Human odors were thick in the air, and a familiar smell was mixed in with the putrid odors of sewage. A strong toxic stench that he had encountered only days earlier. The bessies had taken them to the feeding room above the Leviathan. The same room where he had found his grandfather and Rebecca's mother wrapped in disgusting black cocoons of a substance like a sausage casing. He knew exactly where they were.

He would need to act fast, or they would suffer the same fate.

"We're getting out of here," Michael said.

"Oh shit, man, I can't move," Joey said.

"I'll get you out."

But the bessie had Michael's arms pinned down. He pushed his face forward through the tentacles and took in a deep breath. He forced his hand down, the teeth protruding from the under-side of the bessie's tentacles cutting his forearm, and clutched the edge of the backpack. The bessie didn't like that at all.

Michael yanked his arm up, attempting to pull out the medallion, but the more he struggled the more the bessie tight-ened its grip on him. His muscles ached as the bessie compressed him into a smaller space.

Michael took another deep breath and kicked the bessie with every ounce of strength. It flinched, and he pulled the back-pack's zipper down.

The red glow blinded Michael. The bessie convulsed, throwing him to the ground. Michael tumbled over sideways, knocking his shoulder against the floor. He gripped the medallion in both hands and sat up, holding it above his head.

Michael squinted as his eyes gradually adjusted to the medallion's red glow. The bessie that had carried him and Joey shrieked and hissed as it scrambled to get away, pounding its limbs against the floor and racing toward a hole across the room. Joey had been dumped only a few feet away and stood as if waking from a nap.

Whiffs of black smoke drifted off the bessie's skin as it scurried. It screeched again, more loudly than Michael thought possible, as it sneaked down the hole—the same hole that led to the Leviathan's feeding area below them. Michael covered his ears until the bessie was gone, sure that his eardrums would burst.

Rebecca screamed behind him. The bessie holding her, Lucas, and August had dragged them up the side of the wall toward a dark opening in the stones above.

"Chop its arms off!" Joey yelled as he charged toward them with his hands forming fists as if he'd beat the thing to death.

"I can't," Rebecca yelled back. "I can't move."

Michael hurried toward the bessie, raising the medallion as high as he could toward it. Its skin sizzled and smoked in the red light. Instead of releasing its captives, however, the bessie shrank back further into the shadows above them, finding refuge in a crumbled corner of the ceiling. The bessie hissed and squirmed, lashing its tentacles toward Michael and Joey.

Their only weapon was the medallion. Michael stretched it up toward the bessie, as close as he could get.

Joey dropped onto his hands and knees near the wall. "Stand on my back. Get that thing up higher."

Michael held the wall as he stepped onto Joey's back, raising the medallion a little higher than before. The bessie's flesh blistered and dripped black ooze. It let out a wild, wavering shriek.

Its limbs shuddered and loosened. Rebecca dropped a few inches. She and the others were about fifteen feet from the stone floor. If the bessie let them go at that moment, they'd most likely break some bones.

"Got him!" Rebecca shouted. She grunted, and something metal clinked against a stone surface.

The bessie hissed and lurched out of the corner. It scrambled down the wall and across the room, releasing all three of them at the same time only a few feet above the ground. It scrambled toward the same hole the first bessie had fled through. Rebecca landed on her feet and stumbled. Lucas had crashed down without injury. August wasn't so lucky. He fell sideways and would have landed on his head if Rebecca hadn't lurched forward to grab him before he hit the ground.

"Oh my God," Rebecca said to August. "Are you okay?"

He shook his head. "I'm going to throw up."

And he did. Twice.

"Better now?" Rebecca asked with a hand on August's back.

"A little."

A moment later, a chunk of tentacle slapped to the ground, below the corner where it had held them. Black blood dripped down the wall.

"I did that," Rebecca said with a grin.

"Well done, Bex," Joey said.

In the crimson glare of the medallion, despite the surrounding darkness, August's pale face revealed he'd had a worse time than he'd let on. His eyes moved slowly as he glanced between Rebecca and Lucas.

"You done puking?" Joey asked.

"Yeah," August said.

"Do you know the way out?" Lucas asked Michael.

"It won't take us long from here," Michael said.

He led them out through the doorway into a long hallway. He rounded the corner, and they walked several yards to a crumbled section of the wall, revealing a dark hole not much bigger than a person could fit through. The same hole he had used to escape with his grandfather days earlier.

Michael let out a sigh of relief. "This leads straight down into the temple below the church."

Lucas stepped forward and peered into the dark hole. "Are you sure there aren't more of those things waiting for us down there?"

Michael stared forward and shook his head. "I'm not sure, but I know it's our only way out."

The medallion's glow, their only source of light, faded.

❧ 35 ❧

Michael crouched down and crawled into the hole backwards with his face down. His shoes kicked the walls as he backed in. The walls pressed in and each of his breaths became shallow and quick. As he slid back, slamming his elbows against the hard cold soil with every movement, Rebecca descended after him. Her feet kicked up some dirt and knocked it against his face.

"Easy up there," Michael said.

"Did I kick you?" Rebecca asked.

"Just dirt."

The tunnel angled downward at a gentle slope, but at times it fell away and he slipped for several feet before gaining traction. His backpack scraped against the ceiling and shards of rock and dirt rained down on him. The loose rocks thumped against his backpack, and the sound died away as soon as it hit.

He clutched the medallion in his hands and squirmed backward. If a bessie had wanted to attack him from the bottom, it could have done so easily since not much of the red glow leaked around him because of the narrow walls.

Michael slid down another few feet and paused, giving the others time to catch up. Rebecca groaned and gasped for breath.

"You okay, Rebecca?" Michael asked.

"My elbows are getting banged up," she said.

"We're almost there."

A short time later, the ground dropped away and his feet slid over the edge of the tunnel. He had reached the temple. The toes of his shoes scraped against the wall a couple of feet until he touched down onto the stone surface again. He brushed himself off and glanced around while the others caught up to him.

The temple was the same as they had left it a few days earlier. The stone wheel still covered the well in the center of the room. Streaks of blood on the side of the well reminded him that the man who had helped them rescue his grandfather and Rebecca's mother had given his life for them.

The door leading back into the basement of the church was only a few feet away. As long as they didn't run into any major obstacles on their way up, they would make it.

Michael helped each of them climb out of the hole. They stood brushing themselves off in the dying light of the medallion's red glow. Rebecca nursed her scraped elbows.

Lucas stepped over to the nearest wall with his eyes wide. "So this is what you were talking about."

"This is it," Michael said. "There's a lot of other drawings around the tunnels, but there's a map a little further on. Maybe you can make sense of it better than I can."

"Shouldn't we be getting out of here?" Joey asked.

Michael glanced down at the medallion. It had become the equivalent of a fifteen-watt light bulb.

"Hey, I have some cell phones," August said.

"The ones from the locker room? They're gone," Michael said. "They cleaned out my backpack."

"No, I grabbed a few more." He pulled three large-screen cell phones from his pockets. "Just put the screens in flashlight mode."

"Good man!" Lucas said, walking over to August.

"Do they work?" Michael asked.

August turned on the first cell phone. "Twenty-eight percent charge left." He handed the other two phones to Michael and Lucas. They powered them on.

"Mine is at a thirty-two percent charge," Michael said.

"Mine's almost dead," Lucas said. "Only thirteen percent. Maybe fifteen minutes of light."

Michael led Lucas over to the wall. "Let me show you some of these drawings."

"Do we have time for this?" Rebecca asked.

"We won't be long," Michael said, wandering over to a line of vertical symbols etched in the wall. "Nobody will be looking for us, anyway. They think we're all dead."

Lucas moved in next to him. "Those are the same alchemy symbols, like the ones on the medallion."

"What do they mean?" August asked.

Lucas didn't answer. He ran his fingers along the walls, following the lines as they zigzagged and stopped.

The red glow from the medallion faded away completely, and the others drew closer.

Intricate graffiti covered the wall. Many animal drawings mixed with the symbols and letters. Michael now recognized the Leviathan on the map as the creature with two huge eyes in the center of the largest box. The map made more sense now, but the lines radiated outward to the sides and extended up to the ceiling. If all those lines represented tunnels, and all those boxes represented rooms, they had only seen a small section of the labyrinth. Lots of places for the bessies to hide.

Michael traced the lines of the map around to a box that represented the room containing the pool of Dunamis. Along one wall of the room was the symbol matching the constellation etched into his medallion. Next to that was the representation of a door Lucas had previously explained. Maybe this is why Pastor John wanted the medallion so badly.

Michael pointed at the door on the map. "There's that one

symbol," Michael said. "We can go there now. It shouldn't take us more than ten minutes to get there."

"Michael," Rebecca said, "I don't feel safe down here without weapons."

"The medallion is all we need," Michael said. "The bessies can't get us."

"We should leave while we have the chance," she insisted.

"We'll have time," Michael said. "This is important. There's something at that location I need to find before Pastor John does. He's been trying to get this medallion for a reason. The incident with that thing in the car showed me this medallion can do a lot more than we think. Amazing things I can't even describe. As long as we're this close, we should find out."

"What's that noise?" August asked.

They all stood still. At first, the only sound in the room was their own breathing. Michael's heartbeat thumped in his ears.

Then came the rustling of dirt from the same tunnel they had just exited.

"Something's coming," Lucas said.

"The medallion's not glowing," Michael said. It couldn't be a bessie. Some other creature? Only one other creature popped into his mind. The thing that had attacked him in the car. Pastor John's wasp.

❧ 36 ❧

"Head for the door!" Michael pushed them toward the door leading up to the basement of the church.

Before they took another step, a black twisting form poured out from the hole they had just passed through. It paused for a moment as it consolidated and morphed into the same massive wasp that had attacked Michael the day before. The same six black eyes glared at him. Pastor John's eyes.

The cloud wasp hovered in front of their escape route.

"Son of a bitch!" Joey yelled.

"Get back!" Michael shoved them to the side.

"What the hell is that thing?" Joey asked.

"Pastor John."

"That's definitely not Pastor John."

"It's him."

Blue sparks shot up from the medallion's ruby to the dark patch of skin near Michael's shoulder. The arcs of electricity lit up the room with blue and white flashes. In an instant, his body chilled, and his cloud-self separated, erupting from his chest.

Michael stood with his arms stretched out in front of him as his consciousness split and the dark ghosts clashed. The energy surged through the air and crackled as it smashed against the opposing force. The wasp's power was overwhelming.

Michael stepped back and turned away.

His cloud-self held the thing back as they took off across the length of the temple, circling the pit in the center of the room, stopping at the massive stone door against the wall blocking their escape.

Rebecca and Joey jumped forward, pushing the left side of the stone door so it started pivoting.

"Oh, wow!" Lucas said as the door swung open.

Michael looked back. The wasp hadn't gotten through, but it relentlessly hammered against his defenses. Each clash between them sent torrents of pain through his body.

Before anyone could step through the doorway, a bessie dropped from the ceiling on the other side of the door. Michael's medallion burst bright red. The bessie screeched and backed away, but not before whipping out a tentacle at them, which caught Michael's wrist with the medallion.

Rebecca screamed.

The bessie scraped along Michael's skin, pulling him through the doorway. The bessie's skin blistered and smoked as Michael tried to free himself.

"Good God!" Joey yelled over Michael's shoulder.

Rebecca cried out and sank the hatchet into the bessie's limb. Its black blood exploded across the side of Michael's face and chest. Rebecca swung again and again until she nearly severed off the limb.

The bessie let out a high, piercing squeal and convulsed as it scrambled up the side of the wall dragging its injured tentacle behind it.

Rebecca, Lucas, and August ran through the doorway as Michael wiped his face. He and Joey followed, pushing the door closed again after they passed. Michael wedged some stones into the crack along the bottom of the door. Maybe it would jar the door closed long enough for them to escape.

His cloud-self continued the battle within the temple. The wasp's assault on his energy was wearing him down. His physical body weakened and nausea flashed over him.

Rebecca ran up the stairs first, leading the others. Michael climbed last, keeping the medallion out in case the bessie returned. Their gasping breaths echoed off the walls as they raced. Their stomping feet echoed through the tunnels.

The medallion's red glow faded quickly, and the cellphones lit the way again. At least they had those. Michael searched the floor for anything that might work as a weapon. Anything at all. The small piles of cloth and debris that had been there a week earlier were gone. David must have scooped up everything in sight on his way in and out from retrieving the Dunamis with Rebecca.

Michael's heart hammered in his chest by the time they reached the top of the stairs.

"I need a minute," Michael said. He leaned forward.

"You going to be okay, man?" Joey asked.

Michael shrugged. "I can't breathe."

The conflict with the wasp in the temple was exhausting. He couldn't do it any longer. He drew his cloud-self back. Within seconds, his split consciousness merged into one again.

The wasp had hovered in place as he retreated, forming a strange grin across its face as if pleased he had surrendered. The familiar toothy grin of Pastor John. The wasp still had plenty of strength. It would come at them again.

Michael glanced back into the darkness. Nothing moved. No signs of the wasp. Maybe he had worn it down enough to buy them some time, or maybe it was circling around them to stage an ambush ahead.

"Which way?" Lucas asked.

"Follow Rebecca," Michael said from the back of the line, pausing again as he caught his breath.

A moment later Rebecca screamed and pushed into them as she turned back toward the stairway.

"A bessie!" she shouted.

Shadows moved near the ceiling. The medallion's glow grew brighter as the bessie approached.

The silhouette of a bessie appeared as it scrambled along upside down within the dark corners of the tunnel.

Its tentacles whipped through the air toward Rebecca.

"Rebecca! Hatchet!" Michael yelled.

Rebecca scrambled forward, raising the hatchet to strike the thing, but it eluded her reach. Michael hurried with the medallion, stretching it high into the air. The bessie held its ground and lashed out at them.

"It won't go away," Rebecca said, swinging the hatchet as the limbs swiped down around her.

Michael jumped forward with the medallion still stretched out in front of him. He lifted it as high as he could toward the bessie. A snaking tentacle whipped down and slammed on the floor, missing Michael by inches. He winced as a screeching hiss blared into his ears.

The bessie kept to the shadows, lashing its tentacles toward him as it cowered within the red glare from the medallion. The bessie's flesh sizzled as the light touched it, and the smell of its burnt skin drifted through the air. To one side, a clear path was open for the bessie to escape, but it didn't run this time. It held its position in the corner as if protecting something. It burned and writhed within the red light, still inching toward them. Smoke drifted from its seared and blistered skin.

"Go away, you piece of shit!" Michael yelled.

"Michael," August called out behind him, "something's coming."

Michael looked back. Shadows moved within the darkness of the stairway behind them.

"Go around me," Michael said. "Hurry."

Rebecca brandished the hatchet as she circled around Michael. The others followed her.

As Michael moved toward the others, the bessie inched in

the opposite direction, toward the stairway. It hissed and snapped its beak at Michael while slinking out of the corner, still burning within the red light, and shot toward the stairway as if making its escape. But it stopped and screeched, fanning out its tentacles wide as if about to attack someone.

The black wasp appeared at the top of the stairway, behind the bessie. It floated in the air with the same ghoulish grin as before. Pastor John's grin.

The bessie swiped at it, its tentacle passing through the wasp's body without effect. The wasp's cloud body swirled and reformed.

Michael locked onto the wasp's eyes for a moment before it morphed into a streaming cloud of particles that whipped through the air like a swarm of black insects.

The bessie let out an ear-shattering screech and lunged at the black particle cloud. Its beak snapped open and shut.

The black cloud gathered and then swooped in through the bessie's open mouth.

Tentacles flew in every direction as the bessie swatted the air, clawing at its own face. The black cloud had disappeared inside it. The bessie convulsed for a moment, then settled into a spider-like stance as if it would pounce on them.

Michael backed away. He turned to run along with his friends, but before he circled the corner with them, he glanced back. The bessie was shaking and hissing as if a million volts had surged through its body. Its skin and muscles cracked apart and broke away, slapping down against the stone floor. Each tentacle ruptured and split. The torso flopped aimlessly until it burst open, splattering black blood in every direction.

Within thirty seconds all that remained intact was the black cloud floating in the air, holding the shape of the bessie for a few seconds before morphing back into the wasp.

It turned its gaze back to Michael.

❦ 37 ❦

The crawling in Michael's chest began, and his body chilled. Blue sparks burst from the medallion. He clenched it and moved back. He needed to save his strength.

Michael caught up to the others as fast as he could, which was only a brisk walk. His entire body ached. The medallion's glow had already started to fade. He slowed for a moment and caught his breath. Sweat trickled down his forehead even as the cool air chilled him. Nausea churned in his stomach.

Joey ran to his side. "There's no place to hide up here."

"We'll go to that spot on the map," Michael said. "Something's got to be there."

"We didn't see anything special there a few days ago," Joey pointed out.

"We were too busy running from the bessies to notice anything."

A familiar scent hung in the air. The Dunamis was nearby. If the map was right, the location they wanted was directly against the far wall opposite the pool of Dunamis.

But Joey was right. Why hadn't they seen anything unusual on that wall earlier? If there were something important at that location, it would have caught their eye. Yet any symbols etched in stone could have faded or broken away over time. Either way, they'd arrive in a minute.

As he hurried along with the others, Michael fought against the sensations flooding through him. Another confrontation with that thing would drain his remaining strength. He would delay it as long as he could, at least until the others could defend themselves somehow.

Better be something there. Michael trudged along without pausing.

They came to a familiar wall. A mound of debris led up to a collapsed section of the wall near the ceiling. The last time he, Rebecca, and Joey had been there, bessies had been chasing them. Now Rebecca scrambled up first with her hatchet swinging at her side as if to ward off any bessie thinking of grabbing her.

A jolt of panic passed through Michael. He should have gone through first with the medallion. Anything could be waiting to ambush them on the other side. But the medallion's red glow continued to fade.

Each of them hurried up the embankment of rocks and gravel to the other side. The black cloud would be there in moments.

"Keep going," Michael said as he climbed through the hole. "Look for the symbol. It should be somewhere on the wall to the right."

Michael labored ahead. The stench of the Dunamis was thick. The pit was just to his left. He expected the medallion to burst bright red as bessies might be lurking near the edge of the pit, but the red glow continued to fade. Maybe the bessies had scattered with the arrival of the black cloud.

Michael stared back toward the hole and peered down the hallway into the shadows. No sign of anything approaching. It wouldn't be long.

The wall opposite the pit of Dunamis was a series of interwoven stacked stones, much like other sections of the tunnel.

One flat section stood out. A six-foot tall and wide perfect square. Its surface was flat, without a sign of any inscription—no indication that something special might lie behind it.

Lucas stepped over and wiped the stone with his hand. A single line appeared. He wiped away more dirt. More lines. August joined in. Within a few seconds, their efforts revealed several symbols and engravings covered in a thick layer of dust and black debris like fertile soil.

"Something's here," Lucas said with excitement.

"Look for the symbol," Michael said.

They brushed furiously at the dirt, and within seconds the details emerged. A circle of planetary symbols perfectly matching the inscriptions on the medallion, and the larger alchemy triangle with a dot in the center symbol. In the middle of the wall inscriptions, a gold concave circle the same size as the medallion was set into the stone. Embedded within the gold were several concentric circles of tiny gems of different colors. Red, blue, green, clear, gold. A circle of black gems filled the center, and in a way, the gems' pattern resembled the iris and pupil of an eye.

Michael didn't hesitate. He pressed the medallion into the concave golden eye.

Lucas stepped back.

Nothing happened.

Michael flipped the medallion over and pressed the other side into the stone. Again, nothing happened. The medallion's red glow continued to fade.

"How does this thing work?" Michael asked.

"No idea," Lucas said. "Maybe we're missing something."

Michael held the medallion near the spot on his chest, expecting a spark like he'd experienced when the black cloud attacked him. He shifted it, flipped it, and touched it against the spot. Nothing.

"What the hell?" Michael said, striking the medallion against the golden eye. "It doesn't do anything."

"It must do *something*," Lucas said.

Joey stepped toward the hallway from which they'd entered and stared into the darkness. He turned back to them. "Find a weapon. Something's coming."

Michael pressed the medallion harder against the stone indentation. He rotated it. Maybe it needed to sit at a certain angle. He turned it every way he could think.

The others scrambled around him, scouring the area for anything they might use to defend themselves.

"Grab rocks," Rebecca said.

August walked over to Michael. "Is there another way out?"

Michael scanned the walls and shook his head. "We have to figure this out."

"What should it do?" August asked.

"According to Lucas, a lot more than this." Michael glanced back at Lucas. "What am I doing wrong?"

"I don't know," Lucas said. "Maybe it's not the right spot."

It had to be the right spot. It was the only spot. Michael brushed away every inch of dust and dirt as far up as he could reach. Nothing like those markings on any of the walls nearby. This had to be it.

August picked up a stone the size of a golf ball and stepped to the Dunamis pit at the other side of the room, leaning over the edge and staring into it. "What's down here?"

"Don't go near that," Michael said. "It's the Dunamis."

"Smells like someone died in there," August said.

"Maybe someone did," Joey said.

I almost did. Michael winced and slammed the medallion into the gold eye. "Nothing works."

"What's this?" Lucas asked, reeling in a rope that had been hanging over the edge of the pit. He reeled in an orange five-gallon utility bucket and set it on the ground beside him. "Whatever's in here, it's really heavy."

"We used that to fill the tanks," Rebecca said. "They left some equipment behind."

"Pour that shit out," Joey said.

A faint blue arc of light shot between the spot on Michael's chest and his medallion. He turned and stared at the hole. Either the black cloud was coming or something else had happened. This time felt different. The crawling, nauseous sensations were gone. Only the blue bolts of electricity were there.

Lucas grabbed the bucket handle and began emptying the contents.

"Wait!" Michael said, hurrying over to the bucket. Another blue arc of light bolted between his spot and the medallion. "It's doing something. Maybe—"

Michael stooped and dunked the medallion into the Dunamis. The liquid dripped off the silver metal like chocolate. Another blue arc of light jumped, then several more. Within seconds, the blue arcs became a stream linking him to the medallion. The medallion's red glow had completely faded.

"Grab a weapon," Lucas said. "Something's coming through."

Rubble crackled to the floor down the hallway as a dark shadow passed through the collapsed section of the wall. Footsteps smashed the debris, then thudded across the stone floor. Someone was there, not just the black cloud.

Before the person appeared from the darkness, the shadowy wasp raced into the area first. It charged toward Michael, opening its jaw wide to reveal a massive display of razor-tipped teeth.

"Michael!" Rebecca yelled.

Michael's dark swarm poured out of his chest in an instant and met the wasp halfway across the room. A chill passed through him as he shivered. His consciousness split between his own eyes and the perspective of the black swirling mass emerging from his chest. Arcs of blue and radiant white energy shot between his shadow self and the wasp.

Rebecca swung the hatchet at the wasp, but it passed through the creature without a pause. Lucas threw a large stone, which sailed through its body with ease.

The wasp fell back inches at a time. Michael focused. The wasp moved back further.

The wasp snapped sideways and broke itself from Michael's creature. Instead of attacking Michael again, it lurched toward Rebecca.

It jumped within inches of her face before Michael's creature blocked it.

Rebecca screamed and swung the hatchet frantically as she scrambled away.

It snapped out of Michael's grip again and went for Lucas. Blocked. August. Blocked. Joey. Blocked. Each block drained a little more of Michael's energy. It was wearing him down.

Laughter erupted from the shadows. Pastor John moved slowly into the dim light of the cellphones that Lucas, Michael, and Rebecca aimed toward him as if they were weapons. He stumbled, hunching forward and heaving to catch a breath.

"You won't be saved again," Pastor John said.

The wasp snapped away and jumped over to the bucket of Dunamis, shooting a wide grin back at Pastor John. His own grin was a mirror of the wasp's.

"I couldn't have done it without you," Pastor John said. "Well, I could have, but possibly not in time. Good heavens, if you hadn't led me straight here, I might have *died*." Pastor John chuckled. "I assumed you would run back here to destroy it, seeing the damage you did at The Farm. I guess it was God's will that you survived a little longer. You've served the temple well."

Michael's chest burned as if it were on fire. The stream of blue energy between the medallion and his chest sizzled and spread wider.

Pastor John's eyes followed the blue arc from the medallion to the source on Michael's chest. His eyelids drooped as he sneered. "That device doesn't belong to you."

Pastor John turned his attention to the bucket of Dunamis at his feet. He mumbled a few words and lowered himself to his hands and knees. Lifting the bucket to his face, straining and coughing, he poured the contents into his gaping mouth. It splashed across his chin and down his clothes as he drank.

"Oh, that's so awful," Pastor John said, "yet so refreshing. In moments, my spawn will break your defenses and your will. Each of you will be torn apart and your remains will be lost forever among the rats and beetles in this darkness."

Rebecca lurched forward and heaved a large stone at Pastor John's head. The stone narrowly missed its target, and the wasp shot toward her face. Michael blocked it less than an inch away, and she screamed.

"The Dunamis is making me strong." Pastor John took in a deep breath. "God's gift to me."

August rushed to Rebecca's side and held her. He took the hatchet from her hands and glared at the wasp.

Michael's strength wavered. The wasp bolted over and touched his forehead. The point of contact stung, and Michael winced as it pushed forward, the barrier between his black cloud and the wasp growing thinner with each second.

The image of Pastor John's black cloud ripping apart the bessie popped into his mind. It would do the same to him.

Michael stumbled closer to the wall that bore the markings. With the blue arcs streaming from his chest, he stretched his arm back, holding the medallion, and once more pressed it into the gold eye.

A brilliant burst of energy flashed and blinded him for a moment. The pressure from the wasp fell away. The floor rumbled around him.

His sight was gone, but his cloud's consciousness witnessed the massive wall rising several inches off the floor, its sides scraping and cracking against stone. It hovered above the ground for a moment before a black, ghostly mist crept out from the gap along the bottom, and formed claws stretching like fingers of death. Those ghostly black fingers resembled the same cloudy material from the black spot on his chest.

The slab floated above the black mist, sliding back and then pivoting sideways along an unseen track. When it stopped a few seconds later, it continued hovering in the air.

Michael's eyesight returned gradually, and he stared into a dark doorway beside him.

With the blue arc still streaming from his chest, he moved into the doorway cautiously as his cloud held the wasp outside the door. His cloud's eyesight watched Pastor John's movements. For the moment, Michael had the upper hand, but without weapons to make their escape, there was no point in running.

His friends huddled in beside him.

Michael led the way into the room, as the sound of their footsteps echoed off the walls. There had to be something inside they could use to defend themselves. The glare of metal ahead caught his eye.

He rushed toward the metal object and stopped with a gasp. Inches above the object, a face stared back at him.

They weren't alone.

38

Under the light of their three cell phones, six figures circled the room. Stone gargoyle statues, like those seen at the top of old buildings, sat in a menacing pose. Each held two swords, one in each hand, crossed over their chests to form an X.

If they'd been standing instead of sitting, the gargoyles would have towered over the group of humans. They faced a single object lying on a circular stone table in the center of the room.

A *crypt*? Had they broken into an ancient tomb? If so, where were the bodies? An entire room for six statues? And if it was a tomb, there had to be treasures.

"Grab those swords!" Michael yelled.

Joey pulled at the nearest one and groaned. "Damn, this thing is stuck."

Michael grabbed one, but the sword was firmly attached to the stone hands.

"August," Michael said, "get the hatchet."

August brought it over.

"Sorry," Michael said to the statue before raising the hatchet above the gargoyle's wrist. He swung it down, and the blade clanked against the stone. He brought it down on the wrist again, and this time the hatchet's blade shattered. The pieces clacked across the floor.

"That's it," Lucas said. "That's all we got. No more weapons."

August hurried over to another statue and pulled at the sword with no luck. Nobody could free them.

"Find *something* to use," Michael said.

Lucas, August, and Rebecca scavenged through a pile of items against the wall. Joey continued battling to rip a sword away from a statue.

A stone box the size of a child's coffin sat at the base of each gargoyle. Michael approached one and discovered the top and sides were covered with intricate etchings similar to those covering the temple's walls. The thick stone lid hung over its sides. Michael lifted the cover and slid it to one side. Not nearly as heavy as it looked. He gasped and stared into the box—a stunning assortment of gold and silver treasures.

A surge of excitement flowed through him. At any other time he wouldn't have hesitated to scoop it all up and carry it home, but now it wasn't important.

He combed through the cold metal objects in search of weapons, pushing aside items that sent his heart racing. Jewelry, sculpted miniature figures with gems for eyes, gold and silver coins, gold spheres the size of baseballs laced with a complex web of artwork.

August came over first. "Oh wow! Is that what I think it is?"

The others joined him as August dug his hand into the pile and pulled out a gold cup. He held it up within the faint light of the cellphones.

"That thing must be worth thousands," Joey said.

"Tens of thousands," Lucas said.

"No time," Michael said. "Find a weapon."

August dropped it back into the pile.

Michael's attention was drawn to the center of the room, the focus of the gargoyles. The object on the stone table resembled the medallion in his hand, except for being made of gold. It mirrored the symbols and inscriptions like the gold eye he'd used to enter the room. Along the rim of the new medallion was a ring of amber gems set into the gold.

A blue arc of electricity shot from his chest to his medallion, and then from his medallion to the gold one. The triangle of energy surged through him.

Michael reached out, resting his fingertips against the cold metal. Some unseen force tugged at the medallion in his hand, moving it forward on its own. It wobbled and the closer it got, the stronger the attraction became.

More blue arcs of energy jumped and sparked between the medallions. His own shook, and he gripped it tightly to keep it from flying out of his hand. The gold medallion didn't move at all. It remained still on the table. The blue arcs increased in intensity and frequency as his artifact moved closer. Michael tried stepping away, afraid he'd lose control of it.

"Oh shit," Michael said. He pulled away harder.

"What's going on?" Joey asked, hurrying to his side. "Are you okay?"

"Something's wrong," Michael said. "It's taking the medallion."

Lucas came over. "Let it go."

"We need it." Michael pulled with both hands.

"No," Lucas said, "it's okay."

Michael clenched his teeth and snarled. "What do you mean, it's okay? We need it to get out of here."

Several blue arcs of energy burst from Michael's chest and shot into the gold medallion, bypassing his own medallion now. The pull on it grew like a black hole swallowing a star.

Michael's consciousness shifted to the struggle outside the room. Pastor John's wasp had pinned his black cloud to the floor, but each time Pastor John attempted to step forward, Michael's cloud broke free long enough to isolate him. Pastor John had stood now, and Dunamis streaked down the front of his clothes and neck.

The two creatures flew from one side of the room to the other, slamming each other against the walls and floor. Each collision resulted in a massive electrical storm between them that flashed across the room.

Pastor John's wasp dodged Michael's strikes with greater ease. Michael's cloud slowed as his physical body weakened. Each strike diminished his barrier further. It wouldn't be long now before all his force was gone. The Dunamis had given Pastor John great strength, and that strength had been passed along to his creature.

Michael's legs weakened and he lost his focus. His black cloud had collapsed under the growing power of the wasp. The cloud surged back into his chest with an audible thump as if someone had hit him with a fist. Michael wavered and clung to the side of the stone table in front of him. No more time.

"You failed," Pastor John called into the room. "Face your judgment."

"Michael, he's coming in," Lucas said.

"Grab a rock or something," Rebecca said.

"Nothing here to grab," Joey said.

Michael stood beside the gold medallion, bathed in the triangle of surging energy, his head turned toward the doorway as his friends took defensive positions around the room.

Michael clamped onto his medallion for as long as he could, but it slipped through his fingers, slamming into the gold medallion with a loud clink. The two pieces spun around and flipped, orienting themselves like two powerful magnets as they fused together.

At the moment of contact, a blaze of golden electricity raced through the patch of black skin on his chest and arced out in every direction around the room. Michael shielded his eyes. The golden beams saturated his chest and energized him. Wave after wave of cascading power flooded his senses.

Fingers of golden light raced across every person and object in the room like a giant living Tesla coil. Electricity crackled and encompassed them in a massive web. The waves pulsed and throbbed like a heartbeat.

"Holy shit!" Joey yelled.

A moment later, Pastor John's wasp entered and hovered near the doorway. The golden light reflected off its six bulbous black eyes, and a wide, awful grin stretched across its face. The wasp shot forward toward Michael.

Michael shuddered as his black cloud erupted from his chest and smashed against the wasp. An explosion of light burst out from the collision, snapping the wasp from its insect form back to a snaking black cloud of particles like his own. Pastor John's cloud then whooshed out of the room as if something had inhaled it.

Michael reached out to the fused medallions, the electricity arcing through his fingertips, and lifted them as one piece from the table. The energy coursed through his body, illuminating him in a golden, ghostly glow. The energy streamed up and down his arm and snapped out, clawing at the walls as if attempting to escape.

His friends surrounded him.

"Does it hurt?" Joey asked.

"No," Michael said.

"I can't believe I'm not dead," Joey said.

"You will all be dead soon," Pastor John said.

He stood in the doorway with narrow eyes and a deep scowl. The wasp was gone. He drew a pistol from a holster at his waist and aimed it at Michael.

Michael's black cloud circled in the air between them.

"You do not understand what you're doing with that," Pastor John said. "All your friends will die. Is that what you want?"

Michael trembled with rage, gripping the fused medallion in both hands, and stepped toward Pastor John. "I'm done with you."

His black cloud rushed forward and flew into Pastor John's mouth. Michael merged with his body and his consciousness split. He had control of the gun in Pastor John's hand. His physical body stared back at him as he peered out through his enemy's eyes. Michael experienced Pastor John's rage with his body. His absolute fury at being controlled.

Nothing he can do to me now. Michael lowered Pastor John's gun.

"What should I do with you?" Michael asked.

Michael raised the gun once again, placing the end of the barrel against Pastor John's temple. Pastor John's body shook.

"I will end this," Michael said.

Rebecca gasped.

Pastor John convulsed a moment before Michael intended to squeeze the trigger. Pastor John's black cloud burst out in that moment, forming into the wasp between them. Michael was defenseless as the wasp surged toward him.

Michael separated from Pastor John's body and swooped around, blocking the wasp less than an inch from his face.

Pastor John swung the pistol back toward Michael and fired several shots. Bolts of energy ripped through the air, cracking into each round. The rounds exploded in the air in front of Michael like firecrackers.

Pastor John's wasp swung away and charged at Rebecca. Michael's black cloud intercepted it. It charged at Joey, then August, then Lucas. Each time, Michael blocked it from merging with them.

Pastor John lunged at Michael, grabbing for the medallion. They wrestled for a moment until it slipped from Michael's hand and banged against the floor. Both scrambled to retrieve it.

Pastor John got to it first, triumphantly clutching it to his chest, and ran from the room. The wasp followed.

Michael raced after him. The others followed behind.

His black cloud shot out and merged with Pastor John before he had crossed the room. Once again, he took control of the pastor. The medallion surged with golden arcs of electricity and the bolts shot down into the Dunamis pit.

Bursts of orange and red lit the walls of the pit as if someone had thrown a gas tank on a bonfire below.

Pastor John struggled against Michael's control. His wasp turned its attention back to Michael.

Michael stepped Pastor John to the edge of the Dunamis pit. The pastor resisted.

One foot, then another.

The black liquid below was a sea of molten goo, gushing and spewing over the edge. A stray splash seared through Pastor's John's pants and burned his skin. Pastor John, and Michael within him, cried out in pain.

In Michael's cloud-grip, Pastor John stretched out the medallion over the pit. The electrical current shot furiously between Pastor John, the medallion and the Dunamis. The closer the medallion moved toward it, the more furiously the liquid below erupted.

Another step toward the pit. The pastor's indignation boiled hotter than the pit below them.

Michael gathered all his strength and willed Pastor John to jump.

He jumped.

A jolt of pain broke the connection as soon as Pastor John's feet hit the molten Dunamis. A piercing scream filled the air.

The Dunamis exploded across the room. The golden electrical arcs burst across the walls and ceiling, knocking the stones loose and stirring up a dust cloud. Everything around them rumbled. A flurry of rocks rained down on them as they scrambled toward the exit.

Michael dodged a massive stone that crashed near him, rolling to a stop only inches from his feet. The walls of stone lining the pit of Dunamis cracked apart and caved in. A flow of Dunamis continued to surge up from the pit as they ran, splashing over the edge across the floor. The roar of collapsing stones was deafening.

Michael paused, glancing over to the spot where Pastor John

had stood. He wanted to make sure that the pastor was really gone. Nobody could have survived that fall. Michael searched for any sign of the man who had terrorized them. Some proof that it was all truly over.

"Michael!" Rebecca screamed. "Let's go!"

August grabbed him by the arm and pulled him toward the exit. "Come on."

They ran. The tunnels continued to rumble as they hurried back toward the temple.

The light from Lucas's cellphone died.

❧ 39 ❧

R ebecca coughed, waving her hands in front of her face as if that made any difference.

Lucas groaned. "I can't breathe, and it stinks."

The smell of Dunamis dissipated as they maneuvered over the scattered debris away from the destruction. No sign of the bessies anywhere on their way out. The chaos must have spooked them.

A slow smile crept over Michael's face. Within the devastation, they had not only destroyed Pastor John but also the last of the Dunamis. They had beaten the temple and taken away their most valuable tool. No more miracles. No more deception.

The dust in the air was thick all the way through the tunnels until they descended the staircase and turned into the temple. Michael took a deep breath after they stepped inside. Joey swung the pivoting stone door shut and jammed stones at the base to prevent it from being pushed open from the opposing side.

Within the temple, the air was clearer.

Joey coughed, hunching forward. "Oh man, let's get out of here."

"We'll be home soon," Michael said.

"What if the temple freaks are waiting for us when we leave here?" Lucas asked.

"No way," Michael said. "They don't know we're down here. They think we got eaten by one of those *things*."

The room suddenly became a little darker.

"Oh no," August said, staring at his cellphone. "Phone's dead."

Michael checked his battery level again. Less than five minutes left.

"Michael," Lucas said, "just a minute. Before we go, shine your cellphone over here."

"You got *one* minute," Michael said, walking with Lucas toward a wall.

Lucas examined the symbols and strange language, running his fingers across the inscriptions. "This is incredible."

"Does it make sense to you?" August asked.

"Some of it." Lucas stepped back and took in a wide view. He stepped forward again, pointing to the drawing of a large animal surrounded by dozens of small men. "Do you know what this thing is?"

"I think I killed it a few days ago. We call it the Leviathan."

Lucas studied the drawing again. "How did you kill it?"

"It reacted strongly to the medallion's light, for some reason. Burned its flesh. I forced it back into a hole where we heard it crash to the bottom."

"Are you sure it's dead?"

"No, not sure. Unfortunately."

"Let me borrow that," Lucas said, gesturing at Michael's cellphone.

Michael handed it to him.

Lucas temporarily turned off the cellphone's flashlight mode, then snapped one picture. The flash threw a burst of light across the room. It blinded Michael for several seconds.

"Hey!" Joey yelled. "Warn me before you do that!"

"I'm blind," August said, and chuckled.

Hearing someone laugh warmed Michael's heart.

The room dropped into darkness until Lucas turned back on the flashlight mode.

"We shouldn't still be down here," Rebecca said. "This whole place might collapse."

"I just want to figure this out," Lucas said, shining the cellphone toward another drawing.

Michael stepped beside Lucas and studied the drawings he lit.

"Lots of alchemy and astrology references," Lucas said to Michael. "Take a picture for me."

"We should go," Michael said. "My phone's almost dead too. Let's not push our luck."

"Michael's right," August said. "I don't want to be stuck down here."

"I'd never leave you behind," Lucas said in a distracted voice as he studied a line of symbols along the bottom of the wall.

"Time's up, man," Joey said. "Let's go."

"All right." Lucas groaned, giving the wall one final glance. "Maybe we can come back."

"I am *never* coming back to this place," August said.

They rushed through the door leading up to the church basement, locking it behind them by laying a massive wooden beam sitting nearby across the metal brackets. Someone had built the door to last a long time. Nothing would get out.

At the top of the first staircase, they passed through a small room with stone walls. They turned right through another doorway that led them up another flight of wooden steps toward the church basement. Halfway up the stairs, Michael's cellphone went black. He froze, then continued cautiously.

"Just in time," Joey said.

"Hold the handrail," Rebecca said.

The wooden, shaky steps squeaked below their feet. Rebecca

grabbed the bottom end of Michael's shirt as he carefully ascended. The handrail along the edge of the stairs wobbled and creaked as if it might pull free at any moment, but at least they had something to guide them.

A crack of faint light appeared ahead of them at the top of the stairs. If someone had locked the door from the other side, they'd have no choice but to go all the way back down in the darkness and grab something to smash through. They could use the wooden beam they'd just used to seal the temple's door shut, but it would create a lot of unwanted noise.

Michael reached the door first and turned the handle. The door swung open.

He breathed in the cool, damp basement air. It was refreshing compared to what they had been inhaling.

The church basement was dark, but someone had left a light on in the kitchen. Michael peered at every shadow and corner before moving forward, but the room was clear. No sounds above the hum of the kitchen's refrigerator.

If somebody had been hiding in the darkness, waiting for them, they would have heard footsteps clomping across the kitchen floor as they made their way to the door leading up to the church's backyard.

They went outside through the back door. A clean, warm summer night breeze drifted across Michael's face. Within the moonlight, the branches of the trees around them swayed and creaked. They crossed the back lawn crouching down as if sneaking through a bear's den. Their white clothes had darkened from the dirt and dust, but they still contrasted sharply with their surroundings. Moving with stealth would be difficult.

Michael's legs burned with exhaustion as he led the others past the black garage where they had been imprisoned days earlier. The orchard lay ahead of them. The darkness of the trees would provide no shelter from any bessies that might lurk in there. In the tunnels, it was plausible that the bessies had scurried away during the destruction, but out among the trees they would be easy prey without the protection of the medallion.

"How are we getting home?" August asked.

"I'll take you guys to my house," Joey said in a tired voice. "It's only a few blocks away."

❧ 40 ❧

They scurried along the edge of the streets on their way to Joey's house, careful to avoid streetlights and fanatical temple followers who wouldn't hesitate to report them to the authorities. But even more dangerous than the temple's white vans were the bessies roaming in the darkness. Not a single one in sight. Had the monsters fled the tunnels and the streets as well?

They huddled together as they moved in the shadows. None of them spoke until they reached Joey's yard.

"We got lucky," Joey said. "Maybe those bessies already grabbed their food somewhere else."

"We're not inside yet," Lucas said.

August laughed. "Right you are."

Joey led them around to the side door. He jiggled the door handle, but it was locked.

"That's okay," Joey said. "I know where the key is at. Dad always left one under here."

Joey lifted a potted plant at the side of the steps and plucked up the key under it.

"It doesn't feel right," Joey said before unlocking the door.

"What doesn't?" Rebecca asked.

"Going in there without my Dad around."

Rebecca wrapped her arm around his back. "I'm sorry, Joey."

"At least you're safe," Joey said. "But it just feels weird going in there now. Like it's not my home anymore."

As Joey unlocked the door, a dog barked inside the house. The barking grew louder as it dashed through the kitchen toward them.

Joey let everyone inside, crouching down beside the dog and restraining it by the collar. "He won't bite. Right, Rufus? You won't bite them, will you? No, just be a good old boy now. We've been through enough shit today."

Rufus's tail wagged wildly as they stepped into the kitchen.

After the side door closed behind them, Michael let out an audible sigh. They were safe for now. But his grandfather didn't know that. He needed to call him right away and let him know. But his grandfather's house had burned down, and he didn't know Audrey's phone number.

"We should call my mom," Rebecca said before Michael could suggest it.

"Use anything you want," Joey said. "If you find any booze, and you probably will, I suggest leaving it alone. My old man drank it straight from the bottle, if you get what I'm saying."

Joey let go of Rufus's collar. Far from aggressive, the dog jumped between them, begging for attention. The dog's warmth and joy lifted Michael's spirit. He had never owned a dog, but bonding with this one took seconds. Michael scratched behind its ears as he remembered he should do when petting a dog.

Rebecca got on the phone first. It was an older cordless phone similar to the one Michael's grandfather owned.

"Wait," Michael said. "Don't use that phone."

"Why not?" Rebecca asked, pausing moments before she dialed.

"They'll know we're here."

"But I need to call home."

"No need to worry," Joey said. "Dad blocked our caller ID.

One of the perks of his position at the temple. Nobody can see our number, but you better not say any names, just to be safe."

Rebecca nodded and continued making the call. When her mom answered the line she burst into tears. Her first several words were garbled and full of sadness.

Only a few minutes later, Rebecca handed the phone to Michael. "Your grandfather wants to talk to you."

Michael took the receiver. "Hello, Grandpa."

"Oh, it's so good to hear your voice," his grandfather said.

Michael's eyes watered. "I'm okay grandpa. I'm at—"

"Tell me later," his grandfather interrupted.

Michael winced. The temple listened to every conversation.

"Is everyone okay?" his grandfather asked.

"Yes," Michael answered. "Now we are."

"Let's keep this short. Wherever you are, can you stay there for the night?"

"I think so."

"Good. Do that then. I don't want you taking any more chances. I'm so happy to hear that you're all safe. We were so worried about you."

"Please let the others know."

"I will. We're looking forward to seeing you all again."

"It was pretty bad in there, Grandpa."

"I can imagine. We're doing fine out here, so don't worry about us. You can tell me everything when I see you."

"I'll see you soon, Grandpa."

"Be safe."

Michael let his grandfather hang up first. At least they would both sleep well that night.

Lucas, August, and Rebecca sat at the kitchen table as Joey put a pizza in the oven.

"This should hold me over until tomorrow," Joey joked. "What are you guys having?"

"I'll have a few of those," August said. "Do you have more?"

"A couple."

"I haven't had a good meal in weeks," August said.

"What are you talking about?" Lucas said. "Derek gives us plenty of food."

"Not good food. Not the stuff I want to eat."

"He feeds you just fine."

"You're all welcome to stay here if you want," Joey said with sadness in his voice. "I guess the house is mine now."

The image of Joey's dad being killed earlier that evening popped into Michael's mind. "I'm sorry about what happened to your dad."

Joey paused. "Thanks, man."

Michael stepped over and hugged Joey.

"Soon, this will be a town full of orphaned kids," Lucas said.

"Things will get better now," Michael said. "Their leadership is gone. Their power is gone. Within a few days, everything will be different."

"Some new nutcase will just take Pastor John's place," Lucas said.

Michael shook his head. "We destroyed the stuff Pastor John used to heal people. He's gone. David's gone." Michael looked at each of them. "Except for my grandfather, we're probably the only ones left who know what's down there."

"Then I guess we have to keep this a secret," Rebecca said, "no matter what."

"I ain't telling anyone what I saw," Joey said.

August made a zipper gesture across his lips.

"The bessies are still out there, though," Lucas said.

"Maybe," Michael said. "Maybe not. We didn't see a single one after Pastor John got killed. Maybe they got trapped down there with Pastor John's body."

"I don't ever want to hear that name again," August said.

"You won't," Michael said. "It's over. We won't say that name again. Agreed?"

Everyone agreed.

❧ 41 ❧

Stones crackled and shifted across every part of Pastor John's body. His left leg was on fire. He couldn't tell if the sensation resulted from an actual fire or his nerves exploding from the impact of the rocks. No sensation in his right leg at all. He couldn't move to check if it was still there. At least there was no pain.

He struggled to breathe. Each breath wheezed in. The pain flooded through his chest as it expanded against the weight pressing down on him. His mind wavered on the edge of consciousness. He spent every ounce of strength forcing his chest to rise and fall as he sucked in dirty air from between cracks in the cold rocks. Around him was darkness, but through the gaps a faint, reddish-orange glow filled the air.

Gurgling sounds flooded his ears. Were those sounds from him? Someone or something near him? It didn't resemble sounds a human would make. Or even an animal's. His mind must be playing tricks.

"Help me," Pastor John called out. His lungs burned as the words passed through his throat.

He gasped in another breath. No answer. His body trembled in the barren blackness that encompassed him.

A stone crashed down beside him, knocking some rubble loose. The stones crackled to the floor in a micro avalanche.

He tried to lift his left arm. Pinned to the ground. Pain shot up through his shoulder. Most likely broken.

The odd glow pulsed more brightly and then faded. He peered out between the stones covering his face. The wall of the room came into focus. What had happened to him? The ceiling had collapsed. His mind wasn't so clear. He needed to think.

He didn't feel like himself. Had he gone into shock?

What's my name? Pastor John Crane. What day is it? Friday. What town do I live in? Stone Hill.

His head hurt to focus on details like that, but everything came back to him.

Stay awake. That's how you stay alive.

I am alive.

But the pain.

Oh God, I might pass out. Stay awake.

Every part of his body burned.

Something thumped nearby. A footstep. Or another rock falling? Hard to tell.

"Under here," Pastor John called out with a scratchy throat. He would give a pound of gold for a glass of water.

Another thump.

Someone or something was there.

His guards? They would come searching for him after discovering him missing. His loyal guards wouldn't just leave him there buried alive. Was he even alive? He was breathing. How long had the debris covered him?

He smelled blood. And Dunamis. Not much time left.

The footsteps had to belong to his guards. If only he could crawl out from under the rocks, it would be a simple matter to order one of them to scoop up some Dunamis and pour it over his wounds. He'd be back to health in no time.

The stench of the black liquid was so strong in the air. He must have been only a short distance away from the pit. The smell must have jarred him awake as if someone had placed smelling salts below his nose.

Some stones shifted again above him, and then a few more. He could breathe more easily now. A little, although his lungs still burned. Maybe one of them had collapsed.

More stones rolled off his chest and crashed down across the stone floor beside his face.

"Easy," Pastor John said. His guards should be more careful. "You almost hit me."

No response. They would not dare upset him. He would talk with them later.

More gurgling noises around him. The sounds hadn't come from his throat. They echoed in the air outside his cocoon of stones. Maybe his guards had been injured in the collapse as well, during their search for him.

"Get the Dunamis," Pastor John instructed, his right hand forming a fist. He strained to free his arm, to show his guards that nothing could keep him down.

"Who's there?" Pastor John asked.

Again no response. They hadn't heard him. He would have to wait until they uncovered his face to direct them. If they still couldn't understand, he would crawl to the Dunamis alone.

They removed the last of the stones covering him, yet within the reddish-orange pulsing glow he saw no one. He couldn't turn his head, but the shadow of someone stood at his side within his peripheral vision.

"Dunamis," Pastor John said.

No response. How could they not hear him? Or at least see his lips moving? No flashlights anywhere. His chest was clear of stones, but the heaviness was still there. Pain throbbed through every inch of his body.

A tug on his left leg. The burning sensation burst into a bonfire.

Pastor John groaned. "Not so fast."

They released his leg.

The flame-orange aura across the walls and ceiling faded with each passing moment. The medallion had to be somewhere nearby. Everything he desired was there with him, in the same room, but it remained out of reach. His guards needed to hurry.

"Hurry," Pastor John said.

A dark shape pulled on his left leg again, yanking it harder this time.

"You're too damn rough," he said. "Get me over to the Dunamis."

They dragged him by his feet out away from the bloody mess and across the floor with his arms spread out at his side like Jesus on the cross. He strained to lift the back of his head to keep it from scraping across the stone floor. His arms were nearly useless. His strength was all but gone.

The rubble and shards of gravel dug into his back, and some scraped against his scalp.

"Dammit," Pastor John said. "Slow down. Do you see the Dunamis? It's nearby. Bring it to me. Don't drag me there."

They didn't slow down.

His vision was blurred and only the shadow of his rescuer appeared at the bottom of his sight.

"Brother Steven, is that you?" Pastor John narrowed his eyes to improve his focus, but it didn't help. "Is it you?"

Again, no answer.

Maybe his rescuer had been injured during the search for him. The smell of Dunamis faded, along with the glow. Injury or not, his rescuer was going in the wrong direction.

"Dunamis," Pastor John said, "go back."

He focused on his chest. He drew into himself and attempted to separate his consciousness. His shadow spawn would give him greater clarity. His own eyes failed him. The creeping sensations formed in his chest, but the separation never happened. That last stage of the process eluded him like when his mind clung to awareness before drifting off to sleep. The more he wanted to separate into that realm, the more it sank away.

He had no strength left. Not one part of his body functioned correctly. The cool air pierced him down to the bones. He'd never been so cold in his entire life. Deathly cold.

But he wasn't dead. Not yet. His rescuer needed to reverse course, immediately.

"I need Dunamis," Pastor John said. "For God's sake, do you hear me? Say something."

His rescuer dragged him further without a pause.

"Who are you?" Pastor John asked.

They moved further into the darkness.

The thickness of the void weighed on him as he was dragged down multiple staircases, straining to keep his head from slamming against each step.

If the one dragging him were a guard, they would be safely within the basement of the church by then. This could be no rescuer. The person or thing dragging him had heard his pleas and ignored them.

It could only be a phantom, pulling him along with one of its tentacles, although it made none of the usual sounds. Impossible to know for sure.

It moved him further down into the depths of the tunnels, and long before he arrived there, he recognized the echoes of the room he feared the most. He had been there before. The Leviathan lay ahead.

His clothes scratched across the stone floor as his captor pulled him into the massive room. A low, booming groan filled the air. A little further, the smooth surface beneath him dropped away and transformed into the jarring layer of sprawling shredded animal carcasses and human skeletons. The bones and debris gouged through his clothes and tore open his skin.

His captor stopped and scurried away, leaving him defenseless atop the pile of death, which he had escaped from only days earlier. The Leviathan would be there soon. No chance for escape this time. He was to be another sacrifice to the god of the underworld. If he had any strength left, he would scavenge the pile for a weapon, but that was impossible now.

The piles of bones stirred below him as the Leviathan rose within minutes. Without light, he could only imagine what the beast looked like. He'd never seen it. Never wanted to see it. His imagination filled in the gaps.

So much noise around him and under him as the Leviathan grabbed hold of his legs and hung him in the air upside down. His limp arms dropped as the monster dangled him above what he assumed was its mouth. A wet slurping sound swelled below him.

In an instant, the monster consumed him.

Pastor John's scream came out as a whimper.

Stone Hill: Leviathan Wakes: Book 3 will be available soon!

More novels and stories coming soon!
You can sign up to be notified of new releases
and pre-releases

— PLUS get a **FREE** short story at my website!

www.deanrasmussen.com

★★★★★
Please review my book!

https://www.amazon.com/review/B084T4D52B

If you liked this book and have a moment to spare, I would greatly appreciate a short review on the page where you bought it. Your help in spreading the word is *immensely* appreciated and reviews make a huge difference in helping new readers find my novels.

ABOUT THE AUTHOR

Dean Rasmussen grew up in a small Minnesota town and began writing stories at the age of ten, driven by his fascination with the Star Wars hero's journey. He continued writing short stories and attempted a few novels through his early twenties until he stopped to focus on his computer animation ambitions. He studied English at a Minnesota college during that time.

He learned the art of computer animation and went on to work on twenty feature films, a television show, and a AAA video game as a visual effects artist over thirteen years.

Dean currently teaches animation for visual effects in Orlando, Florida. Inspired by his favorite authors, Stephen King, Ray Bradbury, and H. P. Lovecraft, Dean began writing novels and short stories again in 2018 to thrill and delight a new generation of horror fans.

Bibliography

All Biblical references provided by The World English Bible.
https://ebible.org/web/index.htm

Acknowledgments

Thank you to my wife, Anh, and family who supported me, and who continue to do so, through many long hours of writing.

Thank you to my friends and relatives, some of whom have passed away, who inspired me and supported my crazy ideas. Thank you for putting up with me!

Thank you to my beta readers!

Thank you to all my supporters!